DEAD
IN THE
WATER

B. BASKERVILLE

A ship in the harbour is safe,
but that's not what ships were built for.
- John A Shedd

- PROLOGUE -

He who controls the seas controls the land.

Throughout our existence, humans have settled near the mouths of rivers, as such a location provided access to both fresh water and abundant seafood.

A village or town by the sea could boast better trade than their inland rivals. Transporting goods by land meant manpower, horsepower and the negotiation of terrains from valleys and mountains, to dense woodland and inhospitable deserts. But all one needed to transport goods by sea was a sturdy boat, a competent crew, and favourable winds. Trade via sea opened a state up to richer luxuries and resources. But all wealth comes at a price, and settlements on the coast became more vulnerable to invading forces.

History is riddled with skilled sailors who marauded, raided and raped their way to fortune. The choice was not a simple one: live a safer but more impoverished existence inland, or live by the sea and risk it all for prosperity? For the powerful have always dominated the water. Be them pirates or Polynesians, Vikings, Venetians or mighty Britannia herself, the rulers of the waves were the rulers of the world.

- CHAPTER 1 -

She kicks her feet, her legs searching for a solid surface that they won't find. The water is half a kilometre deep, numbingly cold, and dangerous. She has no life vest, no buoyancy aid, no light.

Freezing water seeps through her layers and she gasps uncontrollably. It's called cold water shock response. Quick, shallow breaths gulp for air, and though she craves oxygen, the shock prevents her lungs from expanding.

In the distance, fishing boats and cargo ships traverse shipping lanes between the continent and the innumerable islands that surround it. They are mere pricks of light and occasional foghorns in the total darkness. Even if they were close enough to rescue her, their engines would drown out her cries for help. She'd be more likely sucked under than pulled up.

Aboard the yacht, a shadowy figure is silhouetted against golden light from the saloon below. Her spirits raise when the figure reaches for a horseshoe-shaped life preserver.

Throw it. Throw it.

Though it makes staying afloat more difficult, she waves her arms over her head and shouts in desperation. She must do everything she can to remain visible and give clues to her location.

The sea is choppy, and though she's a good swimmer, her clothes and shoes weigh her down. Water crashes over her head, and she splutters, coughing up salty liquid. Brine burns her nose and throat and stings her eyes. *Why haven't they thrown the horseshoe?*

Under sail, the yacht moves stealthily. As silent as the North York moors in the blissful seconds when the wind drops and not a blade of grass makes a sound.

She treads water. Her hands move in figure-eights by her sides, and her legs fight the inky abyss with frog kicks. Soon, her body will begin to preserve heat by redirecting blood from her extremities to her core. Her organs will be protected, but her limbs will lose all meaningful movement. And once she can no longer swim, what then?

She slips under the surface only to panic and suck in some water. Adrenaline alone pushes her back up. Her shouts become panicked squeals. She wipes seawater from her eyes in time to see the silhouette return the life ring to its hook.

One final pained plea for help. Nothing more than a shout into the void. Can they even hear her over the sound of the air hitting the sail and the waves lapping against the hull?

The yacht shrinks into the distance; they're not going to help her. It's time to make her peace.

She is alone.

Left for dead.

CHAPTER 2

Two weeks earlier.

Jo.

"Fuck!"

I don't like to swear at work, but there are times when only a curse word will do. Being head-butted by a Great Dane is definitely one of those times. I can picture Lydia, the fuddy-duddy receptionist, tutting and wrinkling her nose from behind her desk. She's probably apologising to the next client and saying something about the youth of today as if I'm some teenage hoodlum and not a partner in the practice. Technically, I'm Lydia's boss, but Lydia's been here twenty years and thinks she runs the place. Granted, she's organised, particular, neat and has a memory like an Indian elephant, but she's also a complete pain in the arse. Lydia isn't one for new-fangled ideas like the cloud, text-speak, almond milk, or women who swear like sailors.

Being a vet seemed like a great idea when I was young and idealistic. I pictured playing with cute puppies and nursing adorable kittens back to health. In reality, I'm peed on twice, bitten thrice and humped at least once before each day is out. I dreamed of specialising in large mammals and finding work in an exclusive conservancy in Kenya or Tanzania. Alas, I found myself at Forest View Vets. If Forest View isn't a case for Trade Descriptions, I don't know what is. There is no forest, no lush vegetation, no towering oaks. We overlook a Sainsbury's car park and a methadone clinic.

I rub my nose where Hercules – that's the Great Dane – got me. I don't think it's broken, but it hurts like a son of a … I shouldn't blame the dog; it's entirely my own fault. My head is elsewhere, which is a dangerous thing when you're trying to give a bad-tempered, eighty-kilo beast his annual vaccinations. He's muzzled, not that he needs his teeth to do me an injury; his head is twice the size of mine, and he can use it like the club brandished by his namesake.

My phone pings, causing my eyes to flick towards the staffroom. The phone is tucked right at the bottom of my handbag which is hanging on the coat peg in the staffroom. It hangs between Dr Green's rather fetching double-breasted jacket and Dr Fenwick's hideous fur coat. Honestly, what sort of veterinarian wears a fur coat? I'm no vegan, but surely there are lines? My phone should be on silent but if Frederick texts I'd like to know. A bit of advanced warning is a good thing. I don't like surprises.

More pings. More images of Lydia tutting and shaking her head. Lydia doesn't approve of SMS messages, Whatsapp or that "Tik-Tok nonsense". She once told me she prefers more traditional lines of communication, which I assume to be telegrams and carrier pigeons.

I remove Hercules' muzzle and lead him back into the reception area where his elderly owner is waiting. She's about seventy-five, give or take a decade, and wouldn't be five feet tall if she stood on her tiptoes.

"He wasn't any bother, was he?"

How this miniature woman controls a creature like this, I have no idea. I consider telling her the truth, after all, my nose is still throbbing. "He was a little nervous."

The older lady gives me a sheepish smile. She knows *a little nervous* was a massive, or rather herculean, understatement.

Once her bill is settled, I ask Lydia about my eleven o'clock.

"They haven't arrive yet, Dr Singh."

She always says *Dr Singh* as if it's an effort. As if she doesn't consider me old enough, or proper enough to be worthy of the title. I bite my tongue. If I were a grey-haired, well-dressed, white man, Lydia would be positively sycophantic over me. I'll call her out on it at some point, but right now I can hear my phone pinging again.

I ignore Lydia's disapproving scowl and head back to the staffroom. I dig my phone out of my handbag and see I don't have a text message from Frederick; I have a torrent of Whatsapp notifications from Esther McPherson.

Esther McPherson has added you to the group Pier Pressure Reunion.

My chest tightens. Esther McPherson? That's a name I haven't encountered in a long, long time.

Hello, darlings,
Daddy wants his beloved Bacchus relocated from Kefalonia to Sicily in time for the spring bank holiday.

Bacchus is the McPhersons' yacht. Esther's dad bought it when we were close to graduating. I've never seen it. Not in real life anyway, but there was a picture of it in Hello magazine last year. Mr McPherson's new wife was standing next to it with the Burj Al Arab in the background. Bacchus is stunning, pure luxury and something even I on a veterinarian's salary can only dream of.

9

Course, he could pay a local skipper to deliver it. But, seeing as his daughter and her besties were the greatest sailing team in the history of St. Andrews, he asked if I'd make the delivery.

I know it's short notice, but how about it, girls? Two weeks in the Mediterranean sun? Free accommodation, Greek wine and a long overdue catch-up. I've missed you all.

Xxx.

I push the phone back into my bag as if it's contaminated with something. I pile my other belongings on top: chewing gum, keys, anti-bacterial wipes, hand sanitiser, spare tights, blister plasters and mood medication. Down, down, down the bag where I won't be able to hear it ping.

Esther's right about one thing: Pier Pressure were a formidable sailing team. Esther, Mabel, Paige, Libby, Verona and myself – Jovitha Singh. We were quite the crew. More often than not, we'd leave other boats eating our sea spray.

I shouldn't think about it, shouldn't cast my mind back to those days. It's not good for me. I twirl my engagement ring around my finger as a distraction, feeling the clean edges of the emerald-cut diamond and the smooth platinum against the pad of my thumb. The ring is a lie. It has been a lie for over a week now. False advertising. A mocking reminder of the life I'd been promised but would never have.

Did I really want to spend two weeks on a yacht with Esther and her mates? The thought makes me

10

feel nauseous, though not as nauseous as the thought of staying in England and explaining to friends, family and colleagues, why the weekend they'd all RSVP'd for was now free.

Given she wasn't invited, Lydia will probably be thrilled.

I run a hand through the length of my ponytail and mutter "bollocks" under my breath three times. What am I going to tell my parents? They adored Frederick. Thought the sun shone out of his Oxbridge arse. Frederick's parents have called about fifty times already. They've tried the softly-softly approach, tried the answer-our-damn-calls-you-rude-cow approach, and the repenting we-just-want-to-know-you're-okay approach. That's rich. They never liked me from the start.

Gathering myself, and with still no sign of the eleven o'clock, I return to exam room three and check the schedule on a computer. Who's next? A Siamese cat with a sore eye, a Yorkshire terrier with diarrhoea and a – oh great – a royal python with heat mat burns. I hate snakes. Lizards I'm okay with, spiders too, but not snakes. I bloody hate them. I close my eyes and take a deep breath but I can feel my skin crawling and tingles running across the back of my neck. I won't need to see the slithering little serpent for at least forty minutes, but the fear is already upon me. I know my fear is irrational, but it doesn't help. Humans have inherited an innate instinct when comes to snakes.

Those who feared snakes, those who knew the dangers, stayed away from them, or spotted them faster were more likely to pass on their genes to the next generations. A distaste for snakes is an evolutionary survival mechanism. Show a child who's never left the safety of the suburbs a composite picture made up of countless species of animals and their eyes will find the snake first.

I shake out my arms to rid them of the prickling sensation. I have to get it together; I'll look unprofessional if I can't treat the animal. But what sort of person keeps a pet snake? One who lacks the inherent fear possessed by others? There's something off about those people – genetic anomalies.

Another deep breath and I'm wondering if I should take one of my tablets. When it comes to the fight, flight or freeze response, I am one hundred per cent a fight person. Fear makes me angry, and no one wants an angry vet.

Or an angry wife.

I've named my anger Patricia. I gave her a name, a face, a body, an entire personality. Truth be told, she looks a little like Lydia. Make of that what you will.

When Patricia gets too close, I raise my hands and gently say, "Not now, Patricia," like she's really there.

Sometimes it works.

Sometimes I feel like a fucking idiot.

Sod it. Some time away will do me good. Even if it is with the Pier Pressure girls. I race back to the staffroom, and despite my trembly hands, I retrieve my phone and type out a quick response.

I'm in. I'll book my flights tonight.

– CHAPTER 3 –

Esther.

The stable door creaks as I close it. That's the muck-ing out finished for one day. I return the shovel to the corner and check the bolt on the gate. Pegasus sticks his head out and nuzzles the underneath of his chin against the wooden planks.

I reach up and scratch his itch. "I'll be back in a few hours, Peggy."

I pat his nose, wrap my arms around his big ol' neck and and say goodbye in a soft voice. I'm sure, that if he could, he'd hug me back.

There used to be many horses on the estate; now there's only Pegasus. He's a beauty. Chestnut and six-teen hands tall. What he lacks on the race track he more than makes up for in grace and companionship. He's been my pride and joy since I was fifteen-years-old – a present from Mummy and Daddy to keep me sweet during their divorce. I try not to think about that time in my life; it was brutal. The words they would use and the things they would throw. As soon as voices began to rise, I would flee to the stables.

I know people think of me as precious, but there are things I find far, far more frightening than getting my hands dirty. Mucking out is a pleasure, not a chore. The comforting smell of cedar mixed with dried dung and leather has always been home to me. I'd take that over the smell of Chanel No 5 any day.

Home is where the horses are. Or horse. Singular. I've cherished the stables more than the studio I rented in St. Andrews or the villa in West Africa where I'd spend those long, hot summers. Amongst the hay and the feed, the stable has been my safe space, and Pegasus my best friend.

The track from the stables traverses heather-covered moorland. My boots kick up small stones as I walk and there's a warmth to the air. The chill of early spring is finally giving way. It doesn't take long for me to to reach the high stone wall that surrounds the formal garden. I let myself in, admire what Peter has managed to do with the hedges, and approach the main house. I remove my blazer and riding boots and leave them in the boot room. My hands smell of fur, and having had the wind in my thick, black hair for over an hour, I am in need of a shower and a deep conditioning treatment.

Before heading upstairs, I move to the kitchen table, where my phone lies faced down. Flipping it over, the screen illuminates to show a number of messages. Pleased that the girls have got back to me, I scroll through the replies. Mabel was the first to reply – no surprises there. There are three things Mabel Sharpe can't resist: parties, cute boys, and holidays. It only took her six minutes to say that I should count her in. Continuing to scroll, I read that Jo is also up for the trip, as is little Libby. It looks like Libby was in two minds but Jo seems to have talked her round. Good ol' Jovitha. Verona says she needs some *vitamin sea* – Good one, Verona – and oh my goodness, even Paige is coming. She has to move some things around but she should be able to make it. Well, I am surprised. I thought Paige might be too busy, or let's face it, too cool for us now.

This thought catches me off guard. How times change.

Daddy will be relieved to know his precious cargo is in safe hands. I'll try to call him later, see if I can get through, and let him know the good news. If I'm tasked with moving Bacchus, I might as well make the most of it, gather the troops and do it properly. Just like the good old days. The six of us on the high seas … Well, not quite the high seas: the Med is tideless. But hey ho, everything will be just as I hoped. I wonder if Mabel is still a wild child? If so, things could get messy. Mabel was the resident Pamela Anderson of our group. Thick blonde hair, big blue eyes and an annoying perfect figure. She looks like the classic airhead, but don't let that fool you, Mabel got into St. Andrews after a lifetime of straight A's. There's a mastermind hidden behind those long lashes.

The sailor in me wants to insist on a dry boat; alcohol does tend to complicate matters. I pout at my phone as I mull it over. No, this is supposed to be a holiday and the girls aren't coming as crew, they're coming as my guests. And if I know anything about holidays, it's that ninety-nine per cent of people like to spend them under the influence. It wouldn't look good if the girls rocked up in Greece and I tell them we're staying sober the entire time. Perhaps, as skipper, I can suggest that we don't drink while under sail. Then, in the evenings, when we're safely moored up, we can pop open the bottles and let the good times roll. That's fair, isn't it? Yes, I might be tasked with making this delivery, but that doesn't mean I can't have a little fun in the process.

I clap my hands together and tell myself everything is going to be fine. Forgetting about the shower I so desperately need, I hunt out some old charts of the Adriatic and Ionian and spread them over the kitchen table. I plan on arriving in Greece twenty-four hours before the others. This gives me time to make sure Bacchus has full water tanks and that her diesel supplies have been topped up. I'll stock up with bottled water, plenty of cheese and nibbles, and a boat load – literally – of Champagne.

I scan the chart, my eyes finding the northern tip of Kefalonia, and I trace my index finger along the route I intend to take. We'll head north, island hopping to Paxos and Corfu before making an overnight passage to Italy. That will be the tough bit. You don't know darkness until you've sailed at night. We'll have to do it in shifts – three hours on, three hours off. Mabel and I are both qualified to skipper at night so we'll alternate, partnering up with the other girls. My finger crosses the Ionian Sea and follows the Italian coast round Calabria. Basically, if Italy were a heeled boot, Calabria would be the ball of the foot. We'll sail down to the toes and across to Catania in Sicily.

I can picture it vividly. Turquoise water, clear blue skies, crisp white wine and great company. It will be heaven.

Almost.

It's a shame I lost touch with the girls after graduating. I still see what they've been up to on the socials, but it's not the same, is it? We all used to be so close. We used to be part of the same sailing team – The Super Six they'd called us in The Courier. Most weekends we'd be out in the laser dinghies, battling the elements off East Sands, but occasionally we'd race yachts. I already had my day skipper qualification by the time I arrived in Scotland, but over the years, the other girls put themselves though their paces, passing competent crew and day skipper themselves. Mabel

18

and I were the only ones to take it further, earning our yacht master certificates.

I smile as I pull up a chair. Sat at the kitchen table, my eyes lose focus until I'm staring through the charts rather than at them. Boy, I used to love taking part in the yacht races. My team, Pier Pressure, dominated the BUSA circuit. Having a background in dinghy racing really gave us an edge. Racing dinghies is tough. Tougher than most land-lovers realise. Not to mention how character building it is. Given its location on the east coast of Scotland, most of the sailors in St. Andrews didn't want to spend too much time in the water. That was a one way ticket to hypothermia. So like all good sailors, I perfected the art of predicting the wind and reading the water.

In contrast, it's pretty hard to capsize a sailing yacht. You have to completely mess things up for that to happen, rogue waves aside. A yacht can be practically horizontal and will still right itself. That's why the yacht purists can be lazy. It's not the end of the world if the mainsail flaps a little. A dinghy sailor would never allow that to happen.

"A flappy sail is an unhappy sail," I whisper to myself.

I lean back in the chair and remember how brilliantly we did in the Round The Island Race in May of our second year. Fifty nautical miles around the Isle of Wight in force five winds. It was magnificent. *We* were magnificent. Not to mention we were one of the

19

only all female crews on the circuit. That's one of the reasons I love sailing so much: it's a great equaliser. The wind doesn't care how much testosterone one has, and the tide doesn't care whether or not one has a penis. It doesn't matter who has the biggest muscles or the greatest lung capacity, it matters who best understands the physics of sailing. Our biggest rivals, Bouys Will Be Bouys, learned that the hard way. I'll never forget the dumbstruck looks on their faces when Pier Pressure zipped past them in our final meeting. We'd competed against each other in Portsmouth and the gents, and I'm only calling them gents to be polite, had tried to compensate for their loss by attempting to seduce us ladies. They were barking up the wrong tree there. The only one they stood a chance with was Mabel, but she'd already set her sights on Finley Livingstone from Ship Happens.

As my mind races – pardon the pun – through a stream of glorious memories, I think of how wonderful it will be to have the team back together. It will certainly help keep my mind off things, and I've missed them all so much, especially Jo. Jo and I were thick as thieves back in the day. We were six-years-old when her family moved to the estate and we went to the same primary school. We were forever riding horses, climbing trees and having sleepovers. Little girlie girls in t-shirts as nightdresses, making tents out of bedsheets and telling ghost stories till we scared ourselves silly. Mummy, my real mother, not the other one, would make us mugs of hot chocolate with marshmallows in to calm us back down.

Sleepovers like that had been a regular feature. Jo would come over every Friday or Saturday, sometimes both, but as we got older, talk changed from ghost stories and ponies to our futures, exams, and boys.

That all stopped when ...

I roll the charts back up and return them to the drawer where I found them. From here, if I crane my neck and stand on my tip toes, I can see where Jo and her family used to live. It's all water under the bridge now. Jo and I are still friends, though admittedly we've never been as close as we had been in those days at Primary School. I turn from the window and realise I'm grinding my teeth. I roll my jaw back and forth to loosen it and use my tongue to massage my gums. This sailing break could be just what the doctor ordered, if I play it right.

An odour catches in my nose. I angle my chin towards my armpit and take a quick sniff under my collar. No, that shower can't wait any longer.

– CHAPTER 4 –

Libby.

Airports always bring the worst out in people, and in my opinion, no airport does that better than London Heathrow. Pack everyone in as closely as possible, ramp up the prices of food and drink and give them nothing to do other than spend money. It's no surprise tempers flare when all anyone wants to do is go on holiday and relax in the sunshine. I'm surprised there aren't more people on no-fly lists. Being from the north, where we're famous for our welcoming ways and friendly accents, I find the abruptness of Heathrow's staff hard to deal with. Yes, it must be difficult to handle people of all languages and cultures while staying vigilant for anything that doesn't look or feel right. Still, manners and a soft tone go a long way. Just because you hate your job, doesn't mean you have to ruin someone's day and talk to them like they're a bloody idiot because they forgot to put a four-gram lip balm in a clear plastic bag.

I flash an enthusiastic smile at the man supervising the x-ray machine at airport security. He resembles a basset hound and has the sagged shoulders of a man who's given up on his dreams.

He doesn't smile back.

I place my shoes in the shallow grey tray, remove my camera from its bag and pat myself down to make sure I haven't left anything in one of the many pockets of my cargo pants.

The metal detector doesn't beep, which is a god-damned miracle. I don't travel often, but I have the uncanny knack of always setting the metal detector off and I've never quite got used to having some stranger pat me down.

The whole airport experience reminds me of a computer game with various levels of difficulty. The goal is to make it to your destination with your sanity intact. Fail and you end up in airport jail with a sweaty man in a loose tie explaining how much you are being fined for punching the Starbucks employee for misspelling your name. Escape London level one: Don't snap at airport security when they ask you to remove your coat, even though it's not a coat: it's a flimsy hoodie and you're only wearing a sports bra underneath. Level two: Remain zen in the departure lounge even though there are more people than seats and half the seats have bags on them. Level three:

Don't lose your shit when the person next to you on the plane has a coughing fit, and the person in front reclines the second you take off.

I pull my Converse All Stars back on and return my clear bag of liquids, camera and phone to my carry on luggage. I'm not sure I've done the right thing in agreeing to this holiday. I haven't seen any of my uni friends since graduating and moving south. I say the word *friends* as if it's in quotation marks. I was always the odd one out in our group. The only northerner, the only non-hetero, the quiet one, the loner, the skint one, the one who goes along with things she shouldn't because she's too damn scared of offending anyone.

A trip to the Harry Potter store brightens my spirits. I'm twenty-four, but once a Potterhead, always a Potterhead. I clutch a yellow and black Hufflepuff notepad and pen set to my chest. Loyal, hard-working, polite, patient, and nice to a fault. Of course I'm a Hufflepuff. I've used fantasy as a form of escapism for as long as I can remember. If it wasn't Hogwarts, it was Middle-Earth, Wonderland, Panem or the USS Enterprise. Okay, that last one is more sci-fi than fantasy, but it's all escapism. Shopping complete, my plan is to head to Wetherspoons for a pre-flight pint.

You can take the girl out of Sunderland …

Ahead, the sea of humans has began to nudge each other. Arms snake out from pockets so that fingers can point and phones can be switched to camera mode.

24

The fingers all point towards a slim woman with a long red ponytail that pokes out from the back of a baseball cap. As she walks, people angle for a better view and snap pictures with their smartphones. Some try to be subtle, holding their phones as if looking for a signal; others don't even bother to switch their phones to silent. Shutter noises *click click* behind her as she walks.

I'd recognise that long red ponytail anywhere. Most British under twenty-fives would.

Paige. She may be hidden behind oversized shades and a trendy cap, but it's definitely Paige.

"Paige. Hey, Paige."

I force my way through the crowd, blinking when a flash goes off ten centimetres from my right eye. The redhead gives me a polite smile and half a wave, but she hasn't even made eye contact with me. *She thinks I'm a fan.*

I increase my pace and have to dodge a pair of dirty old men who eye her as if she's something they'd like to have for dinner. Not that it should matter, but almost every inch of her skin is covered.

"No, Paige. It's me, Libby."

She stops, lowers her shades, and her face bursts into the sort of smile that even airport security couldn't resist. "Eep!" She grabs me into a tight embrace. "It's so good to see a friendly face."

We sway side to side in our hug, neither caring about or noticing the whispers that flitter around us.

"It's Paige Vaughn! The model!"

"She's going to be on Strictly."

"No, it's I'm a Celeb."

"Isn't she dating that singer? The one from X-Factor?"

Paige releases me and takes both my hands in hers. "I don't know about you, but I could do with a break. Are you looking forward to this?"

I shrug. Am I looking forward to this? I look around uneasily. I'm used to taking photos, not being the subject of them. "Erm. I'm looking forward to clear skies and feeling the wind in my hair, but …"

Paige gives me a knowing look. "But you ain't looking forward to the inevitable drama?"

"Something like that."

Paige links her arm in mine and walks me towards an escalator signposted as leading to the business class lounge. When we reach the top we pause to stare down over the railing at everything occurring below. Crowds form into human rivers, carving routes through the departure lounge and branching off towards gates, bars or Gordon Ramsay's restaurant.

I feel a tug on my arm; Paige is heading for the lounge. "Come on, there's breathing room in here."

"Oh. I can't go in." Embarrassed and with my face rapidly flushing, I retrieve my boarding card from the inside pocket of my jacket. "Economy," I say with a pout.

I'm doing okay, financially speaking. I rent a lovely – but tiny – studio flat in Clerkenwell and I earn enough to pay my bills and eat out once or twice a week, but I'm a long way off being able to splurge on business class flights or exotic holidays. That's partly what swayed me to agree to going away with Esther, Paige and the girls. The only other break I have planned this year is a week in an AirBnB in Devon with Danny in the autumn. We're saving for a mortgage deposit and can't really justify anything fancy this year.

Paige removes her sunglasses and shakes her famous red hair free from her cap. "She who dares, wins," she says with a mischievous grin, and before I know what's happening, I'm being marched up to a man in a navy blue suit who's stationed at the entrance to the lounge.

"Miss Vaughn!" he says, his cheeks flushing ever so slightly. "Lovely to have you with us again."

"Thank you, Reg. How's the family?"

Reg? How's the family? I falter at the thought of someone flying first or business class so often that they know the staff by name. Then, Paige has always been good with names. She used to work four shifts a week in the student union bar and never forgot a face. I suppose being personal with the customers means better tips.

Paige and Reg exchange pleasantries a little longer before he turns to me to ask for my ticket. I'm going to have to face the humiliation of being turned away. He hasn't quite finished the question when Paige interrupts.

"Reg, please. This is Elizabeth Bagshaw." She says my name slowly and with a slight raise of an eyebrow as if the entire world should know that name and that if Reg doesn't want to look like a fool he should pretend to know it too. She even adds a nervous look over her shoulder to check her fans from the lower levels haven't followed us up the escalator.

Reg blinks, not wanting to offend the very famous Paige Vaughn, or the not-at-all-famous-but-he-doesn't-know-that Libby Bagshaw. After a couple of seconds of me holding my breath, he waves us through. Paige thanks him with a smile that will keep him going till Christmas.

If I didn't feel like an outsider before, I certainly do now. People who grew up on the same council estate that I did generally didn't end up in places like this. They usually ended up in jail. Okay, that might be a slight exaggeration, but my estate did have the dubious honour of being the car crime capital of Europe for awhile. I follow Paige as she strides confidently to what must be a favourite spot. Around her, people in tailored suits type furiously on laptops, families glide along the buffet helping themselves to hot and cold meals, couples choose from selections of wine and settle into a darkened television room. No one else is wearing Converse All Stars and cargo pants.

28

Paige hands me a glass of organic Prosecco and we collapse into comfortable seats by a giant window that offers views of the chaos in the terminal. It's almost peaceful from this vista. We have plenty of room, and at least ten metres separate us from the nearest family: two dads and their very well-behaved twin girls.

Taking out my wallet, I ask, "What's the damage?"

"It's included in the ticket price, babe."

"But I don't *have* a ticket," I remind her.

"Well I do and it was ridiculously overpriced, so help me recoup some of the cost back in alcohol."

How can I argue with that? "Well, if you insist."

I take a sip and sink back into my seat. I place my bag in front of me and pop my feet up on it. I should be outraged that the haves can buy personal space and quietude while the have nots are forced to exist in the germ-pit downstairs, but right now, I'm with the haves and I want to make the most of it. I sip the bubbly and savour every tingling moment of effervescence.

I might be an imposter, and truth be told, part of me is missing my pint from 'Spoons, but I have to admit, this is the life!

Placing my glass onto a table, I turn to Paige and ask, "How's Graham doing?"

Paige wrinkles her nose. "Same old, same old. Have you seen Esther's yacht?"

I shake my head and wait while Paige whips out her phone and scrolls through some photos until she finds what she's looking for.

"Wow."

"Yeah."

"That's nothing like the one we trained on."

"This is Esther McPherson we're talking about. You think her family would buy something simple commoners like you and I could train on?"

Paige winks.

"You're hardly a commoner," I say, trying not to laugh. "Look where we are for goodness sake."

Paige folds her arms as if saying she wasn't a commoner was a massive insult. "Just because everyone seems to know my name, doesn't mean I've forgotten who I am. I ain't forgotten my roots, luv." She places a manicured hand on her heart. "Don't believe me? I can go full Cockney if you like." Giggling, she takes another sip of her drink before spurting out a deluge of rhyming slang.

I cut her off after apples and pairs. Sometimes I have to remind myself that even though I was the only one in our group at university with a northern accent, I wasn't the only one who grew up poor.

When our glasses run dry, Paige offers to get us refills. "Another one?"

I check my watch; we have time. "Go on then," I say as if she's twisting my arm. "I mean, someone has to help you recoup the ticket price."

She taps a finger to the side of her head and gives me an approving nod. "Indeed."

As Paige walks away, all legs and sashaying hair, I check my reflection in the nearest mirror; sitting next to a model has that effect on people. I smooth my dark brown bob, level my glasses – because they're looking a tad lopsided – and decide that my skin doesn't look as dry and tired as I had feared. I am however, the Velma to Paige's Daphne.

When she returns moments later, Paige hands me a fresh glass of fizz and slaps a newspaper down on the table. "Have you seen this?" Her mouth is pinched and her eyes narrowed.

I think for a second that there's another tabloid exposé splashed across the front page, or a series of paparazzi shots of Paige trying to do something normal like get her groceries. The main headline has nothing to do with Paige; the trial of the year has begun. Rowan Glover, CEO of some energy company was pleading not guilty after indecent images of children were found on his computer.

"Yeah," I answer. "Saw it on the news this morning. Can't believe he's pleading not guilty."

"Not that." Her finger jabs at a column to the left. *Pirates of the Mediterranean. Pirates raid family yacht off Turkish Coast.*

I grab the paper and slide it towards me. "Between Crete and Cyprus … Husband and wife tied up with kitchen string … Took her jewellery, took their cash, cards, passports, everything."

Paiges bite her lip and sinks next to me to read the article in its entirety. "I know. Awful, isn't it?"

"Oh, Christ. They didn't even untie them when they left. The husband tore the skin off his wrists trying to get himself free … Managed to free himself just before they would have hit a rocky reef … Radioed for help … The wife's shook up."

"That sounds like an understatement." Paige puts her glass down, suddenly unable to drink. She wraps her arms protectively around herself. "She must have been terrified."

I feel suffocated. This sort of thing isn't supposed to happen in the Med. It's supposed to happen off the Horn of Africa. The business class lounge no longer feels spacious; it feels exposed, vulnerable even. I'd been wary of going on this trip; worried about how we'd all get on and how the others would treat me.

Six young women alone on a boat? Now I'm worried for a whole new reason.

– CHAPTER 5 –

Jo.

The drive from Kefalonia International Airport to the northern town of Fiskardo takes over an hour. I'm not complaining; the journey weaves its way through sleepy villages and olive groves. The island is hilly, and some of the roads have been carved into the rock. At times I have a cliff face on my right and a beautiful sea view on my left. Forest View Vets, Lydia's scowls, Dr Fenwick's fur coat, and my would-be in-laws seem a million miles away. When we arrive in Fiskardo, I ask the driver to drop me by the Roman Cemetery. While waiting at baggage reclaim, I'd done some Googling and was drawn to the burial ground. I'm a closet taphophile, you see. I find graveyards and cemeteries fascinating. It's not something I can really share with anyone. Taphophilia is a hobby that tends to get you strange looks when you talk about it. Take it from me, if someone asks what they should see and do in Prague, tell them about Charles Bridge, the astronomical clock, and a handful of bars. Don't tell them that they simply must visit the Old Jewish cemetery. They'll take a few steps away from you if you do that. As haunting and eerie as the Old Jewish cemetery is, it's not even in my top three. If I had to pick a favourite, it would be either Père Lachaise in Paris, where Oscar Wilde enthusiasts plant their lipstick-covered kisses on the glass surrounding his tomb, or, the Merry Cemetery in Romania. The words *merry* and *cemetery* don't usually go hand in hand. Still, the site on the northern border of Romania speaks to the sarcastic and dark humour most of us Brits possess. The tombstones are painted blue and are decorated with colourful borders and cartoon-like images of the deceased. Did you like downing vodka shots while you were alive? That would be your tombstone image. Died when a car ran you over? There may well be a cartoon of the accident on your grave. Then there are poems, from off colour rhymes of infidelity to limericks urging visitors to tread lightly and not wake the mother-in-law. That little corner of Europe really has a unique attitude to death.

I thank the driver and take a big breath as I exit his taxi, breathing in the warm air. It's late afternoon, but the sun still heats my skin as I follow a walkway that leads around the cemetery. This beauty, which dates to the second century AD, is entirely different from the Old Jewish, Parisian and Merry cemeteries. It was

34

only unearthed in 1993, and while there are tavernas and cafés all around, it's peaceful here amongst the dead. Some of the graves are lined top and bottom with tiles, others are more like tombs; stone walls with a doorway built into one side. The most impressive, the ones that really catch my eye, are the sarcophagi. Detailed carvings depict some form of battle. I stop and read the description. It's Athena and Artemis chasing Hades as he abducts Persephone to take her to the underworld as his queen. I feel a little shiver run up my spine. Imagine being a young girl, happily plucking flowers in a meadow, when the god of the underworld takes you as his wife. The unfortunate thing is how even today, for many women and girls, this is reality, not the stuff of myths and legends. Not the part about Hades, but the part about abduction and forced marriage. I want to reach out and touch the carving of Persephone, to stroke the white stone and warn her not to eat the pomegranate seeds that will keep her bound to Hades for six months of every year. Leave the seeds alone, and you can be free of your captor and marry the person of your choosing. It was too late for Persephone, but it wasn't too late for me.

Leaving the historical site, I bite down a little anger – *not now Patricia* – and follow the path towards the bay. White yachts stand out on the blue water like giant seagulls, and jovial music and sounds of merriment carry on the breeze. The music is coming from a

35

bar called Panormos. It isn't loud and obnoxious like a club on one of the busier islands. Maybe I'm old before my time, but I never liked having to yell and scream to be heard. It's Greek music, quiet but upbeat in tone. The perfect antidote to the mood I'm trying to suppress. A chalkboard advertises happy hour cocktails for seven euros.

Well, don't mind if I do.

Peering down the stairs, I watch guests drinking Mythos and feasting on mountains of fresh calamari. A group of women are sat on cushions by a low table that looks out over the cliff. They're leaning towards each other, heads bowed as they share stories. One head pops up, and an arm waves frantically at me. It's Paige. I recognise her instantly; most people do. She has millions of followers on Instagram, and there are rumours she'll star in the next season of *I'm A Celebrity … Get Me Out Of Here!* She looks every bit as glamourous as her photographs. Slim and toned, with impossibly bright skin and a curtain of luminescent auburn hair. Between working all the hours the lord gave me and getting engaged, I've piled on the pounds. I'm not obese, but I am overweight, and every picture of the perfect Paige Vaughn that pops up on my feed has me reaching for the biscuits. Jaffa Cakes and Penguins. If it's not chocolate covered, is it really a biscuit? I suppose it is, just not a very good one.

I try not to be bitter. I'm happy for Paige. If I could earn a living doing what she does, I would. We all would.

The girls jump from their floor cushions and run up the stairs to engulf me in a group hug. There are high-pitched pleasantries and speedy catch-ups while I'm shepherded towards their table. Then Mabel, who never misses a thing, grabs my hand and squeals at my engagement ring.

Mabel is all curves, but unlike me, she absolutely owns hers. She looks healthy and bubbly; I feel dour and too sore in the knees and hips to be in my mid-twenties. What I try to hide, Mabel flaunts.

"Jovitha! Look at the size of that rock." She pulls my hand close to her face and tilts it back and forth, examining the cut and clarity. "Who's the lucky man?"

I yank my hand back, rather rudely and push it into the pack pocket of my trousers. "Actually," and I hate that I have to say this because it's not exactly a happy tone to start the holiday, "it was called off."

Heads tilt and lips pout in sympathy.

"I … I just can't face taking the ring off yet."

"No? What happened?" Mabel asks, her hand coming to rest on my arm.

"He was cheating on me."

This isn't true, but I'm not ready to tell anyone the truth. Not yet.

Mabel looks offended on my behalf. "Someone cheated on our Jojo? Unacceptable. Keep the rock," she says, eyes darting back to my hand. "Have it reset as a necklace or a bracelet or something."

Not a bad idea. I can't wear the ring forever.

"Do me a favour," I say, voice lowered. "Don't say anything to Esther. You know how she is. She'll find a way to …" I look around. "Where *is* Esther. I thought we were going to meet at the yacht?"

Mabel raises the biggest piña colada I've seen in my life. "Liquid courage," she says, and we exchange a knowing smile.

"We thought we'd meet here," Verona explains. She looks different from how I remember. Gone are the flower-child clothes and the long, wavy locks. Her hair is cut into a sharp, poker-straight, platinum bob and she's dressed like she's on her way to a board meeting, not a sailing holiday. "Thought we could run the gauntlet together."

Something else is different. She's more confident, I can see it in her posture. Verona used to cling to Esther like her life depended on it, but now her shoulders are back, and her eye contact is infallible. I sense these things. I'd put it down to working with animals but its something I've always been able to do. They say dogs can smell fear, well I can sense anger. I read it in a person's body language, and right now, I'm picking up a serious vibe from Verona. Beneath her sleek exterior, she's furious with one of us.

38

Libby, with her dark brown hair and those thick-framed glasses that are so popular with the geekerati, gets the attention of a waiter. He returns moments later with five shots of something very alcoholic. I don't even ask what it is. We clink and drink.

"Urgh," says Paige.

Grimacing, I couldn't agree more. *Urgh* indeed.

After a Greek Mojito made with Metaxa instead of rum and a couple more of whatever Libby keeps ordering, Paige springs to her feet with the athleticism of a gazelle. "Right. Shall we?"

Verona looks at her watch. "I guess so. Time and tide wait for no man."

"Nor do they wait for slightly drunken women," laughs Mabel.

It only takes a minute or so to walk down the bank. When we round the corner, Fiskardo reveals herself. When I picture Greece, this is what I imagine. Buildings of pastel pink and baby blue are separated by crisp white tavernas. Old wooden shutters line windows, and wrought iron balcony surrounds are painted in delicate hues. Combine the pinks, whites and blues of the buildings with the sea-green water, and you have a scene worthy of a postcard. I'm struck by the lack of drain pipes on some of the older houses; I guess it doesn't rain much in these parts. Old-school lampposts are painted the same green as the water and trees with hundreds of purple flowers cling to walls. There is colour every which way I look.

Sailing boats of all sizes are moored to the quay, their owners sitting on deck, watching the world go by. Across the bay, more yachts use long lines to secure themselves to rocks and trees. Anyone on those boats will need to row to shore on smaller inflatable dinghies. I wonder for a moment, if I took my savings, sold my car and sold the diamond, could I buy a small yacht and come out here? How long would my money last if I didn't eat out and made sure I stuck to a budget? The thought of escaping, or simply never going back home tugs at my heart. Could I? Do I dare?

A superyacht glides into the bay. Some crew must have gone ahead because there are people with the boat's logo on their polo shirts waiting to help moor her up. The nearest restaurant has tables set up in some sort of shore-side VIP section. I wonder who they are? I wonder if they know who we are? I mean, Paige isn't the only famous face in our crew.

There's commotion ahead. The sound of a glass breaking on the pavement raises my hackles. People move, chairs are pushed back or pulled in. A man and woman, each with heavy shopping bags, drag a non-compliant toddler at full speed towards the port.

"Me synchoreís. Me synchoreís."

Their eyes are wide as they try to run.

I raise my eyes at Verona; she speaks more languages than I've had hot dinners.

"I think she's asking people to get out of the way," she tells me just as they almost run us over.

We turn, watching them continue their sprint until the thunderous horn of a ferry leaving the port gives us all the explanation we need.

Mabel laughs, rather cruelly. "Oh. So close."

Libby looks gutted for the family as their run slows to a defeated walk. There's visible water between the ferry and the dock. "Will the captain turn back for them?"

We all doubt it and shake our heads at her.

"But what will they do?" she asks. "Is there another ferry? Are they stuck for the night?"

A voice from behind startles us. "Don't know. Don't care."

We spin. Arms outstretched and glowing with pride, it's Esther Bloody McPherson.

"Ladies," she beams. "Welcome to Bacchus."

Her arms gesture to a mightily impressive yacht. Much bigger and shinier than anything I've ever sailed before. Easily fifty, maybe even sixty feet, and duel helmed. Bacchus is a beauty.

One-by-one we hug and kiss Esther. She's still as striking as she ever was. Her father is a minor royal, and when I say minor, I mean barely. He's the cousin of a viscount or something like that but the way Esther used to tell it, she's practically best mates with William and Kate. She even got to go to one of their children's Christenings. Charlotte's, I think. My parents worked for her parents when I was young, and part of the job involved living on site. We had a cot-

41

tage on the estate but Esther would have me over to the big house all the time. The games of hide and seek we used to play in their grounds were beyond anything you could imagine. I used to like hiding in the orchards in summer. I'd eat the apples while waiting to be found.

Esther's mother is the daughter of a Nigerian oil tycoon which means she has money coming at her from both sides of the family tree. Her parents are divorced now – nasty business that I won't get into right now. After uni, we all seemed to move on and start our adult lives, but Esther did the opposite and moved back home to live with her dad. Strange. But when *home* is a stately home, it probably makes moving back in with your folks a bit easier.

Between Esther and Paige, I'm feeling horribly frumpy. I tug at my t-shirt, making sure no part of my midriff is exposed.

It's my turn to hug Esther. Great. I was hoping I could hang behind the others and get away with no physical contact. She pushes her thick black hair behind her ear, and the setting sun glitters off a gold earring that runs from the lobe all the way up the helix. She moves in and hugs me tight.

"Jo, I've missed you," she says, and when she pulls away, I can see the earring is a word. I squint. It says *feminist* in cursive writing.

What a joke. Esther McPherson is the worst victim-blamer I've ever met in my life. When Deana Nichols had her skirt pulled up in full view of the entire school assembly, Esther gave her no sympathy whatsoever. I remember it like it was yesterday. Deana ran from the school hall in floods of tears, and Esther turned to me, rolled her big, brown eyes and called them crocodile tears.

"She was asking for it. Wearing those red knickers. She obviously wanted someone to see them."

If Esther is a feminist, I'm a fucking astronaut.

CHAPTER 6

Libby.

It's hard not to be intimidated by Bacchus. It's huge. I mean, *she's* huge. Are boats still referred to as *she* when given a male name? I guess they are. Hey, it's the twenty-first century: Bacchus can be any gender he or she wishes. I'll stick with *she*. That's what Esther does, and I don't want to – Sorry, I can't resist – I don't want to rock the boat.

Bacchus screams wealth and indulgence. My first thought when we stepped on board was, *I don't belong here*. The saloon's kitted out in white leather and pale, bleached wood. Beech perhaps? Maple? Shimmering white tiles cover the floor and spotlights twinkle above. Long windows run the length of the saloon and galley. On the far side of the saloon, above the chart table is a framed photo of Esther when she would have been nine or ten years old. She's with her parents outside St. Mary Magdalene's Church in Sandringham. It's a well-known photograph. A number of other young royals, ones much higher in the line of succession, are in the background, and it was printed in *Hello, OK!* and *Take a Break* magazines to name a few. A bookshelf runs under one of the panoramic windows. It's filled with hardback atlases, The Oxford Dictionary of Quotations, Jack London and Agatha Christie.

When we were training for our competent crew and day skipper qualifications, we used a boat named Juniper. The saloon area was tiny; there was barely enough room to fit four people around the table. The kitchen area was made up of a stove and a sink and not much more. Having never been on a yacht before, I thought Juniper was spectacular. Bacchus has blown her out of the water – so to speak. I don't know why my brain keeps insisting on all these water idioms. I must be nervous. This saloon has space for at least twelve, and the table can expand to triple its size. There's a separate galley area with all the mod-cons and high-end appliances.

Esther has put on a real feast. Locally sourced olives, sun-dried tomatoes, all sorts of cheeses, hummus and dips. Gleaming wine glasses are handed out and filled to the brim with something labelled Petrakopolous Mov. The diamond-cut crystal twinkles under the spotlights, casting tiny flickers of light all around us.

"Daddy knows the growers," Esther says when she sees I'm reading the label on the bottle. "The vines are from the sixties." She holds up her glass and pauses until we all do as she does. "In vino veritas."

That was our old way of saying cheers. It's pretty lame hearing it now as a grown-up, but back then I thought Esther was oh so sophisticated with her Latin words and cut-glass voice.

"In vino veritas," we echo as our glasses touch.

In wine, there is truth.

* * *

With bellies full and heads foggy, thoughts turn to the sleeping arrangements.

"There are four double berths," Esther tells us. "Plus the saloon. It converts into another double."

Verona begins to tidy our glasses and dishes to the galley.

"Leave those, V. We'll get shipshape in the morning. Now, I already claimed the port aft cabin," Esther says, pointing to the rear of the yacht. "It has an ensuite."

Mabel cranes her neck. "I spy another bathroom. Bagsy the aft starboard."

Jo picks up her holdall and tosses it into a cabin to the front of the boat. "Bow port side."

Paige and Verona both race to hoy their bags in the remaining cabin at the front on the left-hand side. Paige gets there first.

"That's fine," Verona says. "I don't mind having the saloon." Though it certainly sounds like she does.

That leaves me. Last again. One of these days I'll assert myself rather than letting everyone else go first, but today is not that day. "Okay, who can I bunk with?" I ask, feeling awkward.

There's an uncomfortable silence. Of course no one wants to share. Why would they? Even on a yacht this size, space is limited.

Verona's the first to answer. "Not me."

Eyes flicker to each other as everyone picks up on her tone. I guess I'm not forgiven.

"I'd offer you half my bed," says Mabel. She has the look on her face that she gets when she wants to make the conversation all about her. "But I'm not sure you'd be able to keep your hands to yourself."

This is typical Mabel. She thinks everyone is in love with her. How wrong she is. Unlike Paige, who can be one of the sweetest people imaginable, Mabel's beauty is only skin deep.

Paige opens her mouth and I hope to God she's about to say I can bunk in with her. Of the six of us, she's probably the one I trust the most, but before Paige can save me from this embarrassment, Esther pipes up, "How silly of me. There's the crew cabin. It's a single birth, so a tad on the cosy side but you'll easily fit, Libs. What are you? Five-two?"

I hate being called Libs. My mother used to call me that, but I can let it go, given Esther's offering me a lifeline. My own space? That sounds perfect. It might be cosy, but having to share a cabin would be difficult in this heat. Not to mention awkward. There's no way to share a double berth and not have your legs touch during the night.

"Slight catch," starts Esther, "you have to access it through a hatch on the deck. Think of it as your own private entrance. Follow me."

I can practically feel Verona smirking as I follow Esther on deck. It's dark now. Fiskardo has gone to sleep. Across the bay, an old lighthouse emits a beacon every few seconds, and mooring lights reflect in the still water. "You should be clipped on," she says as we traverse past the saloon's portholes and head towards the bow. "Safety first. I'll get you some cables in the morning." She opens the hatch, and I peer in.

Cosy is obviously code for *tiny*. The crew cabin has the smallest bed I've ever seen, a plastic toilet, a mirror and that's about it. Trust the McPherson's to house crew in a cabin that's smaller than your average dog crate. A lightweight ladder folds down, and as I descend, I feel for a moment like I'm going caving. Not that I ever would. I'm not good with confined spaces, or the dark for that matter, so potholes would be my idea of hell. Wow. Now that I'm in here, my instincts were right; I'm in a subterranean, windowless hell.

Esther smiles down at me. "Sweet dreams, darling. Light switch is on the left."

And with that, the hatch closes, and I'm plunged into darkness. My hands scramble across the cabin wall. Did she say left? My left, or her left? Why wouldn't she say port? For all her blasted sailor speak … Faster my hands move, banging against a shelf and who knows what else. I can't even find the clasp to open the hatch again. I'm trapped. I'm ready to scream for Esther to come back when my fingers find something smooth and round with a small pin poking out of it. I flip the pin sideways, and harsh light floods the room. I cover my eyes with my hand as I adjust to the brightness.

I'm such an idiot for coming here. I knew I shouldn't have. I thought these girls were my friends, but I was always the outsider, the one on the fringe of the group. I was too different to really be one of them. They'll be lying in their cabins now, or having showers in their ensuites before bed. My hands are still pressed into the walls, arms not fully stretched, back hunched, the crown of my head brushing the ceiling.

My vision blurs at the edges. Darkness creeps into my peripheral.

It's a panic attack. I can't breathe.

This isn't a cabin.

It's a coffin.

– CHAPTER 7 –

Paige.

I didn't sleep well. In fact, I'm not sure I slept at all. Bacchus bobbed back and forth all night. She was secured correctly, but you'll never get a yacht to stay completely still – the sea doesn't work like that. Then there's the heat. I've worked in some hot places before: Abu Dhabi, Cancun, Seoul. But in destinations like those, you hop from one air-conditioned building to the next. Man, I'm starting to sound spoiled. I need to nip that in the bud. I have a television opportunity coming up, one that I can't afford to screw up. If I do well, it could really help my family out. I could pay off my parent's credit cards, get Grams an upgrade on her sheltered accommodation, and we have some medical bills that need taking care of. It won't go down well with the public if I go on like a princess and complain about things like heat, bugs or humidity. So what if it's warm on Bacchus and I couldn't sleep? It's not like I sleep well when I'm away from home anyway. Plus, I know fine well it ain't the temperature or the movement of the boat in the water that kept me awake – it's the feeling of exposure. I don't feel secure without bricks and mortar. I've *glamped* in some lovely places: yurts, tents, houseboats, shepherd's huts. But I've never had a full night's sleep in any of them. Perhaps Mum or Dad read The Three Little Pigs to me one too many times. If a place doesn't have stone walls and five locks on the door, I won't feel safe. Bacchus is a beast, but it wouldn't take much to force open the companionway doors, and I'm not even sure Esther locked them correctly before we all went to bed. We were all hammered by that point. But who would want to break in? The local population rely on tourists coming by boat, and last night it looked like most people left their boats open and unattended. The thought of anyone trying to board Bacchus suddenly reminds me of the newspaper headline about the pirates. Jesus, if pirates boarded Bacchus, we'd be done for. Suppose they realised there was royalty aboard, or me, or even Verona – she's CEO of a big brand. In that case, they wouldn't merely steal our belongings, we'd be taken as hostages.

Good grief. I need to get a grip. I'm going to give myself anxiety, and as for these giant bags under my eyes, there's nothing caffeinated eye cream can't fix.

After my turn in the shared bathroom, sorry, *the heads* – got to get used to using sailor speak again – I find Esther and the girls on deck. Esther unfolds the table and spreads some charts of the Ionian Sea in preparation for a morning briefing. This is where Esther shines. If I know one thing about Esther McPherson, when she takes on the role of skipper, she makes sure things go to plan. She'll be prepared.

Jo lifts two silver containers and with a warm smile she mouths, "tea or coffee?"

I yawn before I can answer, which turns out to be all the answer she needs.

"Coffee for my favourite Cockney."

Jo seems more relaxed than she had yesterday at the bar. Perhaps she's already feeling the benefits of being away from her cheating fiancé. Maybe she just got a good night's sleep.

"Right, ladies," Esther begins when we've all taken our seats. "We need to be in Gaios by tomorrow evening. So, we can either go slightly further today and head to Lefkada town, or we can have a more relaxing first day and only go as far as Nidri."

We lean in and follow Esther's index finger as she traces a route that heads north, then east, then north again up the eastern side of Lefkas. Her index and middle fingers tap on our options of Nidri, halfway up the island, and Lefkada Town which sits at the northernmost point.

"Wind?" asks Mabel between sips of tea.

"Northwesterlies today. Twos gusting threes, increasing to threes gusting fours in the afternoon. Tomorrow's better with westerlies starting at fours but getting up to fives after lunch."

Mabel nods as she takes in the information, a slight curl to her lips at the thought of force five winds. Force five tends to be the sweet spot. Fast enough to have fun, not so fast you're holding on for dear life.

"You're the boss," she says with a shrug, "but I think the answer's obvious."

"Then it's settled," Esther says. "We take an easy jaunt up to Nidri today, then put in the hours tomorrow when the wind is on our side." She points to some dotted lines on the chart. "We have some major ferry dodging to contend with early on, but that will ease when we pass Arkoudi island, and you should be aware there's a one-metre swell."

Jo pours everyone a top-up. "We're Pier Pressure. Since when were we afraid of a bit of swell?"

* * *

With us all agreed on a destination and a course, Jo unties Bacchus from her moorings while Libby raises the anchor. We're off! Mabel hoots with excitement as we head east into the channel between Kefalonia and Ithaca. It's been a few years, but the sensation of being on the water again feels like a homecoming. This is what we do.

There are two lighthouses on the headland: a modern one, and one from the Venetian era that sits closer to the shore. We haven't even passed the first one when Mabel strips down to her bikini. She's wearing one of those micro bikinis that just about cover your nipples and require you to have had a Brazilian wax. I've had to wear some tiny swimsuits on photoshoots before but nothing like that. I watch her as she scans about to see who's looking. When Libby looks up from securing the bow locker, Mabel presses her boobs together and winks at her. This is standard Mabel behaviour; she's never been shy about showing a bit of skin. I turn just in time to catch the look on Libby's face. She has dark brown eyes, but I swear they just turned black. She looks like she could throttle Mabel.

I love Libby, but I'm not sure what her problem is. Luckily there's a lot for us to be getting on with, so I don't need to worry about whatever's going unsaid between my friends. I'm tasked with bringing in the fenders. Fenders are basically portable bumpers that look like bolster cushions. They're used to absorb the impact between boat and jetty when moored side to, or to protect one boat from another.

"Esther," I call from the starboard, "I thought you said it was a one-metre swell?"

"It is," she calls back.

Beyond the safety of the bay, it looks as if the water rises up like a concrete wall of darker blue. That's no one-metre swell. Jo was right earlier; I'm not afraid of a bit of swell. Not two metres of the stuff anyway. But I do need to move quickly and get the fenders in before I start getting thrown about. They're heavier than expected. I suppose a big boat needs big fenders.

"No one said I'd have to do weight training," I joke.

Esther's at the helm. She looks the part in her navy and white striped shorts and an anchor-shaped necklace. "Don't be dramatic, darling. I've seen you carry two four-pint pitchers in each hand before."

I laugh at the memory and just about get the last fender in the locker as the swell kicks in and sends me tumbling into Jo.

"Woah. I've got you," she says, catching me. "Trouble finding your sea legs?"

I'm out of practice.

I form the warp ropes into neat coils and store them under the seats in the cockpit, wobbling as I do so. Jo and Verona unfurl the mainsail, and Libby heads below deck to wash up our breakfast items.

Once the basics are taken care of, I can relax into a seat, knowing most of the sail trim work will be handled by Mabel and Jo. Bacchus may be rising up and down like the front car on a rollercoaster, but I'm safe in the cockpit, so I think it's time I strip down to my bikini as well. It's too lovely a day not to feel the sun on my skin. I take my time applying sunscreen, making sure not to miss anywhere. I use factor fifty. Most of the girls will end up with lovely tans but not me. My skin can't handle the sun; I'm a pale redhead. I was teased mercilessly for it at school. I was called Little Orphan Annie, Carrot Top, Freckle Face, I was even called Lamppost because I was tall and skinny and orange on top. Kids are cruel. Hell, adults are cruel. The mean kids don't grow up, they just get bigger. One boy who made life hell when we were thirteen had the cheek to contact me on Instagram last year to *see if I remembered him and if I'd like to get a drink one evening*. I replied with a string of laughing emojis and took great delight in blocking him.

Within a couple of hours, we've safely traversed the straight between northern Kefalonia and the southern tip of Lefkada. Esther wasn't kidding when she said we'd be ferry-dodging. I counted at least twenty passenger ferries, but we managed to avoid them all and remain under sail. We're hoping to reach the island of Meganisi by lunchtime, but it seems like the wind is beginning to drop. Jo tightens the mainsail, trying to get the most out of the little breeze that we have.

Esther curses – which always amuses me because I'm sure there are rules about her swearing in public – and twenty minutes later, Bacchus comes to a stop.

"Doldrums," she growls as if it's another swear word. "This wasn't in the forecast."

"Unbelievable," says Jo with her usual dry sarcasm. "I can't believe the weather forecasters got it wrong. I mean, what are the chances?"

Esther, frustrated, goes to switch the engine on but Verona stops her.

"Wait. It's so peaceful. Let's just enjoy the silence for a moment. No wind, no engine. It's almost magical."

Esther scoffs. "Magical? I knew behind that boardroom haircut and shoulder pads you'd still be a hummus-loving hippy. Okay, sweetheart, we'll enjoy the magical silence for a while."

If Verona objects to being called a hummus-loving hippy, she doesn't show it. Esther is clearly itching to get going again. I don't know why she's in such a hurry; we're not in a race. But, Esther's a perfectionist. Race or no race, if she has a time in mind, she'll hate not achieving it. The rest of us lay back, and you know what? Verona's right; it is sort of magical to be here in the quiet. None of us will admit it, but even after just a few hours of swell, it's nice to have a rest from it. There's no lapping of water against the hull, no wind in my hair, not even the distant squawk of a gull or a tern. It's tranquil.

I catch Esther's eye. "Hand me the binoculars, Skip."

She loves being called Skip or Skipper. The binoculars are excellent quality – like everything on Bacchus – and they must weigh a good kilo and half. I scan about enjoying the scenery and hoping to spot pelicans or – pretty please – a dolphin. Meganisi rises out of the haze, as do two other islands that lay behind it: Kalamos and Kastos. It's so green. I wonder how much water falls here to support so much flora. I can see another yacht off in the distance, and I play with the focus until I can see the people on board. Four men. Three are busy furling their sails, and the fourth is—

I gasp. The fourth man has his own pair of binoculars, and he's looking straight back at me.

The binoculars fall into the cockpit with a bang.

"Careful!"

"Sorry, Esther. It's just the guys on that yacht are looking at us. It freaked me out."

Mabel grabs the binoculars, looks, waves and blows a kiss in their direction.

"Stop it," I hiss.

I feel exposed again. Who are they? They could be perverts, or worse, paparazzi.

Instinctively, I pull on a baggy t-shirt and shorts, but Mabel doesn't look impressed.

"Relax, Paige. They're just tourists. Probably in the same boat as we are. Excuse the pun. Bored in the doldrums."

That's probably the case, but if they are paparazzi they'll ruin this trip, and that's not fair on the other girls. I feel nauseous, and I know it can't be seasickness. It's the god-awful love-hate relationship I have with the press. We need each other. They get clickbait; I stay in the limelight. But fuck me, they can be so intrusive and rude at times. They're like vultures, feeding off the moments when I'm most vulnerable.

Is Paige Vaughn pregnant? They wrote after I gained a mere kilogram. It drives me crazy. They'll write a headline like that one day and accuse me of setting a bad example to young girls and encouraging eating disorders the next. *Paige Vaughn's Acne Hell.* Urgh. I'd had a terrible breakout last summer due to stress. Stress those damn vultures had caused by camping outside my apartment building for three days straight. *Paige Vaughn Crashes Car.* I was trying to lose the journalist that was tailing me to a hospital appointment.

The sickness moves further up my throat when I think about that one. I guess what it comes down to is that I need the paparazzi to stay relevant, that doesn't mean I have to like their methods. They're like stalkers, no actually, at least stalkers have the decency to hide most of the time. Those close to me – my family and friends – know how I feel about this, and yet they're the ones most likely to sell a story for a quick buck. I have to turn my head away and keep my eyes on the sea while I focus on not welling up. I can put up with a lot of things, betrayal isn't one of them.

– CHAPTER 8 –

Jo.

Once the water calmed and our passage smoothed, I'd made my way to the bow of the boat to have a little space to myself. With legs danged over the edge and the latest Mari Hannah thriller in my hands, I felt peaceful for the first time since wandering around the Roman cemetery. Paige, Verona and Libby like romance, Mabel doesn't hide the fact she reads erotica, and Esther's more about the classics, but I prefer murder, mystery and things that go bump in the night. I'm sure Paige is just being dramatic about our neighbours on the other yacht. Still, curiosity has got the better of me, so I put the thriller down and make my way back to the stern.

"It's probably nothing," I say as I take the binoculars.

Despite my reassurance, she repositions herself, turning her back in their direction. I count four guys.

They're youngish, mid-to-late twenties I'd say. The one securing the sheets is dark and very fetching, like a young George Clooney in his ER days. Another looks to be reading at the bow of the boat, just as I had been doing. He's broad, tanned, and has a shaved head. The guy with the binoculars has sandy hair and a good build. He's wearing a pair of green shorts and nothing else. He must have lost interest in us because his gaze is pointed towards the island of Meganisi. I watch as he tilts the binoculars slowly upwards, looking from flat waterline to the tree-covered crest of the hill.

"They're not looking at us anymore," I tell Paige.

"Good," she replies, but she still doesn't look back or remove her extra layers.

The sandy-haired guy, lowers the binocs, wipes his brow, and turns to speak to the George Clooney look-alike.

I stifle a shriek.

My mouth dries up. He looks just like Frederick. It can't be, though. Can it? I must be seeing things. How could Frederick possibly know where to find me? I vowed I wouldn't go to the police if he promised to stay away from me.

I hand the binoculars back to Paige and swallow. "They're just tourists."

I hope.

Esther.

Zephyrus, the west wind, must have heard my prayers as the sails are filling once more. We don't need a lot of wind to get going. The girls and I are more than capable of getting the most out of what little wind we have. If the wind is only two knots – but it's coming from the right angle – guaranteed we can get Bacchus to do three, maybe even four knots. I'm not one for science, I was always more of an arts or linguistics kind of girl, but physics really is marvellous when it comes to sailing.

It's comforting to see everyone falling back into their old roles. Jo is already tending to the mainsail, and Mabel reads the water like a charm, pointing out the gusts as they approach. We'll need to tack soon, which in plain English, means we'll be turning. It's not as simple as turning a car, you don't just slow to second, check your mirrors, indicate and go.

"Ready about?" I call.

"Ready," they answer.

I turn the helm, Paige waits for the right moment to release the genoa sheet and Verona pulls as fast and as powerfully as she can on a purple rope. When the sail has switched positions, she wraps it around a silver drum, attaches a wrench and tightens the sail until I say stop. They execute it seamlessly, and I swell with pride. I'm glad I got the old crew back together.

It takes another hour to reach Meganisi. I've always wanted to visit the Papanikolis cave on the peninsular, so seeing as we're here and have plenty of time, I drop anchor about twenty metres from the mouth of the cave. I lower a ladder from the bathing platform into the water and ask, "Who's up for a swim?"

With all eyes on me, I slide out of my t-shirt and shorts, turn and dive into the turquoise sea. Within seconds, Mabel has jumped in next to me. Libby and Paige exchange a look, run, and cannonball into the water, causing a huge splash that forms a tidal wave over my head.

Libby hollers up to Jo, "You coming in? The water's not too cold."

Jo shakes her head. "Not today. You enjoy. I'll fix us some lunch."

Jo's wrapped up in a palm-print kaftan. I hope she's not still giving herself a hard time about her figure. You should have heard the way she'd describe herself when we were at uni. When we went dress shopping for prom, she said she looked like a transvestite Mr Blobby. I know it's easier said than done, but she should focus on her positives. Do you know how many people would kill to have her brain or her work ethic? Hey, some people would kill for her eyelashes.

It hurt when Jo got engaged and didn't tell me. I only found out because I read the announcement her parents put in the paper. It stung to not hear it from her, and now I find out from Mabel that the engagement's been called off. Am I the last to hear everything? Her fiancé, this Frederick chap, well I only met him a handful of times, and that was a few years ago now, but he didn't really seem her type. He's one of those slicked-back city types who use phrases like *let's circle back*, *I just wanted to touch base,* and *let's park that project for now*. Also, he's a year younger than Jo and Jo has always preferred older men, even when we were little kids. When we were six-years-old, I found her in my treehouse showing eight-year-old Andre Parker her swimsuit area. Jo would be much better suited to an older, more rugged and rural type.

Libby dives under the water and emerges seconds later. "This place is brilliant. What did you say it was was called again? Oh, look at all the fish!"

"Papanikolis. It's named after a submarine that used the cave to evade the Germans in the first world war."

"Cool."

This time it's Mabel who takes a deep breath before rolling forward and diving under while the rest of us swim further into the hole.

I can't imagine what it must have been like for the men on the Papanikolis. The cave is impressive, but it hardly seems big enough to hide a submarine. It must have been terrifying.

Paige is so far into the cave her feet reach the bottom. She stands and looks to the roof of the cave. "There aren't any bats in here are there?"

"God, I hope not," says Libby. "I hate bats."

Treading water, I scan around me. Mabel's been under the water an awfully long time. Well over a minute, maybe two. "Girls, where's Mabel?"

"MABEL?" Paige calls, only for the name to echo around the cavern walls and scare a pair of bats out from their roost. Libby squeals and covers her head as they zoom past.

"This isn't funny. Where is she?" I brought everyone here; I feel a sense of responsibility to make sure they go home in one piece. I'm about to dive under when I feel a sudden pull on my big toe and almost wet myself with fright. I kick out in wild panic, trying to shout *SHARK*, but only managing, "Sh – Sh – "

Mabel pops her head back out of the water. "I just saw an octopus! Must have been a foot long."

I slap my hands into the water and splash her over and over. "You. Scared. Me. Half. To. Death."

As we swim back towards Bacchus, Paige, Libby and Mabel hum the theme from Jaws over and over.

"Did you really think I was a shark?"

"No."

"You did, didn't you?"

I splash her again. "Maybe for a millisecond."

When we reach Bacchus, Jo hands us towels as we climb aboard, and lunch is ready and waiting. A tasty-looking Greek salad with feta cheese and plenty of red onion and olives. Lovely. Verona is at the bow, waving her phone around as she looks for a signal. She was the same before bed last night, checking her share prices and replying to emails from board members. I hardly recognise her anymore. She used to be so clingy and shy. She needed me.

In our university days, Verona wouldn't say boo to a goose, but now she's some powerful businesswoman? She used to dress like a … How can I best describe it? Like a monochrome hippy? Imagine watching a documentary on the hippies of the seventies, only it's filmed in black and white. That was Verona. Long flowing skirts and vest tops, baggy cardigans and floral prints, but always muted greys and faded beige. I often wondered if she was trying to be invisible with such an austere colour palette. Now when I look at her, she seems chic in her designer labels. Nothing brash or anything that screams *look at me*, just timeless elegance and quality fabrics. Blacks, golds and clean, sophisticated cuts. She has her own brand of vegan ice cream and was doing well on her own, but things really took off when she went on Dragon's Den and three of the Dragon's started fighting over her. She had them in quite the bidding war and ended up with twice the investment she'd initially asked for. The publicity helped her seal a deal with Tesco, Sainsbury's and ASDA and I heard some of the US stores are interested too. Verona was even featured on the posters and in the television adverts, which I guess makes her sort of famous. People don't stop her in the street like they do with Paige, but they do a double-take. They know they know her from somewhere, they're just not sure where.

I pat myself dry and wring the excess water from my hair. At uni, I was the one people looked at and had hushed conversations about. I was the one people called exotic and regal. Not anymore. Have I really become the plain one?

CHAPTER 9

Verona.

It's gone five when we approach Nidri. We could have arrived much earlier, but it was lovely to drift in the low winds for a while. There's something quite freeing about letting the current take you where it pleases, to give in and let the water make the decisions. I check the charts. The island off our starboard side is called Skorpios, which makes it sound like the lair of some sort of Bond villain if you ask me. As we near, I take a closer look. Signs warn against mooring, and … is that an armed guard patrolling the beach? It is. I recoil at the sight of the heavy-looking machine gun. I grew up in the countryside, so I'm used to shotguns, but semi-automatic weapons are not part and parcel of everyday life in Britain. I've only seen them in airports up until now. I wonder how many bullets that thing can fire in a single second.

"What's the deal with Skorpios?" I ask Esther, nodding my head towards the island.

"Russian billionaire," she says matter of factly while inspecting a fingernail.

Interesting. Couldn't be more Bond-villainesque if they tried.

"He clearly likes his privacy," I say.

"Hmm. I heard they have frogmen patrolling the water around the island."

"Whatever for?" I ask Esther.

She shrugs. "Keep out the hoi polloi?"

This seems excessive, but I can't muse on it for too long. The water around Bacchus is lightening through various shades of blue, meaning we are leaving the deeper waters and are entering the bay. Esther radios ahead to arrange a berth for us on one of the pontoons. Within seconds it's clear there's a language barrier, so with big, pleading eyes, she hands me the VHF radio. "Can you do the honours, darling?"

Once I've said "Out" – it's always *out* and never *over and out* – I call across to Esther. "End of the jetty opposite the chandlery. Set up stern-to."

She winks at me. "My favourite polyglot," and I actually glow inwardly at being called her favourite anything.

The sails are furled, the fenders secured, and the anchor dropped. As Esther brings us in, I jump ashore and connect us to the nearest cleat. The sun is lower now, and I take a moment to appreciate the slight drop in temperature and the subtle change in the colour of the sky. Most people won't notice, but there's the tiniest hint of orange.

While the others finish off the jobs onboard, I nip to the nearest bar and buy six cans of Mythos from a cheerful young man with dreadlocks and a tattoo of the ban the bomb logo. He probably thinks I'm some stuck up Brit given my pasty skin, sensible haircut and grown-up blouse, but unbeknownst to him, I have the same tattoo. Yes, Verona Appleton, of Lazy Llama Foods, has a ban the bomb tattoo on her butt. I giggle to myself as I walk back to the marina – the cans uncomfortably cold in my hands – and think of a time not too long ago when I couldn't dream of buying a round of drinks. I could never afford it. I grew up in the outskirts of Cambridge, in a small village called Cottenham. It was an affluent area overall, but not so for my family; we struggled and often relied on government subsidies. At university, I stayed out of rounds and usually bought myself the cheapest cider available. Esther wouldn't hear of it, of course. She'd buy me a glass of fizz here and a bottle of bubbly there, and I'd always pull this *I'm-grateful-but-you-shouldn't-have* face, then she'd hug me and say, "Sweetie, it's nothing. You can buy me a drink when you're rich and successful."

When you're rich and successful. Never *if*. It was like Esther always had faith in me.

I look at the green can of Mythos, condensation trickling down the sides, and burst into laughter. I will have to buy her some Dom Pérignon at some point, but for now, a can of perfectly chilled lager will do.

We gather on a patch of grass between hotels and sit cross-legged in a line. The whooshing noise as we open the cans flutters from Libby on the left to me on the right, like a Mexican wave of thirst-quenching goodness. A boy and girl jog along the road in front of us, kicking a football back and forth between them. Two men in their sixties are fishing from the shore, and a boy on a bike goes door-to-door selling sea urchins to the tavernas.

"Ooh, they've got a bite," Libby says, pointing to the fishermen and we watch, holding our breath as they reel it in.

Mabel's eyebrows shoot up into her forehead. "Look at the size of that!"

"That's what she said," Paige taunts only to be punched on the arm by Mabel.

The taller man pulls the fish from its hook – it's over a foot in length – grabs it by the tail and whacks it off a rock to stun it before going to work with his knife.

I cover my mouth. "Oh, Jesus."

"Urgh," says Mabel, scrunching up her nose.

"You *urgh*, but I bet you order fish tonight," Esther says, draining her can and going to find a bin.

71

She's right. She usually is. I bet all the girls order seafood. Why wouldn't they in a place like this?

"Jovitha?" Mabel's eyes hone in on Jo. "You're a vet. What's it like killing an animal?"

What a question. I shudder at the macabre query and at how easily she asks it. Jo does too. She's quiet, as if stealing herself or as if she's fighting a memory.

"It's … draining," she finally answers. "You can tell yourself that you're doing it for the right reasons, that the animal's in pain, that you're ending its suffering, but it's still fucking draining."

I watch Jo's face as she says all this and I can relate. I don't say anything, but I know how she feels. I know how it feels to take a life.

* * *

Esther's chosen a cute little taverna for dinner, but apparently, we have to nip into somewhere called Tree Bar first. She says it's the law – a local institution. Mabel is thrilled to hear we're going to a bar and changes into a little black dress and a sparkling pair of heels. The rest of us opt for flat shoes and clothes that keep the mozzies off us.

Tree Bar doesn't seem like the sort of place Esther would usually be seen. Perhaps that's why she's so keen to go there. With no elders here to watch her every move and critique how it will affect *the firm*, she might want to make the most of it. I could do with a little of that spirit myself. The bar is, as you may have guessed, built around a tree. A roulette wheel is marked with a variety of drinks from tomato juice to a bottle of prosecco. As if the wheel is possessed, it somehow awards me – the purveyor of vegan foods – a tomato juice. Paige – the model – gets a glass of water. Mabel – the party girl – spins the wheel and is handed a rum and coke. And Esther – royalty – beams when the pointer lands on prosecco. Jo and Libby both win pints of lager. Libby shares hers with Paige, and Jo shares hers with me. Despite my fondness for salad, I have no time for tomato juice. I think it tastes of dirt.

Drinks polished off, apart from the tomato juice, we make our way to dinner. A waiter sits us near the window and tells us it's the best table in the house. As the sun lowers towards the horizon and lights begin to twinkle across the bay, I have a feeling he's right. From here we'll be able to see the moon and stars reflecting on the still water of the anchorage.

"Do you have any organic wine?" Esther asks.

"Yes, madam. From Santorini, very nice with shellfish."

"Two bottles, please, and can we get a seafood sharing platter to start, oh and your best salad." She squeezes me on the shoulder.

This is classic Esther, just going ahead and ordering on our behalf. I'm not offended or anything; I like organic wine, and I'm pleased she remembered to order something I can eat. Still, Mabel may have liked another rum and coke, and I think Jo wanted another lager.

When my salad arrives, it turns out to be vegetarian rather than vegan, but I just pick out the cheese and put it to one side. I'm not the sort to make a song and dance about it or start manically tweeting the Vegan Society. I'm not a militant vegan; I drink lager and I've been known to have honey now and again. The salad is delicious and compliments the wine. It's funny, I feel so much more like my old self here. Don't get me wrong, part of me still wants to nip to the loo to quietly check my emails and make sure the entire company hasn't fallen apart in my brief absence. Still, it's a part that's getting smaller and smaller with each passing hour. I never used to be so obsessed with work, but it's become a bit of a comfort blanket of late – a distraction – something for me to focus on, because the truth is, I'm lonely.

Our waiter clears our plates, and I catch Mabel checking out his rear as he walks away.

"What?" she asks, placing her hand on her chest and feigning innocence.

Somethings never change.

He returns in a while with our mains. "Erm … the, how you say … aubergine?"

Mabel points in my direction. "That would be our vegan friend." I see the fire in her eyes begin to burn as her wicked side kicks in. "But wait, aren't you vegetarian as well, Libby?"

Libby puts her drink down. "No. You know I'm not."

"But we all know you don't like a good piece of meat."

Libby's face flushes with hurt, or maybe it's anger. I don't think Mabel is deliberately acting homophobic. In her head, she's just being a tease, but that's the problem with Mabel, she never thinks what it's like to be in someone else's head.

"Sorry, I don't understand," says the waiter. "Did I bring the wrong meal?"

Mabel places her hand on his arm and beams at him. "No, dear. I was just making a joke about my friend not liking …" she lowers her voice to a stage whisper, "penises."

Esther coughs. "Oh, Mabel. Do behave."

The waiter goes a little pink, but Mabel just can't contain herself. "I do though," she adds with a wink.

I roll my eyes and look away. I can't watch. Plus, I kind of feel sorry for Libby. I've always hated teasing and bullying, and for a moment, I think about saying something, she's gone all quiet, stabbing at her food with her fork and I think I can see a tear in her eye – but I won't. Mabel might be a piece of work, but Libby isn't the innocent little northerner she likes to make out she is.

CHAPTER 10

Paige.

Dinner was fab. I really enjoyed it. Most people think I don't eat, or that if I do eat, I throw it up afterwards. Most people are wrong; I have an incredible appetite. We feasted on prawns, lobster and scallops, but it was actually the grilled sardines served with nothing but olive oil and a lemon wedge that stole the show. They tasted so fresh. I wouldn't be surprised if they were caught less than an hour ago. That's one downside to living in London. We think we have good seafood – we certainly have some outstanding restaurants – but the second we get somewhere like this we discover the truth; there's nothing quite like being at the seaside.

As the meal went on, we seemed to naturally fall into pairs. Libby chatted with Esther, and Jo and Verona were deep in conversation about politics and the economy, and I had a good chinwag with Mabel about – you guessed it – boys. I can fully understand her attraction to Jorge, our waiter. He's broad with inky black hair and a chiselled jawline. With smooth skin and full lips, I'm sure my agent would scoop him up in a heartbeat. He's also twenty at the most and possibly as young as seventeen. God, I hope he just looks young for his age. It's creepy otherwise.

As we finish up our fifth, yes fifth, bottle of wine, Esther announces, "I'll get this, ladies. To say thank you for a great day's sailing."

"You don't have to do that," Verona says, reaching for her purse.

She puts her hands together in prayer. "Please. Let the skipper treat her wonderful crew."

Verona puts her purse down. "Okay, but tomorrow we should form a kitty for meals and the like."

Esther claps with glee and asks Jorge for our bill. He brings it promptly and returns to the bar to pour drinks for other diners. Almost as soon as Esther drops the euros onto the little silver tray, Mabel swoops in and scoops it up. She heads for the bar with an actual spring in her high-heeled step. I chuckle then listen into Jo and Verona's conversation about the recent collapse of a FTSE 500 company.

"The marine energy sector's worth over seventy billion worldwide. It's no wonder people are fighting to invest. Everyone wants a slice of that pie," Verona says between sips of what remains of her wine.

Jo shakes her head. "Imagine securing the bid to make the biggest tidal energy project in UK history and having it all pulled out from under you?"

"With images like that found on company servers? Rowan Glover's getting what he deserves." Verona turns to Esther. "DYH Triton are stepping in to finish the Solway Barrage. Isn't that one of your father's assets?"

I'm half listening, half watching Mabel. She's leaning over the bar suggestively. Jorge is blushing and tugging at the collar on his shirt.

Esther frowns. "Who knows, darling. He buys this, sells that. I can't keep up half the time."

"Well, according to the Financial Times, DYH Triton is going to make a fortune now Gimenez Energy has folded. All their existing sites will need to be maintained, there're the contracts they can't honour …"

Mabel beckons Jorge closer with a curl of her index finger and whispers something in his ear. The poor boy runs a hand over his face and looks unsure, then he turns to a coworker to ask something.

"Might have to buy a few shares myself. Renewables are only going to keep rising."

Jorge picks up his jacket and comes out from behind the bar. He slips a hand around Mabel's waist, and they share a flirty kiss.

"Are you seeing this?" I ask the others.

"We can't miss it," jokes Esther.

Libby drains her glass and says in a low voice, "Un-fucking-believable."

Esther nudges her and gives her a smile that infers *chin up*.

"She's going to take him back to Bacchus," Libby warns.

Esther shakes her head. "No, she isn't. She'd ask us first."

"Then why are they walking off towards the marina?"

"Oh for goodness sake," says Verona at the exact same time as Jo grunts, "Shit."

We grudgingly get to our feet and follow the love birds, cringing when they squeeze each other's butt cheeks as they walk.

* * *

It's cold on deck, but Esther retrieves some blankets from one of the many storage compartments and rustles up a round of gin and tonics. It's not like we can sit in the saloon below deck; yacht walls are thin, and we'd be able to hear everything. As it stands, we can still hear a fair amount. At least the companion-way doors do a reasonably good job of muffling the louder grunts and groans.

"They sound like they're killing each other," says Jo. She looks at Libby – who's shaking like a leaf now that the temperature has dropped – removes her blanket and tucks it around the little brunette.

"Stop it," laughs Esther, "I just managed to zone them out. In my head, I'm singing sea shanties on repeat."

"At least it's a clear night," says Libby. A pale arm slinks its way out of her double layer of blankets and points towards the sky. "There's Orion. See the three bright stars? That's his belt, and the hourglass shape around it is his body. If you follow that line of stars, that's a sword he's holding above his head, and in his other hand, he has a shield. And there's the big dipper—"

"Ursa Major," Verona corrects her.

Esther nods and jingles the ice around her glass. "The Great Bear. I remember that myth from school. Do you remember, Jo?"

"Oh, yes. The pretty little nymph, Callisto, is dedicated to Artemis, goddess of the chaste. Of course, nothing is more attractive to dirty old Zeus than a woman who says she's not interested in sex. He gets Callisto pregnant, causing Artemis to banish her from their circle. When Callisto gives birth, Zeus's wife is so enraged that he's had yet another bastard child that she turns Callisto into a bear."

I laugh. "Little harsh. Shouldn't she punish her husband rather than the nymph?"

Esther shakes her head, but her eyes are still on the sky. "It's complicated. Gods can't really punish other gods." She adjusts her weight before continuing. "Callisto's son grew up to be a hunter. Naturally, one day he was out hunting and crossed paths with his mother in bear form. He was about to spear her when Zeus intervened, turning her son into the Little Bear – Ursa Minor, and cast them both into the sky where they could be together for eternity."

Libby's brows raise. "How do you know all this?"

"Classics," Esther explains. "Jo and I were in the same class at school."

"Oh. Classics wasn't on our curriculum. I thought it meant classic novels. Jane Austin, stuff like that."

Esther, Jo and Verona laugh. "Bless," Esther says condescendingly.

I'm with Libby on this one. I went to an inner-city school in London where we were being groomed for jobs in call centres and supermarkets. We didn't get to study classics; the teachers were too busy making sure no one got stabbed at the school gates. I hid all this when I got accepted into St. Andrews. I toned my accent down and, as far as anyone there knew, I went to a great school in Kensington. Once I did my first Paris Fashion Week, all the stories came out about my humble beginnings. I was rumbled. It taught me two valuable lessons: you can't hide from your past, and people can't keep secrets.

An epic groan erupts from below deck and we all wrinkle our noses. To distract us, Verona points to the heavens again. "I see your Ursa Major …" Her finger casts an arc across the starry sky. "… And raise you Venus."

"That's Venus?" I ask. I don't think I've ever seen another planet before. Not knowingly anyway. "It just looks like a really bright star."

"That's Venus, all right. Roman goddess of love and beauty." She pauses. "Do you speak French?"

"Enough to order room service."

"Well the Greeks and Romans named the seven days of the week after the seven brightest celestial bodies, and it's pretty much stuck for French, Italian and Spanish. Monday is the moon's day, or luna day, *Lundi*. *Mardi* is Mars' day. *Mercredi* is Mercury's day. *Jeundi* …"

By now I've got the point, but she keeps going, her voice increasing in volume to cover whatever is occurring below deck.

"And *Samedi* is Saturn's day. *Dimanche* or *Domingo* is the odd one out as the church didn't like all that sun worshipping and changed it to the Lord's day."

"But we kept Sunday as the sun's day?" I say it like it's a question but its really kind of obvious.

"We did," she says, her voice almost a shout. "Us Anglo-Saxons kept Saturn's day, sun's day and moon's day but we changed the others to honour of the Norse gods. Thursday is literally Thor's day, and another name for Odin is Wodan—"

"Wodan's day," I finish, just as Mabel and Jorge do so as well.

82

"Well, thank Wodan that's over," Libby grumbles. "Hopefully they don't go for round two."

Esther, perhaps out of some sense of duty – we're all here because of her – tries to keep the mood light. "Okay, so we know all about Mabel's love life. What about the rest of us? I'll go first. Single. Don't feel sorry for me, ladies, I'm single by choice. Focusing on my career."

I try not to scoff. *What career?* Esther's not cut out for real work, she never has been. Not that I can talk, all I have to do is smile when I'm told and walk and in a straight line. I know I offend other models when I break it down like that, and there is a lot more to it, but we're super fortunate to do what we do so I'm not going to pretend it's a chore. I worked three jobs at uni; *that* was a chore. But Esther lived off her parents. It's all she's ever known.

"Paige? Anyone special in your life?"

I squirm, because there is, sort of. "An on-again, off-again thing. I like him but …" I think how to word it, "… he wants to keep things casual."

"What's his name?"

"Omar," I answer and they all coo, all except Verona who gives me some sort of side-eye.

"Libby's turn. Fess up, darling. What's going on in your love life."

Libby's eyes flick across to either Jo or Verona then turn back to the sky for a moment. She huffs. "Cohabiting. We've been together a while now."

"Ooh!" Esther is beside herself with curiosity. "You never said! How romantic. What's her name?"

Libby shakes her head. "That's all you get for now."

"Oh, you tease. Come on, your secret's safe with me."

Bullshit. That's total bullshit. I don't blame Libby for wanting to hold something back from Esther. I swallow and realise I'm gripping my tumbler so hard I'm afraid it might shatter. I place it on the table and sit on my hands to stop them from shaking. I might not have studied the classics, but I am one for quotes, and Benjamin Franklin once said, *three may keep a secret, if two of them are dead.*

* * *

Jorge avoids eye contact as he manoeuvres his way up the companionway, through the cockpit and across the gangplank. Once on the jetty, he doesn't turn back, disappearing into Nidri's night.

"What have you done to him? The poor boy looks exhausted," Jo asks.

Mabel, looking pleased as punch, is stood in the companionway in a floaty silk nightgown. Her skin is already coloured from a single day at sea, and her golden hair is tousled and wild.

"Well, that was fun," she says with a roguish smile.

"We've been taking bets," Esther tells her. "How many men can you get through on a single holiday? I bet five."

We haven't been doing anything of the sort. Esther's just trying to rattle her cage.

Mabel pours herself a gin and tonic from the jug and downs it in one. "You're just jealous."

Esther laughs. "Jealous? You don't think I could have a man in every port if I wanted to? I just consider the needs of the group before my own. Besides, one should have standards."

Uh oh. Here we go.

"Standards?!" Mabel gasps incredulously. "You call sleeping with Hugo Snowden having standards?"

"Hugo was an angel."

"Herpes Hugo? I don't think so …"

Jo seems to be enjoying the show, but I'd like to go to bed. There's some tension building and it's making me uncomfortable. By the way Libby and Verona are looking into their laps, I think they feel the same.

"… And what do you mean *consider the needs of the group before your own?* The girls don't mind me having a little fun, do you?"

Great – she brought us into it. "Erm … I don't have a problem with you hooking up with someone," I say diplomatically, "but, I mean, we've been stuck up here for over an hour, and it's pretty cold, Mabel."

"And we don't know anything about this guy. What if he was dangerous?" Jo adds.

"Or underage?" Esther mutters.

Verona puts her hand over Esther's mouth. "At least tell us you were careful."

Mabel recoils looking half angry, half disgusted. "I can't believe you're all slut-shaming me." The disgust flitters away until she is a giant ball of fury. "No one forced you sit up here in the cold. You could have gone back to the the bar—"

I try to smooth things; I can't stand shouting. "We wanted to be here in case you needed us. He was a total stranger."

"So what? I'm quite capable of taking care of myself."

"I know you are, Mabel, but—"

Esther cuts me off. "Listen, darling. You've had your fun with the local boy. We chose to come back here because we love you and didn't want you getting hurt, so don't go redirecting your post-coital regret on to us."

Mabel makes a noise like an angry cat; the fact her hair looks like a lion's mane also adds to the image. She grabs one of the tumblers and throws it at Esther with all her might.

The tumbler sails past Esther and shatters off the helm. I scream at the noise and the velocity as shards of glass explode behind me. Mabel calls Esther something I won't repeat and storms down the companionway. We sit, the silence only broken by the sound of Mabel's cabin door slamming. A warm sensation creeps down the back of my neck. I reach behind and massage my fingers through the hair at the bottom of my head. When I bring my hand back in front of my face, it's completely covered in blood.

CHAPTER 11

Libby.

This cabin sucks. There's no other way to say it. I might as well give up on trying to get any sleep while I'm here. Forget counting sheep, I should count how many times I've hit my head or bumped my elbow. The mattress is lumpier than Mam's mashed potatoes, and I can't even stretch my arms up without my hands hitting the ceiling. There's not enough room to swing a cat.

Fun fact, that saying actually comes from sailing. There's a whip type thing, favoured by sadists, that's called a cat o' nine tails. It's called that because of the nine strips of leather attached to the handle; I wouldn't be surprised if Mabel has one in her suitcase. Anyway, back in the day, the captains of Royal Navy vessels would use one to punish sailors who misbehaved or just weren't up to scratch. So when someone says there's not enough room to swing a cat, they're not talking about an actual cat. It was also kept in a little bag, hence its sister saying, *to let the cat out the bag*.

Man, I know some useless crap. Didn't know what classical studies was though. Nope, everyone had a nice laugh at the northerner's expense on that one.

I sit up and wince. My head hurts from the wine and gin, and my back aches from this mattress. I wonder if the beds in the other cabins are any better. Of course they are, this is a McPherson yacht. They'll be luxurious. Probably hand-stitched by virgins in the Peruvian mountains using wool from alpacas who've been fed on a diet of the rarest grass known to man. I should have a word with Paige, see if she minds me bunking in with her for a night or two. Anything's better than this.

I've been claustrophobic for as long as I can remember. Apparently, my brother locked me in the cupboard under the stairs when I was two or three. I was in there over four hours. I don't remember it, but it probably explains my hatred of confined spaces. I had panic attacks because of it up until about the age of sixteen or seventeen. I'd managed to control them until the night before last. For over an hour, I pressed my feet into the ceiling (because they reach, believe it or not), covered my mouth with one hand and pulled at my hair with the other. I ugly cried until I got a series of text messages from Danny. Having to focus on the words on the screen gave me something to centre my attention on, and I calmed down after a little while. It was awful. I felt like I'd never be able to breathe properly again.

I pick out a navy bikini, wash in the little sink and brush my teeth. I pull on a pair of denim cut-offs and a vest, push open the coffin's hatch, and poke my head out into the fresh morning air. Some seagull poop misses me by half an inch and splats on the deck. Apparently, it's good luck if a bird craps on your head. But that might just be something people say to make you feel better, like when we tell kids head lice only choose people with immaculately clean hair. The sun is up, and the weather looks glorious. It's early, but I guess the mercury's already at twenty-two, twenty-three degrees. Esther is spreading the charts on the table in the cockpit. She's wearing a stylish gold chain over a red and white striped t-shirt. Very nautical. Her hair is formed in perfect, soft, black curls and a pair of Chanel shades are perched on her head. She catches my eye and waves.

"Morning sleepy head. Come join me. Jo's got the kettle on. Coffee?"

I nod and climb out of my hole, sidestepping the gull crap. Esther looks so poised and noble; she always does. In fact, I don't recall her ever looking scruffy. I guess it's not the done thing in her circles. To think we were on the same course at uni, and yet our childhoods couldn't have been more different. She grew up on the Crown Estate; I grew up on a council estate.

Did I mention my home suburb was the car crime capital of Europe? Well, we were also the teenage pregnancy capital of Europe. I found that statistic out the hard way. I had an absent father and a mother who may as well have been absent given the amount of vodka she could put away. I remember one night, not long after my brother – yes, the one who'd locked me in the cupboard – had been sent to a youth offenders institute for his part in ram-raiding an off-licence. Mam was so upset at her little prince being sent to the clink that she drank enough to both piss herself and spew all over herself. Nice. Once I'd cleaned her up and got her into bed, I just thought to myself, *No, I'm not getting stuck in this spiral as well. This isn't the life I want.*

I was thirteen years old.

The next day I threw myself into school and studying like I had never done before. I knew it was the only way; no one else was going to help me. I studied all day and all night, hoping to get good enough GCSEs to get into St. Margaret's sixth form. I ended up with the highest grades in our year according to our headteacher. I had to get three busses to get to St. Margaret's, and it meant leaving home before seven most mornings. Still, it was worth it to have access to the best teachers and the finest facilities in the area. I didn't know what I wanted to do at university, or what job I'd like as an adult. So I selected art, physics and business thinking they'd give me a good spread. I spent my commute head bowed with eyes burrowed in my physics textbooks, but art was something I could only do at school. I didn't have the space to work at home and didn't have the funds to buy my own materials.

Anyway, two A's, an A-star and a heart attack later, and I had offers from St. Andrews, Bath and Oxford. I couldn't believe it. My teachers were thrilled and had been so supportive. Meanwhile, my brother was saying things like, "Oh, off to university are ya? This place not good enough for ya?"

I had a feeling I wouldn't fit in at Oxford or Bath, I mean I can't even bring myself to pronounce Bath like it has an R in the middle of it. *Barrrrrth*. So I chose art history at St. Andrews. When I got there, I quickly realised it was primarily populated with the same Oxbridge types, only these had ventured north of the border for some "life experience."

How many times did I have to hear some toff with a cut-glass accent joke about needing a booster vaccination to journey north of the Watford Gap? They were the embodiment of Pulp's *Common People*. Oh, you've run out of money? Call Daddy. You don't like your student accommodation? Call Daddy. You need the professor to change your grade? Just call Daddy.

I chose art history because I had this dream of working in a gallery. We'd been on a school trip to the Shipley Art Gallery in Gateshead, and I found it shockingly peaceful and serene. An antidote to my chaotic home life. I fell in love with galleries completely. I ended up going into photography, but I don't see it as settling; I love my career. On weekends I shoot weddings and Christenings as they pay the bills, but during the week I go exploring and get as far from the city as I can. Being outside in the country, snapping pictures of barn owls and harvest mice brings me the stillness I'd always craved from that one day at the gallery.

"I made it extra strong," Jo tells me as she hands me a coffee and I take a seat in the cockpit. It smells like the perfect remedy to last night's overindulgence.

Where was I? Oh yes, art history at St. Andrews. There was this one girl who just didn't belong there. I felt like I didn't belong because I'd never heard of Bollinger, but at least I knew I deserved to be there. This other girl, she was intelligent, of that, I had no doubt. She was always saying things in Latin to impress her groupies, but she didn't know the first thing about art. She thought Monet and Manet were one and the same. One time when she was boasting about seeing the Mona Lisa, a boy on our course asked what she thought of *Victoire de Samothrace*, and she stared blankly at him.

"Oh, we only popped in to see the Mona Lisa. It's Paris, darling. There was shopping to be done."

I couldn't believe how flippantly she spoke of just popping into the Louvre like it was nothing. I'd never been abroad, didn't even have a passport, and the

93

closest I could get to visiting the Louvre was scrolling through the pages of their website. I was sure she was only there because Kate Middleton had studied art history at St. Andrews. She even styled her hair the same: side parting, curled under at the ends. When I visited the new photography suite and darkrooms, it suddenly all made sense. It was the McPherson Suite. Daddy's donation had been the ticket Esther needed to get on the course.

Verona carries a big, crystal serving bowl up to the cockpit and places it on the table. It's full of fruit. She dips below deck and returns with a stack of toast, honey and Greek yoghurt. Mabel and Paige follow. Mabel has her arm over Paige's shoulder, and they're giggling about something. I take it all has been forgiven. If it had been me, and my neck was the one to get sliced open, I'm not sure I'd be so quick to forget. Actually, I'm the sort of pushover who'd say they were okay with it. *Oh, it's no big deal. Honestly, forget about it.* I'd still be pissed off, but I'd pretend otherwise if it meant avoiding conflict.

I grab a slice of wholemeal toast and add lashings of butter and local honey. I don't even pause for breath before taking another piece. I'd forgotten how hungry sailing can make you.

Once we've swept the crumbs away and our coffees have been topped up, Esther coughs to bring our attention back to her. "Right ladies, full disclosure, there's been another piracy incident."

94

Silence.

My breakfast feels lodged in my oesophagus.

More silence. Then, "What?" we all gasp. "Where? When?"

She holds up her hands to shush us. "In the Messenian Gulf."

I stand up and lean over the charts. "We're here," I say, pointing to Nidri, "and the Messenian Gulf is … just over here."

"That's not that far away," Paige says, fear flashing over her pale face.

"It happened in the middle of the night," Esther tells us. "They targeted a motor yacht that was anchored about two hundred metres off the coast. They took the usual: money, laptops, jewellery."

"Fucking hell," says Jo, folding her arms, and looking about as if they could be moored next to us.

Two middle-aged women on the yacht next door look across. They have a Swedish flag hanging from their halyard, and a spaniel is running up and down their deck. I don't know what modern pirates look like, but I suspect they aren't mumsy, dog-loving Swedes.

"Are the people on board okay?" I ask.

Esther shakes her head. "The report said the teenage son was taken to hospital as a precaution, but that's all I know."

Hospital? Did that mean the son was in distress, or did it mean – and this is more worrying – that the boat invaders had been violent? There's a real unease in the atmosphere as we sit around the table, then Paige says what I think most of us are thinking.

"Should we check into a hotel? At least for a couple of nights? There's one right there. It looks all right. Nice pool."

Esther leans across and kisses Paige on the top of her head. "Poor bunny. Stop worrying, everything's going to be fine. First, we have a schedule to keep. We're supposed to be in Catania by next Wednesday. And secondly, think about it, the coast guard are going to be crawling all over this area today. Trust me, this is the safest part of the Med right now."

– CHAPTER 12 –

Verona.

I made a giant fruit salad for everyone for breakfast. Fruit would have been more than enough for me, but I know some of the girls need more sustenance, so I rustled up a bit of toast and yoghurt and it seems to have gone down a treat. It's a good thing too; Mabel can be a nightmare when she's hungry, and we don't need a repeat of what happened last night. I'd have thought she'd make some sort of apology, but no, nothing was said over breakfast. She must have apologised to Paige for injuring her, as they're behaving like best buds now, but there's been no hint of remorse otherwise. She's acting as if nothing happened. It's not like Paige was the only one affected by it all. We were all stuck out in the cold, we were all made to feel awkward, and we all know it was Esther she was aiming for. Weird. Maybe she doesn't remember half of it.

I push thoughts of last night aside. It was dreadful, and I'm trying to embrace the holiday version of myself that I touched on yesterday. I want to be more in tune with the environment, and Gaia, and Mother Earth, but it's not easy with all this talk of pirates. I haven't been able to find much in the British press about this latest incident. Fortunately, my language skills are good enough to read the Greek and Italian sites. From what I could find out, it's a group of four men, and they all wear masks, so no one knows what they look like. White moulded masks, like the kind you get in craft kits. The police aren't giving much away to the news sites, but one journalist said the pirates are *forensically aware*. I assume by that he means they wear gloves, don't leave any fingerprints, hair samples, or bodily fluids. I grimace thinking about it.

There's a definite air of dread and foreboding about the cockpit since Esther's announcement. Poor Paige's aura has turned a greyish-yellow – not good – and Jo is scrutinising every vessel within fifty feet of us. I think we're all wondering how we'd react if something like that happened to us. Bacchus, even with a top speed of over ten knots, would be no match for a speed boat. They'd be clipped on and boarding before we could even reach for the radio. Mabel and Jo would fight tooth and nail. Esther would start reciting nautical regulations and how they were in breach of this and in violation of that. I don't think she's silly enough to pull the *don't you know who I am* act. Well, I hope she's not. Paige would lock herself in the bathroom, Libby would just start crying, and me, well I'm not sure what I'd do. Not sure at all.

Esther's taking charge and trying to keep us all rational. Of course, she's taking charge. It's not only because Esther's the skipper but because she's … What's the right word? She's … Esther. It's in her nature. She took charge the very first time I met her.

My parents own a farm just outside of Cottenham. From a very early age, I was involved in all aspects of farm life. By six, I knew how to milk a cow and sheer a sheep. I couldn't do it unsupervised, that would be ridiculous, but I understood it and could carry out the basics. I still remember my favourite dairy cow. She was called – of all things – Mabel; she had the sweetest temperament and had the biggest, brown eyes. It might seem strange, naming cattle, but farmers swear cows with names produce more milk. And it's true! There have been studies. At eight, I knew how to hold a rifle and could hunt rabbits and pheasants with my father. I shot my first rabbit at nine, and by ten, I understood more about butchery than ninety-nine per cent of the city dwellers.

One day, when I was twelve, I made dinner from scratch. For most people, that means grabbing the raw ingredients from Tesco rather than heading straight to the ready-meal aisle, but for me, it meant I selected a chicken and snapped its neck. I plucked the entire bird by myself, butchered it perfectly and roasted it in the oven. I picked carrots and parsnips from our vegetable patch and rosemary from our herb garden. I even made a gravy from the chicken juices. My parents were thrilled that they'd created such an independent and industrious young woman, and truth be told, it was one of the nicest meals I've ever had. Food earned always tastes the best, don't you think? I was so proud of myself and couldn't wait to tell my school friends on Monday morning.

Monday arrived, and I told my best friends, Martha and Jenny, what I'd been up to. Unfortunately, they weren't impressed; they were horrified. They wrinkled their noses, took a step away from me, looked at me like I was a freak and never spoke to me again.

A week later and everyone called me Farmer Freak at best, and Miss Murderer at worst. And you know what? Not one of those horrible little name-callers was a vegetarian. They'd sit there in the school dinner hall, scoffing down sausage and mash or lamb and peas and call me a chicken-killing-freak. They were so detached from what they ate, and yet I was the weirdo.

From then on, every time I ate meat, I'd have some form of PTSD. I'd see the snarling faces of all those bullies, feel their eyes burning into me, hear the whispered insults and cruel jokes. I'd feel their shoulders barging me as I walked down the corridor to English class, feel the bumps and bruises from being pushed to the ground outside the school gates. To me, meat had never equalled murder, but from that day on it equalled bullying and feeling so alone. I never ate meat after that, and I never had another friend until I met Esther.

I was stood queuing in a café called Peas and Carrots just round the corner from the university. I'd loaded my tray up with a slice of vegan pasta bake and a bottle of kale and pineapple smoothie and was waiting to pay. To my left, a group of French students were chatting animatedly. One, a girl with a blonde pixie cut, pointed to the St. Andrews logo on some paperwork she had with her and said how she must have been misled. That she'd been told this was a top university, on a par with the ivy league schools in America, so how come they couldn't even remember to put an apostrophe in Andrews? Being fluent in French, I knew exactly what they were saying. I caught the eye of a remarkable girl on my right who must have been listening in as well because she turned to them and loudly proclaimed …

"Actually, darlings, St. Andrews doesn't have an apostrophe. It's never had one, nor will it ever need one. The town of St. Andrews got its name long before the sixteenth century when the English language first made use of apostrophes."

She continued with some additional facts about the town's namesake to fully cement the notion she knew what she was talking about.

"St. Andrew, as you might know, is the patron saint of Scotland but he never actually set foot in it. Not when he was alive anyway. Relics from his body, including his knee cap and shoulder blade, were given to St. Regulus, who was told to take them to the *ends of the Earth*, so he brought them here, to Scotland."

She said all of this in perfect French without so much as an *um* or an *er*. She finished it off by saying that if they were going to go to a prestigious university with as much history as St. Andrews, that they should at least do it the honour of some basic research and respect.

The girl with the pixie cut got up and left after that, and the striking woman with the black hair and impeccable posture turned to me and introduced herself.

"Esther McPherson," she said, extending her hand. "That looks *délicieuse*. What is it? The vegan bake? Think I'll get one of those myself."

And somehow, without even doing anything, I'd made a friend. We sat together and talked about how difficult, and yet exciting, it was to be away from home.

"I'm going to the freshers fair after this? Care to join me?"

I wasn't in a position to turn down friendship, so I shrugged and agreed.

"I'm going to sign up for the sailing club. Do you sail?"

I laughed. "I grew up on a farm over an hour's drive away from the sea."

"So, that's a *no* I take it."

"Yeah, that's a no."

She got all excited. "A sailing virgin! Oh, you are going to love it. There's nothing like it. Say you'll join too."

I didn't know what to say or what to do. I felt as if I was being swept along by the tide and that I should trust the water to take me wherever it wished to go. "Okay," I said.

After we finished our meals, we walked arm-in-arm to the freshers fair and joined the sailing club. That day I met so many people, and not one of them judged me for growing up on a farm. Not one of them turned their nose up at my vegan diet. In fact, a lot of them said they longed to spend more time in the countryside, and a fair few told me they admired my discipline in abstaining from meat.

I wasn't a freak at St. Andrews. I could finally be myself again. If I could just remember who she'd been in the first place. I owed it all to Esther. Without her, I think I would have spent the entire first year in the dorms, only venturing out for food and lectures.

Esther claps her hands twice, and I stop my daydreaming. The noise bring me back to reality. I'm on Bacchus, the sun is shining and the birds are singing.

The double clap is a habit of hers, it either means *look at me* or *chop chop*. Right now, it means chop chop. There are a couple of tasks that need taking care of before we can set sail, the first is getting ship-shape. The breakfast items are washed, dried and stored securely. Seagull excrement is scrubbed from the deck, the table is wiped down, and the charts are returned to a drawer in the saloon. We shower, dress and apply sunscreen. Paige and Libby nip to a local shop to pick up bottled water and some freshly baked pastries that smell delightful but probably contain butter or cheese, or both. Esther adds our coordinates to the electrical chart plotter, and Jo cleans the lines.

We're headed for Paxos today which I'm beyond thrilled about. White sand beaches, turquoise water, quaint tavernas and gorgeous olive groves. Now I know you're all thinking, *that sounds like everywhere else in the Ionian, Verona*. Still, there's something truly special about Paxos. The sands are that bit whiter, the lagoons are a touch more turquoise, and the olives are that bit earthier. We're under sail quite quickly, but it will only be this way for an hour or so. To reach open water, we need to pass through the Lefkas canal. I make the most of the time we have without engine power, relishing the sounds of nature and keeping an eye out for passing shoals of fish. Before long, the waterway between Lefkada and the mainland narrows, and we're funnelled into the canal.

"The bridge opens every hour, on the hour," Esther informs us. "But it only stays open for a few minutes at a time. If we miss it, we'll have to wait around for almost another hour, and I don't think any of us want that."

I wouldn't mind. As much as I love racing along at high speeds, I equally love the bobbing about. You need one to appreciate the other.

Ahead, sailboats and catamarans – or *twatamarans*, as Mabel likes to call them, form an orderly queue. This is as close to rush hour as you get in the sailing world. The straight becomes increasingly narrow, and when we near the boat ahead of us, we furl the sails and switch the engine on. We keep within a channel marked by buoys, noting the speed of cars as they race by on my left as they try to get over the bridge before it closes to them.

A siren echos through the air, denoting that road traffic must stop and give way to water traffic. The bridge is quite impressive. Its sides fold upwards before it begins to rotate and tuck itself into the eastern bank. Esther checks her watch, she looks fidgety. I bet she's itching to get out of this queue and start some real sailing. She stretches her arms above her head, then pulls her neck to either side and twists her hands back and forth to stretch her wrists. I really do owe Esther a lot. I wonder who I'd be now if I'd never met her.

Another siren sounds, and as if a race has started, Esther floors it. There's a speed limit of five knots per hour, but Esther isn't going to hang around for the next opening. She squeezes Bacchus through with seconds to spare. We're off!

An ancient and expansive castle flanks our starboard side, but before long we're free of the canal and the other vessels and can unfurl the sails once more. As promised, there's a decent wind coming from the west which will help us greatly. The sky is speckled with clouds so white and fluffy they look like they've been painted on. Mabel adjusts the mainsail ever so slightly, and as we catch the wind just right, the boat leans to around thirty-five degrees. We're flying.

"Woo!" shouts Mabel and we all hoot with excitement.

Strictly speaking, you should try to keep your yacht vertical to get the best performance out of it, but heeling does make the ride more exhilarating. And what's life without a bit of adventure? This beats meetings in the boardroom any day of the week.

"I see Pier Pressure still have what it takes," Esther beams. She checks the monitor and gasps. "Seven knots, ladies. Let's see if we can get her up to eight."

I freaked out the first time I was on a boat, and it heeled like this; I thought we'd capsize for sure. I've since learned to trust the keel and trust the skipper. Like I said, it can be fun. Esther could have Bacchus practically horizontal and we'd still be all right. She wouldn't let anything happen to us. We're her girls. Her crew.

– CHAPTER 13 –

Paige.

We're avoiding a long sand bar that extends north of the island. I wonder how many inexperienced crews have beached themselves here over the years. Mabel takes no chances, watching the depth gauge closely as we gain a little more speed.

"Take her another ten degrees port."

My fingers find the plaster on the back of my neck. It's stopped stinging, but there's still a dull ache where the shard of glass caught me, and I'm still shaken up. The sight of all that blood really scared me.

Mabel knocked on my door at about five this morning. She'd clearly had a rough night; her face was all blotchy from crying, and the remnants of her mascara had stained her cheeks black. "Hey," she'd said sheepishly, before coming into the cabin and sliding under the covers next to me. "I'm sorry. You know I wasn't aiming for you, right?"

The uncomfortable feeling I'd felt when Mabel cuddled up to me diminished quickly. She seemed unusually sad, like a child apologising to their mummy.

"You were aiming for Esther," I reminded her. "What were you thinking? We're on her dad's boat. It's going to be a nightmare getting home if she kicks us all off."

She buried her face into my hair. "She won't kick you guys off. Only me. I'm such an idiot. I never learn. Never."

She sighed deeply, and I felt every drop of air leave her lungs. I've never craved men the way Mabel does. She's like a bloke at times. Once she gets horny, there's no stopping her. Yeah, I like men. It would be nice to have a boyfriend, but not for sex; I want someone to hold me, someone who'll make me feel safe and secure. But now's not the right time for me to be looking for love. My brother's sick and my work schedule's all over the place and—.

Mabel kept sniffling and taking tiny panicked breaths. I couldn't stand the thought of her torturing herself, so I tried to lighten the mood. "At least tell me he was worth it."

Her eyes brightened instantly. "Oh my God," she said, blowing her nose on a tissue, "he was amazing. Wait till I tell you what he could do with his …"

I got every disgusting detail after that, but at least she stopped crying. When she was done, I sent her over to Esther's room to apologise. Whatever she said, it must have worked because, although there's a bit of tension between Mabel and Esther, no one has been kicked off Bacchus. Yet.

At the end of the sandbar, I spy a tiny island. It can't be more than fifty metres long and is only big enough for one building – a church by the looks of it. There's a large white cross erected outside. I wonder how people attend church services there. Presumably, they'd have to go by boat. Perhaps it's a pilgrimage site? I have a phone signal, so I do a quick check, but all I can find out is that a poet lived there and that his wife, his muse, liked to be naked all the time – each to their own.

It's not long before Pier Pressure begin to strip down. No one here will go naked, or I hope they won't, but t-shirts and shorts are peeled away. I'm wearing a silver, cut-out bikini. It's asymmetric with both straps coming over my left shoulder. If I tanned, it would leave ridiculous tan marks, but I'm pale and covered head-to-toe in sunblock so I can get away with it. It's made by this little label out of Sydney, Australia. This time last year, no one had heard of them, but they aligned with some up and coming models, and now everyone in the industry is talking about them. The second I posted that I was going on a sailing holiday, I had offers for promotional posts. They sent me a link to all their swimsuits, asked me to choose my three favourites, and they were with me by the end of the week. That's over six hundred Australian dollars worth of bikini and another grand in my bank account if I post at least one photo and one story in each of the swimsuits. The world's a crazy place. At one time, I wouldn't have been able to afford something like this. Now I have the money, I get it for free. Nuts.

I love this bikini, it won't be hard for me to gush about it when I post. It really suits my frame. I know, I know, I'm a model, and most people think everything will look good on me, but that's simply not true. I'm flat-chested. An ironing board. A pancake. The Netherlands has more curvature than I do. I used to be so self-conscious about it; I still am sometimes, truth be told. Those secondary school insecurities don't always leave us. I wish I could say they do, but they don't. All the other girls got boobs and boyfriends, but I was the tall, skinny, androgynous one. At least the tall, skinny, androgynous one grew up and got a modelling contract – ugly duckling: one, school bullies: nil.

Esther lowers her shades and takes a good look. I think she's about to compliment me until she grunts, "Urgh. You're so skinny."

"I'm not skinny. I'm athletic," I reply, knowing that Esther hates it when people answer back.

"Same difference, darling."

It ain't the same. Ain't the same at all. To be skinny, all you have to do is starve yourself. To be athletic, you have to eat all the right foods and do all the right exercises. I have to train hard, like really hard. Like my life depends on it sometimes. I run sprints as if I'm being chased by zombies. I cycle as if I'm trying to out pedal a runaway train.

Esther can be snarky all she likes, but I want my thousand dollars, so I take a stand for my phone from my bag and use its suction cup to secure it next to the winch. Esther is at the port helm, so I aim my camera at the starboard helm and set the timer for ten seconds. I strike a pose and Esther chooses that moment to steer Bacchus hard to port. There are no apparent obstacles, so I assume her only reason to do so is to ruin my shot. The sudden movement causes everyone's heads to turn in her direction. Their faces morph into quizzical expressions at the sudden change of direction. All she succeeds in doing is making the sail flap. It sends a gust of air billowing through my hair, and the sun catches it just as the camera's shutter noise sounds.

I remove the phone from the stand, place it back in my bag and move to the shade to crop and choose the best filter.

Our skipper – our childish, bitchy skipper – sets Bacchus back on course but can't resist saying, "Hashtag attention seeker."

She says it in a tone and with a smile that suggests she's just fooling around. It's her way of provoking me. I've seen it a thousand times before. If I take the bait and rise to it, I'll look overly sensitive. I mean, she was *just kidding, darling. One doesn't need to get her panties in a twist.*

I select my usual filter and play with the settings until the shot is just right, and it fits with my regular theme. It might not sound like a big deal, but it's important to have a consistent approach to your Instagram account so that your profile always has a great aesthetic. My aesthetic has always been plenty of green-blue hues with white. I love teal and turquoise accents on a predominantly white background. Today's photo works like a charm. I have a perfect tropical-blue sea behind me, and Bacchus brings plenty of white to the shot.

Getting some vitamin sea with my besties from uni, I type. *Pier Pressure back together again and ruling the waves. Beautiful bikini by Eucalyptus Designs, fits perfectly and makes me feel wonderful. Whatever you're doing today, I hope you feel wonderful too.*

I add *hashtag ad* to the caption because it's in the terms and conditions if I'm being paid to promote a product. I provide the link to Eucalyptus Designs, then I look over my shoulder for a moment. Screw it. I add *hashtag attention seeker* as well. If Esther looks at my feed, and I know fine well she will, she'll see my dig and won't be able to say a thing because *it's just a joke, darlin'. Keep your Alans on.*

– CHAPTER 14 –

Libby.

It's lunchtime. Esther and Mabel offered to stay on deck while the rest of us shelter from the midday sun. In the galley, Verona has whipped up a Greek salad to stuff into pitta bread halves. The look of it already has me salivating. She fills her pittas first then adds plenty of feta cheese to the remaining mix for the rest of us. She's one of those people who seem naturally gifted when it comes to food. I'm the opposite. If the cooking's left to me, eighty per cent of the time, I'll open a tin of something and hope for the best. And the other twenty per cent? That's when I dial the Thai place around the corner. I'm that hopeless in the kitchen. I didn't even know how to boil an egg until I met Danny.

"Score," says Jo as she finds a bag of salt and vinegar crisps in one of the lockers. We share them out between our plates. Usually, I'm not a big fan of salty foods, but I could do with the electrolytes. Since arriving in the Ionian, I've been sweating like a dyslexic on Countdown.

Sorry, dyslexics. The gym I go to is pretty rough and ready – a real spit and sawdust type. I can't afford one of the squeaky clean private gyms that the celebs go to. The men at my gym are always *sweating like a whore in church,* or *sweating like a priest in a* … Best I keep that one to myself.

When I've had my fill, I leave Verona, Jo and Paige to their discussion about some Eastenders actress and decide to take advantage of the empty heads. I've been using the crappy little sink and shower in the coffin room. It's basically a hose pipe attached to the wall, and I need the skills of a contortionist to get myself clean without soaking my bed or suitcase. I fetch my wash bag and towel and use the shared shower at the bow. Shower rooms on sailing yachts are almost always a cramped affair, but Bacchus isn't any old sailing yacht. I'm amazed; the cubicle is bigger than the one I have at home. In fact, it's bigger than my excuse for a cabin. It heats up quickly, and the water pressure on my shoulders feels magical. I hadn't realised how much tension I'd been carrying in them until I felt the spray massaging my deltoids. I stretch my arms and upper back, lift my foot up behind me to stretch my thighs and take my time washing my hair. If fresh water weren't such a valuable commodity at sea, I would stay in here all day.

Clean and refreshed, I emerge feeling much better. I actually feel awake. Esther and Mabel are in the saloon. They're tucking into the food Verona prepared. Everything seems all right between them until I hear Mabel ask if they should open a bottle of bubbly.

Esther gives her a stern "No."

I catch Mabel wrinkling her nose at Esther then climb back up the steps and into the open air.

"Feeling better?" Paige asks.

"Much."

"You should just say whenever you want to use the heads, you know. There's no point you fighting with that tiny thing you have in your cabin. We don't mind sharing, do we girls?"

Jo immediately answers. "Not at all."

Verona simply doesn't answer.

I thank Paige, but she waves my gratitude away as if it's nothing. It's not nothing though. Paige is kind. She said she hadn't forgotten her roots and I believe her. Fame might have changed the clothes she wears and the amount of money in her bank, but it hasn't changed her as a person. She's the same sweet but paranoid girl I remember from uni.

She picks up the binoculars and scans about. We're quite far from the mainland; I'd guess we're about four kilometres offshore.

"Anything good?" I ask.

"The scenery's as pretty as ever. Thought I saw a dolphin for a second, but it hasn't come back."

That's a shame. I'd love to see dolphins in the wild. Not that I've seen one in captivity either. I've never been able to afford one of those swim-with-dolphins holiday experiences, and I'm not sure I'd go on one even if I could afford it. I'm not like Verona when it comes to animal rights, but there's something about keeping animals in cages that makes me uncomfortable. I wonder if it all stems back to that time I was locked in the cupboard? I pull out my phone and make a note of it to ask my shrink when we have our next telephone appointment. Free anxiety consultations. God bless the NHS.

Paige's arm extends and points at a cluster of yachts in the distance. "Those guys are back. The ones from the other day."

Jo shoots to her feet and joins us. She's left Verona at the helm, not that it matters because Esther is back above board and she doesn't look pleased. For crying out loud, I hope she and Mabel aren't going to have another fight. Last night was a dumpster fire. If that's what we can expect every evening, I think some of us will bite the bullet and book flights home from Corfu rather than wait until we get to Sicily.

"Are they staring back at us?" Jo asks.

Paige nods.

"You don't seem too bothered," I say. Paige was really tense when we saw them last time.

"I'm trying to – pardon my French – chill my tits. I mean, binoculars are a normal part of sailing. They're not doing anything I'm not doing."

"Very Zen of you."

"I just get a little distrustful sometimes."

I give her a coy smile and dryly reply, "You don't say."

"Sometimes I just need to give myself a slap and remember there isn't a pervert hiding in every bush or a photographer lurking around every corner." She lowers the binoculars to look at me. "Oh, sorry, Libby."

I nudge her. "It's okay. I only photograph animals, newlyweds and newborns, and I definitely don't sell to the tabloids."

"Glad to hear it. They're the worst."

She hands the binoculars to Jo, but before she can put her shades on, I'm sure I see her eyes glisten. "You okay?"

She nods and walks away just as Mabel joins us.

"Are they looking?"

Jo raises the binoculars to her eyes and scans the water until she finds the boat. Her body stiffens. "Yip. They're looking back at us."

Mabel grins, pulls her bikini top down and flashes them.

I can't see their faces from this distance. But I can hear cheers and whoops carrying across the sea.

I snort and turn so Mabel can't see the look on my face. What I saw in that woman, I'll never know.

Yes, I Elizabeth Bagshaw, was once upon a time, madly in love with party girl, Mabel Sharpe.

I'd been burning the candle at both ends at uni, working my fingers to the bone and a whole host of other idioms to describe working my arse off. No one in my family had been to university before. I'd sacrificed so much to be there and had plunged headfirst into upwards of forty grand's worth of debt. There was no plan B. Everything was invested in plan A. I was going to ace my degree, spend summers volunteering in art galleries, graduate, and with any luck, work my way up to curator at a top European gallery. It was a long shot, but as far as dreams went, it was actually possible.

My lecturers were concerned that I didn't appear to have any form of social life. Apparently, I'd turned the sickly, pallid white associated with being a hermit. It was suggested I should talk to one of the guidance counsellors. To my rough-around-the-edges upbringing, it sounded like some hippy nonsense from an American high school drama. I'd always been told shrinks were for the self-indulgent, for people who liked the sound of their own whinging. But, I did what I was told and found it surprisingly … therapeutic.

My counsellor was named Dr Nell Lancaster, and her office smelled strongly of lavender. I suspect the lavender was used to mask the smell of the fish and chip shop that was located downstairs, but it mainly made me sleepy. It took a few sessions, but she got me to open up.

"No boyfriend?"

I shook my head.

"Girlfriend?"

I wrapped my arms around my chest as if I was cold.

"Libby?" she pressed, then it all came out, or rather, I did. I'd never told anyone this before. Not a living soul. I couldn't.

There was a boy at my school who everyone called gay. I don't know if he was or not, but he was thin and freckly, his voice still hadn't broken by the time he was fifteen, and to top it off, he didn't like football. That alone was enough to make him a target. He'd be beaten up at least once a week, and I remember him being taken to hospital twice when we were in year eleven. All because some of the bigger lads *thought* he was gay. If anyone knew what Courtney Smith and I did during our sleepovers, we might have been beaten to death. My school wasn't exactly progressive.

Shit, I'm making the northeast sound like the dark ages. I promise it's not. Newcastle Pride is immense! It's the UK's second-largest Pride event and the area around Times Square has some of the best gay bars in the country. The northeast, on the whole, is a very welcoming, open-minded sort of place. But my estate? All those years ago? No. Being out wasn't an option.

After the allotted hour was up, Dr Lancaster asked me to speak to a member of Saint's LGBT+. She said I didn't have to join or sign up to any events, she just wanted me to talk to a representative. I agreed, and before the week was out, I was at something called QueerFest. Yeah, little ol' me, from the backwaters of Sunderland, where even my own mother didn't know I was … I was … What was I?

A Japanese drag queen handed me a beer. It was my fourth of the evening, and though I wasn't drunk yet, everything was starting to seem a little blurred around the edges. The Drag Walk event was the highlight of the evening.

"What am I?" I asked for the second time. "I'm not straight, I know that much, and I'm not a lesbian." I said the last word in a whisper. "It's like I don't *see* gender …"

Okay, maybe I was drunk. *I don't see gender?* What was I on about?

"… I don't see if someone's male or female, I just see the person as a whole. I'm attracted to the person, not their body parts."

Yeah. I was definitely drunk.

The queen hugged me. I've completely forgotten his name, his real name that is – his stage name was Sue She. Never forgot that. Not that I'd recognise him out of the full gothic Lolita attire he'd worn that night. By the way, before you accuse me of anything, he told me he preferred male pronouns. Earlier in the evening, I'd been pathetically awkward. I'd been skirting about using *they* and *um* and *ah* until he rolled his gorgeous eyes and said, "I'm only *she* when I'm on stage, Libbykins." He had this black corset and a black, frilly, lace skirt and these patent leather boots that laced all the way up to his thighs. Anyway, he hugged me, then grabbed me by the shoulders, looked deep into my eyes and told me to stop looking for labels.

"The only label you need is this one." He pressed a finger against a necklace I was wearing. It had been a gift from Courtney before I moved schools for sixth form. It was silver and dainty and shaped into my name: Libby.

Dr Lancaster was thrilled I'd not only left my dorm for something other than lectures but that I'd actually socialised. I'd mingled and allowed myself to have fun. I accepted that I wasn't going to squander my education by enjoying a couple of nights out.

The second challenge she gave me was to get more fresh air and counteract the stale, musty air of the library. Next to admitting who I was, getting some fresh air would be easy. We had a flick through a booklet that outlined all the societies and clubs at St. Andrews and kept a lookout for any outdoor ones.

"Archery?"

"No."

"Rugby?"

"Absolutely not."

"Sailing?"

I paused. "Sailing?"

The thought conjured up images of rosy-cheeks, wind-swept hair, teamwork and a sense of achievement. I agreed to give it a try but wouldn't promise more than that.

Fast forward a week and a half, and I was on a beach, dressed in a wetsuit and buoyancy aid. I looked like a shapeless slug. So did everyone, to be fair. Everyone bar this blonde girl who was pulling her ponytail through the hole in the back of a black cap. I'd never seen anyone so glamorous, and my lecturers were usually brimming with Kate Middleton wannabes. She had golden hair that bounced with every movement, and huge, green eyes that looked like emerald pools. She had wide hips and a small waist, and everything about her was captivating. I felt like a beached whale, but she looked like her wetsuit had been custom made. In hindsight, it may well have been.

She saw me staring, and I looked away in horror. *Shit.* Did she know what I'd been thinking? Then she bounced over, all smiles and energy.

"You must be Libby. I'm Mabel. Welcome to dingy sailing. I'll be showing you the ropes today."

Happiness seemed to beam out of her, and her enthusiasm was infectious. She bounced on the balls of her feet, so eager to get in the dingy.

"It's a tad rough out there," she said, pointing to the water. "I'll do my best to keep us upright but be prepared to get wet."

I said nothing, drawn in by her charm and friendly demeanour.

"Oh, don't look so scared. You're going to love it. It's a total rush. Then afterwards, you'll have the most satisfying shower of your life."

I still couldn't find the words. I just stood there like a gormless fool.

"Do you drink?"

I nodded.

"Great. We usually go to the wine bar after practice. I'll introduce you to everyone." She put her arm over my shoulders and guided me to a small white boat.

My life had changed so much in such a small amount of time. QueerFest, drag queens, wine bars and wetsuits?

"Sounds good," I managed to stutter. I couldn't explain it. I'd only just met Mabel, but she was so lovely, warm and welcoming. Everything about her made me crave more. It was completely irrational and nonsensical, but in that instant, I was in love.

– CHAPTER 15 –

Esther.

We're approaching the southern point of Paxos. Goodness, this place brings back some memories. Good and bad. I'm watching Jo. She's sat with her legs dangling off the bow end of Bacchus. The book she's reading is so thick and heavy she could probably kill someone with it if she hit them over the head with it. If she were so inclined. She's still covered up in that palm print kaftan. It's really not my style, and I suspect it's a supermarket brand, but you know what, it does kind of suit her – green complements her skin tone.

"Jo, sweetie," I say. "You remember the story of Paxos, don't you?"

She looks up and closes her book. "Which one?" she says with lowered brows and a bit of a chuckle. "The one where Poseidon created the island by striking Corfu with his Trident? Or the one where you were caught skinny-dipping, and the royal family had to pay a small fortune to hush the whole thing up before the press get hold of it?"

My mouth falls open, and I notice all the other girls have turned to stare at me. Of course, they have, they don't know this story, and it's not one I'm ready to share with them just yet. In fact, the memory makes me blush with both shame and excitement. Shame, because I know how disappointed Daddy was when I phoned him from Paxos police station. And excitement, because I know how much fun I had getting in that much trouble. You have to abide by many rules in families such as mine. Even minnows such as myself have to remember a whole host of regulations and etiquette. Certain indiscretions, like wearing the wrong colour nail varnish, or crossing your legs at the knee rather than the ankle, can be overlooked. However, being caught with one's boobs out at the Tripitos Arch is not one of them.

"Do tell," says Verona in a pleading tone.

If this were a story about Mabel no one would bat an eyelid – she's already gone topless twice today – but because it's about me, they're all ears.

"That's a story for another day," I tease. "But I will show you where it happened." I point westerly. "Want to take a look?"

There are nods of agreement all round, so we tack and I steer Bacchus towards a beautiful natural stone structure on the south-west of the island. We have

126

time – I'm meeting someone at seven, but that's still three hours away.

"Get your camera ready," I tell Libby. She scrambles to her feet and scurries towards the crew cabin at the bow, emerging a few moments later with a camera almost as big as she is.

The girls move towards the front of the yacht, ready to view the arch – all except Paige, who stays in the cockpit reading a fashion magazine. Although, come to think of it, I don't think she's actually reading. She's been on the same page for over half an hour now, and she hasn't said a word all afternoon. She lightened up this morning, but something is clearly bugging her. I hope it's not me and what I said earlier about being an attention seeker. If it is, then it just proves I was right – I must've touched a nerve. Unless it's not me, and she's really just upset because her swimsuit post didn't get as many likes and comments as she'd hoped. But if that's the case, I suppose I'm still right.

Tripitos Arch is magnificent. Just how I remember it. A thick column of land, around twenty metres in length, is connected to Paxos by a thin archway. The arch sits high above the water, but I'm not sure I could fit Bacchus under it. Bacchus's mast reaches twenty-two meters, so one had better not risk it – demasting would be a humiliating and expensive mistake. Libby coos about the azure water and how it contrasts with the off white of the stone cliff faces. She snaps away, occasionally stopping to show Jo what she's captured on the digital display. I steer us slightly to port to give a family of kayakers space as they paddle east, away from the arch and towards a cave system.

Verona points to the peak of the arch. "There's someone up there."

"It's wide enough to walk over," I tell her. "Assuming you can walk in a straight line, it's not that dangerous."

She shakes her head. "You wouldn't catch me up there. Mabel?"

Mabel lowers her shades to take another appraising look. "I've cliff jumped from higher."

"You're crazy," Verona tells her.

"You're not the first to call me that."

I think back to being a small child and my youthful fascination with mermaids. When I was six or seven, Mummy and Daddy brought me here for the first time, and I was convinced that mermaids lived in the caves that line this beautiful island. With Poseidon having created the island and him being Triton's father, I guess it makes sense. Even now, I find myself gazing into the water, hoping to catch a glimpse of a human-fish hybrid.

When the sighs of admiration die down, and the girls have stopped talking about how the arch would be covered in guard rails and health and safety notices if it were in England, I know they've had their fill. I start the engine to get us moving again. We may as well finish the journey this way. We're not far from Gaios where we'll be mooring up for the night.

I call a quick meeting as Gaios has an unusual approach and natural harbour. It won't be difficult for us, but we need to be aware of a few things. The inlet where Gaios is situated also houses a few small islands. They form the harbour into a narrow horseshoe shape. Because of Bacchus's immense size, we won't be permitted to moor in the thinner part of the canal; we'll need a space near the northern entrance. I'm glad I secured our berth in advance. Otherwise, we'd have to free swing off the coast. Although it sounds like something Mabel would do, free-swinging is when you drop anchor in the bay and spend the night there. To get to land, you need to use an inflatable dinghy. Some of them have motors, but most people just row and after a few glasses of wine, they can be absolute death traps. Back when Mummy and Daddy were still together, we had a sailing holiday in the south of Italy, and this horrific event occurred. A couple who were dining at the same restaurant as us were free swinging in the bay of Otranto. They had too many glasses of Puglian red and were rowing back to their yacht in the pitch black when the husband dropped the oars. Within a minute they'd been carried out to sea and were never heard from again.

It still gives me shivers.

I want the girls to have fun, but I also want them to be safe, and if we're not careful, things could go very wrong indeed.

We moor stern-to and hit the showers. As we still have a bit of time before dinner, I suggest we go our separate ways. We don't want to suffocate each other, and one has a few things to attend to. I unfold a piece of paper in my pocket and type the number into my phone. I ask the voice on the other end to relay a message to Daddy: We've arrived in Paxos, and all is well. I would have liked to have spoken to him directly, but that's not always possible.

Libby and Paige have popped to a local gallery. The owner and artist is a fascinating Scottish lady who specialises in mixed media, coastal views and beaded jewellery – I know her well. Mabel, Jo and Verona have wandered off to see the statue of George Anemogiannis at the south end of the harbour. If I remember correctly, he was a Paxos-born sailor who attacked an Ottoman ship. The locals view him as a revolutionary hero. Though, it's not like he succeeded in burning down the Ottoman navy. He was captured, executed, and his body hung in the streets for days as a warning to other potential rebels.

There's a lesson in there. One shouldn't rise up against the ruling class. One will lose.

By the time Libby bounds back over the passerelle, I'm still thinking about Daddy. I hope he gets my message tonight. He sounded stressed the last time I spoke to him, but he needn't worry, I have everything under control.

"Check it out." Libby's bought a selection of seascapes painted onto pieces of driftwood. "Do these colours remind you of anyone?"

I study them. "Should they?"

"Mary Cassatt?"

I look at her blankly.

"We studied her in our second year," says Libby with a piercing look. "She was one of the three great ladies of impressionism."

It rings the vaguest of bells. "Oh *that* Mary Cassatt," I say sarcastically. "*You* studied her, sweetie. *I* partied."

She pouts.

With everyone back aboard and busy with make-up and hair, I make my excuses. "Just nipping out to pick up a few things for Bacchus. I won't be very long." And I'm not. I'm back within ten minutes.

"What's in the bag?" Libby asks me.

The littlest of our group has scrubbed up well. This might be the first time I've seen her in a dress. Very rockabilly. If only I could have convinced her to try contact lenses.

I throw the holdall on my bed and fish out the topmost item. "Sat phone," I say, lifting the state of the art gadget to give them a better view.

Jo whistles. "Nice. They don't come cheap."

I hand her the phone, and she inspects the smart orange casing and rubber edging.

"Global coverage, water-resistant, hundred and sixty hours standby …" I rattle off its features until Libby interrupts.

"Why'd you need a sat phone? The radio coverage's great in the Med."

"I don't," I tell her. "Daddy does. He told me to pick one up. Probably just wants the latest gizmo. Though, I think I heard him say something at Christmas about a transatlantic crossing." I shrug. "He might be getting adventurous in his old age."

Mabel doubles over, ruffles her hair to give it volume, and flips it back. "Are we going to talk about your father all night, or are we going to get some grub?"

* * *

Agatha's must be my favourite taverna on the island. There's plenty of outdoor seating, which is perfect on a warm night like tonight. The wind has died down, and as the sun lowers, it colours the sea with a hint of burnt orange.

Wooden chairs, painted white, surround tabletops made of old barrels. Candles in wine bottles, the soft strumming of live guitar music, and the sound of the head chef singing in the kitchen. Cats, both domestic and stray, wind their way around chair legs, their tails caressing the legs of patrons in the hope they'll receive leftover fish. Jo, ever the animal lover, stops to pet them and is instantly surrounded by ten undernourished felines. She makes soothing noises as she gives their ears a quick check. I get why she cares, they're enchanting little creatures, but you wouldn't catch me stroking them.

Agatha recognises me instantly. She wipes her hands on a tea towel and runs over, only stopping to curtsy. I wave away her formal greeting and extend my arms. She hugs me and strokes my hair in a maternal manner.

"Miss Esther! It has been too long. Too, too long. How have you been? How is Mr McPherson? How long are you staying?"

She doesn't give me time to answer.

"And you bring guests? Come. Come. Any friend of Miss Esther is a friend of mine. Some aperitifs?"

Again, before I can answer, she runs off and returns with a tray of Metaxa and settles us into a table for six overlooking the bay. Good ol' Agatha. Her back may be hunched, and her joints may creak, but she moves like a Thoroughbred. She's been kind to my family over the years. When Mummy and Daddy separated, Daddy stayed on Paxos for a month while he gathered his thoughts. Agatha always made sure there was a table ready for him come dinner time. She even had the chef teach him how to make hortopita: moreish pies made with filo pastry and stuffed with aromatic herbs, crumbly cheese, dandelion and fennel. They taste heavenly, but they're devilish when it comes to one's waistline.

When Agatha has finished fussing over us, I raise my glass of Metaxa and wait for the girls to do the same. I can't use our usual toast as we're not drinking wine. Yes, yes, technically it is made from wine but let's not be pedantic, besides it's always fun to break out a new Latin phrase.

"*Dilige amicos.*" Love your friends.

Everyone leans in to clink glasses, but I notice not all at our table can meet my eye.

– CHAPTER 16 –

Paige.

The lamb cutlets are still sizzling when they're served to me. Feta melts into the juices as the aroma of fresh thyme and oregano wafts upwards. It looks gorgeous, like something out of a food magazine, but as I take my first bite, the feta goes claggy against my dry pallet. To compensate, I begin sipping more wine than I should, slurping it down like apple juice. A lean cat circles my right calf. She's a ginger tabby with big blue eyes; a feline version of myself. Her fur feels nice against my skin, but the poor little thing's ribs are protruding. I feel bad for her, and I wonder if the other cats make fun of her for being a slim redhead. Of course not, cats have better things to do than taunt each other: taunting humans for one. Agatha has asked us not to feed the cats, so I wrap up what remains of my lamb in a napkin and pop it in my handbag. I can't face finishing it, and it would be a shame to waste it. I'll wait until we're off the property to feed my new furry friend.

Across the restaurant, a blissfully happy couple can't bear to let go of each other's hands. They're in their early twenties and have the swarthy complexions of those who work in the sunshine. Everything they do is a display of loved up teamwork. She places her fork in the meat while he cuts. He holds the bottle while she unscrews the lid, and she stabs a few chips on to her fork to feed him. If it sounds like I'm mocking them, I'm not. It's genuinely cute.

Young love.

Must be nice.

Jo wrinkles her nose. Perhaps it's a public display of affection too far after her recent break-up. I should distract her – engage her in conversation – but I don't know what to say. In truth, I'm waiting to be distracted myself.

Behind the love birds, a family with two children – a boy and a girl – put their forks down and swap their dishes one place to the left before continuing to eat. I smile briefly. My brother, Graham, and I used to do that with ice cream sundaes. Dad would drive us down to Bournemouth and we'd sit on the beach eating fish and chips, play in the sea, and get ice creams before coming home. We could never choose which one to have so the three of us would each get a different flavour, and we'd swap when we'd eaten a third. *Simpler times*.

If I tried that now … I can just picture the clickbait article about me binging on dairy. Bile rises in my throat. I can't win. In one breath, they accuse me of not eating, and the next, say I'm letting myself go when I do. The thing is, I'd take every nasty headline, unflattering paparazzi photo, and pathetic bit of clickbait if it meant I could have one more day on the beach with my brother.

I push the remaining feta around my plate and try to zone in on Mabel and Verona's conversation about the America's Cup. It's hard to concentrate now my head's a little woozy. The wine is going down far, far too easily, and my stomach is practically empty. I'm distracted by a group of men who've just arrived. They look like the men from the other boat – the ones with the binoculars. I turn my eyes away and hope, if it is them, that they don't recognise us. After Mabel's X-rated antics earlier, they'll think we're all like that and might come over in search of a good time and a repeat performance.

"Hey."

I feel a gentle nudge in my ribs from Libby.

"You okay?" she asks, as her glasses slip down the bridge of her nose.

I shrug. "Yeah. Sorry. I just a have a dark cloud following me this evening."

She curls the corner of her mouth into a sympathetic smile and pushes her glasses back into place.

"That feeling when you're sad, but you don't know why?"

"Oh, I know exactly why," I grumble.

Her face creases.

"Oh, God. No, not you, Libby." *Shit*. "I'm just in a bad mood. It's not you. We're cool," I say. "We're always cool."

She nods, raises her fist, and we bump our knuckles together.

Esther, who's at the head of the table – make of that what you will – sees and loudly says in her cut-glass accent, "Fist bumps? How urban."

I bristle and glance at Libby. We both came from run-down, neglected areas, abandoned by the government and local council alike. We made it. We survived school and got good – no, great – educations. We graduated with excellent grades and have absolutely nothing to be ashamed of whatsoever. Libby could become the world's most sought after photographer; I could be the next great supermodel. None of that matters to the aristocracy. With them, it's less about achievement and more about good breeding.

"What, darlings?" Esther asks, her face plastered with fake innocence. "I was only teasing. Trying to bring a little life to the dinner table. You've both been so quiet. I mean, Paige, you've hardly said a word."

I surge to feet with such speed Esther actually flinches. I have to admit, it feels good seeing her on the back foot for once. "That's because everything you say, can and will be used in evidence."

I pick up my handbag and march to the toilets to calm down. I enter a cubicle and lock the door behind me. I want to lash out and thump my fists against the toilet door until it shatters. The words *she sold you out, she sold you out,* play in my mind on a loop. They're words that have followed me most of the afternoon and evening. I'm not sure what triggered it, but the words seem here to stay.

Esther McPherson, my good friend and confidant, has sold at least three stories about me to the press. Not shitty little pieces of clickbait like I was moaning about earlier. I mean real stories.

The sort that makes your grandmother disown you.

It was our last year at St. Andrews, my modelling career was really starting to take off, and for two months, I was pregnant.

It was an impulsive night of stupidity, and yes, I knew better, but I was caught up in the heat of the moment. Peter, his name was. He was sweet and romantic and wonderful. I heard he's married now. Anyway, I told myself I'd take the morning-after pill, but once I'd seen off the last of my hangover, I did some calculations and decided I was probably fine.

Probably fine. How many disasters have followed those words over the years?

I went to my new doctor in St. Andrews and arranged an abortion. I never told Peter, but I did tell two friends: Libby Bagshaw and Esther McPherson.

Libby was terrific; she was really there for me when I needed her. She admitted she'd been through the same thing when was sixteen and she talked me through what I should expect. She'd hated not understanding exactly what was going to happen, how much it would hurt, how long it would take, the clots, the sweats. She made sure I was prepared. She even came with me on the day and read a novel to me while I was curled up in pain. It was a Harry Potter one. I can't remember which but it was one of the earlier ones, and she even tried doing some silly voices.

Libby's attitude couldn't have been further from Esther's; she just wanted to know how it would affect her.

You're not going to keep it, are you? It'll ruin your body. You'll lose all your friends, you know? No one wants to go partying with someone who only wants to talk about how the last PTA meeting went.

When I told her I'd arranged a termination, she was happy. I mean the big-fat-smile kind of happy. I'm not ashamed or remorseful about what happened but its not a happy thing. Not by a long way. Esther took me by the hand and practically dragged me to the Champagne bar.

Three weeks later and there was a story in a low-brow gossip magazine. They had a photo of me walking out of the hospital hand-in-hand with Libby, in sweats and a beanie hat, with greasy hair and bloodshot eyes. Within two hours of circulation, word had got back to my Catholic parents and grandparents.

I steady myself on the wall of the cubicle and dab a tissue against the corners of my eyes. It was only when Graham got sick that Gran actually started acting civil around me again, and I think that was only because Graham told her to.

A quiet mewing makes me jump. I open the door to the cubicle and see the ginger tabby with the blue eyes sitting with her tail wrapped around herself. She stares up at me and meows again.

Smiling, I reach down to pet her. "You came looking for your lamb, didn't you?"

I open my bag, unfold the napkin and watch as the little cat demolishes her dinner. Hopefully, Agatha doesn't walk in on us.

"Don't worry," I whisper to the cat as I stoke her spine. "I'll get my revenge."

She flicks her tail.

"Because, the thing is, I know a dirty little secret of Esther's. I'm just not sure what to do with it yet."

– CHAPTER 17 –

Jo.

There's an uneasy hush around the table.

Mabel finishes the last of her wine, waves to a waitress and asks for our bill. "What was that about?" she asks.

Esther shrugs. "No idea, sweetie. Hormones perhaps? PMS?"

Ah, the return of Esther-the-feminist. To her, Paige's display of emotion can't possibly be valid. It must be her menstrual cycle making her irrational.

The bill arrives, and Verona takes charge of the kitty. We each put a hundred euros in earlier so it should last us a while. I cast my eyes to the group of men on the far side of the bar. I saw Paige staring earlier. Her brows were dropped like she was trying to work something out. If she was wondering if they're the guys from the other yacht, then she's right. It's definitely them. What I am unsure about is if the man on the left is Frederick. You'd think I'd be able to recognise my own fiancé – sorry, ex-fiancé – but he's sat at a right angle to me, meaning I can only see his profile. A baseball cap casts a shadow over his eyes, and he's more tanned than when I last saw him. Of course he's tanned; it's the Greek Isles. Even Esther and I are a shade darker than when we arrived. I turn my chair, angling it so I have my back to the men. The way I see it, if it is Frederick and his being here is a coincidence, he'd have caught my eye, we'd have shrugged awkwardly and agreed to keep our distance. But that hasn't happened. So, it's either not Frederick, and my mind is running away with itself, or it is, and he's avoiding my eye because … because he doesn't want me to know he's here. He broke our agreement and has followed me to Greece. Why? What's that bastard's end game?

I'm fussing with a napkin when Paige returns. She pulls her handbag higher up her shoulder and holds the strap as if it's a safety cord. She has a stern expression on her face, but she still looks pretty despite her serious eyes and stiff lips. When I pull that face, I look like a witch.

"There you are," Esther says with an over the top smile. "You okay, dear?"

"Fine."

We all know this is a lie. People who are actually fine don't just say they're fine. *Fine* is nothing more

143

than a socially acceptable way of saying *No, but bugger off, I don't want to talk about it.*

Esther apparently doesn't know this code because she places a hand on Paige's arm and purrs, "Good, because I'd hate to think I'd upset you."

Paige says nothing but her arm is rigid, every muscle tensed like a dog about to attack. I chance a look at the far side of the restaurant and rub my own arm, massaging the spot where Frederick snapped it in two. It still itches from time to time. Broken bones are like broken hearts: they never mend quite right.

Once the bill's settled, Esther gives Agatha a good-bye embrace, and we head back towards the harbour. It's eerily dark along this stretch. There's no street lighting, only the twinkling lights from the top of masts. I have a sudden vision of one of us slipping off the harbour wall and falling into the murky water.

Paige lags behind. A dozen cats have surrounded her, all purring and trying to outdo each other as they try to win her affections.

"Shoo, shoo," she says with a little slur in her voice. "Yes, I know you're cute, but I don't have any lamb left."

"We should hurry up," I say, trying to hide the tension in my voice.

Esther sidles up to me and puts an arm over my shoulders. I can smell wine on her breath, though I could say that about all of us. "You're not still afraid of the dark, are you Jo?"

"Not since I was fourteen," I say.

It's true. I'm not scared of the dark; I'm scared of those who lurk in it.

A noise behind us makes us all jump. The cats scarper in different directions, and we instinctively move closer to one another. Whatever our differences, there's a survival instinct – safety in numbers. You see it in other species too, not just humans.

Verona pulls her phone from her bag, switches on the torch function and aims it south, back towards Gaios town. A shape is silhouetted against the sky.

People.

Big people. A group of four or five.

"Is it the guys from the restaurant?" Paige asks, her pupils widening to absorb as much light as possible.

"I think so," I say loud enough for only her to hear. "They're the group from that other yacht."

"Let's get out of here."

We move as one along the darkened quay that leads back to where Bacchus is moored. After thirty seconds or so, we stop to look behind us.

Verona raises her torch again. "They're getting closer."

"Are they following us?" asks Mabel. She stops and turns, staring back in the direction we came from. Shoulders back and chin up; she's a vision of confidence.

Verona snorts. "If they are following us, it's your fault."

145

"Excuse me?"

"You flashed them for fuck's sake."

"Ladies!" I hiss. "Now is not the time." I look again. They're definitely getting closer, but oddly I can't hear them talking. If it were a simple case of a group of lads walking back to their boat after a night out, they'd be chatting and joking. They'd be making a right racket if experience is anything to go by. But not these guys; they're as silent as the water. In the animal world – and we're just well-groomed animals at the end of the day – creatures stay quiet because they're avoiding detection. And why do they want to avoid being detected? Because they're either the hunted or the hunter.

"Fuck this," mutters Paige, and we speed up again.

The marina comes into view. Behind all the darkened yachts full of sleeping sailors, Bacchus looms tallest. Her mast stands several feet taller than those around her. Libby goes first, traversing the plank onto the stern. She removes her shoes and manoeuvres her way towards the bow. Like a spider monkey, she practically swings from shroud to shroud, using the metal lines to steady herself.

"You should clip on," Esther warns.

She reaches the bow in no time. The hatch to the crew cabin opens, she drops inside, and the hatch closes behind her. Not even a wave good night.

"She should sleep in the main part of the boat," says Paige, boarding Bacchus. "It'll be scary in there by herself."

Verona follows. "She'll be fine. It locks from the inside."

Once we're all below deck, Esther locks the companionway, checks it, then double-checks it.

Even though we're all back on board, my heart is still racing. I don't know if we were actually being followed, but the whole thing has me gripping onto the galley's worksurface. My fingers need something solid, something tangible, to ground my thoughts and prevent my imagination from getting away from me. I swallow and look at the others. They all look how I feel. Paige doesn't say a word as she joins me in the galley. She retrieves a chef's knife and sharpens it on a honing steel. The high-pitched swishing noise of metal on metal goes right through me. She stops, admires her work and goes to bed, taking the knife with her.

Esther blinks, shakes her head in disbelief then raises a bottle of Gordon's. "Gin?" she asks.

"Not for me," says Verona. "Too much already." She picks up her pyjamas and heads to the bathroom to change.

Esther lifts her brows at Mabel and me.

"Oh, go on then," I say as if she's twisted my arm. I could use an extra tipple to take the edge off. Otherwise, I'll never get to sleep.

I fill glasses with ice and follow Mabel into Esther's cabin. It's luxurious, with a full king-size bed, satin sheets and a built-in dressing table. Back home, my dressing table is cluttered with perfume bottles, hair-brushes, makeup and hair ties, but Esther – ever the skipper – has her room shipshape. Everything is neat and tidied away; every surface clear and dust-free.

We exchange a look of relief as we clink our glasses. Esther begins to say something in Latin, but I clamp my hand over her mouth. "Can we, for once in our bloody lives, just say *cheers*?"

She sweeps thick black hair over her shoulders and lets out a soft sigh. "Cheers, Jovitha."

Mabel and I clamber on to Esther's bed and get comfortable. Mabel lies on her side while I sit cross-legged. Esther changes into her robe, then jumps on the bed to join us, causing Mabel to almost spill her drink.

"Isn't this nice?" Esther beams. "Like a sleepover. Jo and I used to have them all the time back in the good ol' days."

My body stiffens, but the others don't seem to notice. It's the word *sleepover;* it turns me into one of Pavlov's dogs. The dogs would salivate at the sound of a bell; I tense up when I think about – never mind. While Mabel and Esther fall into a natural conversation, I lay back on the soft bed; my thoughts turn to Paige in her room with that sharpened chef's knife. Is she really capable of stabbing someone if they broke in? I know everyone likes to think they're capable of doing whatever it takes in a situation like that, but you never really know. Not until it happens. Fight or flight. What most people don't realise is that there's a third option – an outcome a lot of people find themselves in – freeze.

Fight, flight, or freeze.

I always pictured Paige as a freeze kind of girl. I mean that in no disrespect. We're talking about instinct after all, something you can't help, something you can't plan for. I wonder what group people would put me in? They might think I'd freeze up too. Nice, sensible Jo. And they'd have been right if we were talking about the old me. The girl whose parents worked for the McPhersons. The girl who was only popular at primary school because she was friends with Esther. I don't freeze any more, but my muscles do harden, braced for whatever may come my way. I know exactly where I fit in this hypothetical situation: I'm a fighter. I can't help myself these days. If someone puts their hands on me, I lash out. Whenever Frederick hit me, I'd hit him back. Then he'd hit me harder. I'd pick up a chair. He'd choke me.

My arm tingles again, but enough about that.

I'm trying to say that you don't have to hurt me to see my merciless side. Hurt someone I love … then the real Jo Singh shows herself.

– CHAPTER 18 –

A man in a black hood cracks his knuckles as he towers over a man tied to a chair. Steely, unemotional eyes peer out from two holes that have been cut in the dark material. Black Hood isn't tall: five-eight at the most. But he's heavyset, with arms as thick as a basketball. They stretch the material of his long-sleeved t-shirt, and his ballooned pectorals balance on top of a well-fed belly. Though he carries an excess of fat, it would be a mistake to think Black Hood didn't have strong, powerful muscles underneath.

The man tied to the chair rolls his jaw from side to side. It isn't dislocated or completely shattered, but he's sure the last punch has cracked it. His tongue bleeds where he bit it, flooding his mouth with the taste of warm copper. He spits bloody saliva down his own shirt, one that used to be white, before letting the tip of his tongue roam from tooth to tooth, gently prodding each molar in turn until he feels one give. Top left, third from the back. His tongue can't leave it alone now. It fixates upon it, gently rocking the tooth back and forth until it loosens further and eventually pops free from the gum tissue, crown, neck, roots and all.

He spits the tooth to the floor and tongues the gaping hole it's left in his aching mouth.

"Was that necessary?"

Black Hood doesn't reply. He never does. The beefy man hasn't said a word in three days.

He's used to the silent treatment at home, but this is something else. He isn't sure what's worse: the physical torture, or the mental torture. His ribs sting whenever he takes a deep breath, and his little finger has been throbbing ever since they pulled his fingernail off. Maybe they'll take the whole finger next.

Black Hood takes two steps, his steal-capped boots thudding against the concrete floor. He picks up the tooth and lifts it until it's level with the holes in his face covering. The corners of his eyes crinkle as he examines it, turning it this way and that as if he's never seen one before. There isn't much light in the room. A lone bulb hangs from a greasy cord in the centre of the room, but Black Hood has secured him in the darkest corner. It's also the corner furthest from the doors. Not that anyone beyond the doors would help him anyway.

Black Hood throws the tooth away, and it skims across the dirty floor like a smooth stone on flat water. The tooth kicks up dust as is slides and tiny particles dance in the only area of illumination.

"I was hoping to keep that," he calls after Black Hood, who's heading towards the only exit. He knows the torment isn't over. Black Hood will be back in the morning. "You know, put it under my pillow. Wait for the tooth fairy?"

The metal doors slam and the sound reverberates around the cavernous room. The man in the chair sighs. He has more chance of the tooth fairy being real than of getting out of this mess.

- CHAPTER 19 -

Esther.

It's coming up to six a.m. when I'm woken by the dawn chorus. A symphonious mix of larks, warblers, pipits, and buntings plays over the beat of a green woodpecker rat-a-tatting into a nearby tree. I wait until I can hear Verona folding her bed away in the saloon, before emerging from my cabin. I have to admit this trip isn't shaping up quite how I'd hoped. Between Mabel's temper tantrum and Paige's outburst, I don't know what's got into everyone. Jo seemed distracted all day yesterday, and something is definitely bugging Verona. I may have been naive in thinking we'd pick up where we left off, but it's what I'd been hoping for. It seems we haven't only distanced ourselves physically since graduating, by moving away and beginning our new adult lives, but we've distanced ourselves emotionally. We used to open up to each other about everything. We were close and had no secrets. Now, well, it's like I can feel the walls between us growing higher each day. Hopefully, I can raise everyone's spirits at our morning briefing.

"Morning," Verona greets me as she disappears into the bathroom she shares with Jo and Paige.

"Morning," I reply through the door. "Sleep well?"

She opens the door ajar. "Mostly. I had a nightmare about those men breaking in here, then I couldn't get back to sleep for an hour because I was worried about Paige sleepwalking with that chef's knife."

"You don't need to worry about anyone breaking in here, V," I reassure her. "Bacchus is safe as houses."

She doesn't look convinced.

"Besides, Paige is just paranoid."

"Wouldn't you be? She went home one day and found a fan in her bed. I know he's likely not the first fan she's had in her bed," she adds with a snide smile that doesn't suit her at all, "but that one was uninvited. It must have been terrifying."

She shuts the door again. I hear the rhythmic thud of the water pump followed by running water coming from the shower. Paige never told me about someone breaking into her bedroom. No one tells me anything these days. Still, it sounds horrific. If I've heard the story of Michael Fagan and the Queen once, I've heard it a hundred times, and it never sounds any less awful. And, I'm not sure what Verona meant by *not the first fan she's had in her bed.* That's not Paige's style. Besides, she should be dating film stars and lead singers of rock bands. I heard the Viscount's eldest is single. No, he'd be a terrible match for Paige, doesn't like to be outshone. Also, one shouldn't matchmake, one only gets blamed when things turn sour.

"I'll get the kettle," I call through the bathroom door. I notice our glasses from last night have been cleaned and put away. Jo must have washed them before bed. I use our gas kettle as we're not plugged into the shore power and wait patiently for the water to boil. Once the kettle begins to whistle, I fill a large cafetière with my favourite Ecuadorian roast and breathe in the invigorating smell.

One by one, the smell of a fresh brew draws the girls from their slumber, and we meet in the cockpit to go over the plan for the day. I've already studied the charts and checked the weather report. Still, it's my duty to communicate all of this to the others.

Paige's luminescent hair is held back by a silky eye mask. She pours a cup of coffee and sits next to Libby.

"Is that woodpecker going to knock it off any time soon?" she says, glancing at a small green bird with a flash of red across the top and back of its head. "It's doing wonders for my hangover."

Mabel's golden locks are sopping wet from her shower; she takes a seat dressed only in a towel. Verona and Jo stifle yawns as I spread the charts on the table.

"Good news or bad news first?" I ask the group.

"Good, please," Libby answers before the others can object, and I know they will. Who picks *good* first? It's an unwritten rule, is it not, to have the bad news first, then soften it up with the good?

"As you wish. Well, darlings, the good news is that there have been no further reports of piracy. Nor have there been any reports of creepy men getting up to no good here on Paxos. I think we let our imaginations run away from us last night."

Paige pouts, but Libby comes to her defence. "Better safe than sorry. So what's the bad news? You said there are no pirates, but I'm guessing marauding zombies await us in Sicily? Vampire attacks in Puglia?"

"Very funny," I say, tilting my head in her direction. "No. It's way less interesting than zombies and vampires. It's the weather."

Everyone eyes the perfectly blue sky, then they turn as one to question me.

"What about it?" asks Mabel, water dripping from the ends of her curls to create wet patches on the towel.

"It might look wonderful right now, but there's a front moving in. You can see the mackerel sky on the horizon." I point into the distance and heads follow my arm to ripples of thin, white clouds that resemble its namesake's striped scales. "It's going to get pretty nasty. We need to get under sail as soon as we can while there's good wind and try to get to Othonoi before noon."

Mabel blows a raspberry. "Pfft. We've sailed in worse. Remember that race around Bute during the blizzard?"

Libby shudders and Jo rubs her arms as if the memory alone is enough to chill them to the bone.

"It was minus eight if I recall," Verona adds.

"Minus eleven if you count the wind chill," says Jo.

"Ladies," I say, "I know we're not scared of a little rain, or a little snow for that matter, but this is going to be one heck of a lot of rain. Even if you don't mind getting drenched, the problem is the wind." I lift my finger from a small island that sits north-west of Corfu and run it across the chart. "The wind's coming this way. It's going to pick up, bringing the storm clouds with it. It's going to get up to force seven, gusting eight."

Eyes flick left and right until Jo says, "Yeah, that sounds a bit shit."

The others nod.

"I say we aim to get to Othonoi by noon at the latest. Then we'll have about an hour before the storm hits. We can fit in a quick drink somewhere near the harbour; there aren't many choices if I'm honest. Then we should grab some goodies and hunker down in Bacchus for the night. Nice cosy night in. Sound good?"

Shrugs.

157

"Come on, it'll be lovely. Champagne, olives, the sound of the rain on the deck? I have some battery-powered candles around somewhere. We can put face masks on, paint our toes? A proper girl's night in."

Libby drains her cup. "Would sound lovely if I didn't have to clamber across the deck in gusts of force eight to get to my cabin."

"Oh, shh, Libby. You can bunk in with me tonight."

I don't like sharing a bed. Never have. That's why I had two beds in my room at home: a queen for me and a double for any friends who spent the night. But Libby's right, and as skipper, I shouldn't have her traversing the deck during a storm. Even clipped on, it would be a bit sketchy.

She smiles, and I ignore Mabel's wiggling eyebrows.

"So we're in agreement? No handsome young waiters?" I look at Mabel. "No bloody cats, and no weirdos following us back from tavernas?"

Verona tops up our empty coffee cups. "Sounds like a plan, Skip."

– CHAPTER 20 –

Verona.

What a beautiful morning. The air smells of seaweed and pine, and I'm mesmerised by the glittering effect the morning sunshine has on the ripples of the water. It looks like it's alive with thousands of sparkling creatures. I'm finding it hard to believe there's a seventy-five mile per hour storm coming when all is so calm and fair here. But, I've checked all my apps, and it's true. They're called medicanes, which is a portmanteau of Mediterranean and hurricane. I stare at *weather.com* in disbelief. Esther's right; we're in for a bumpy ride. Not that I didn't believe her. You know what else is hard to believe? That I have such a good signal out here; back home, I have to go upstairs if I want to send a text message. I shouldn't grumble. I should be grateful to have a three-storey property in London. I'm mortgaged up to my eyeballs of course, and it's a lot of space for one person, but somewhere between the noisy neighbours, the rising damp and the expensive heating bills, yes, I'm grateful. I say it three times in my head as an affirmation. *I'm grateful. I'm grateful. I'm grateful.*

That's right, Verona. Say it enough times, and you might start to believe it.

Even with favourable winds and a mainsail the size of Bacchus's, I think we'll be pushing it to get to Othonoi by noon. Time is precious. The fenders are in, and the sails are up before the clock hits half six.

Esther seems tense. She says she wants to be in Sicily by Thursday, which means getting to Calabria tomorrow. She sets herself these challenges then gives herself a hard time if she doesn't achieve them. She was the same in Bute. She could have picked a harbour on the western coast of Corfu for tonight, it really wouldn't make a difference, just a few extra hours on the overnight passage. But now she's said Othonoi, she'll have to stick with it. She never changes. Her voice is snippier than usual, and she's barking orders at everyone. I can see Mabel rolling her eyes. I've checked our horoscopes and Leos are warned to tread carefully with those in authority today. I wouldn't exactly say that Esther is in a position of authority over Mabel. Still, I hope she can tame her predatory, passionate and powerful instincts for the sake of group harmony. If I can manage to keep a lid on my feelings, everyone should be able to.

160

"Paige," Esther snarls. "Heave faster. Oh, for the love of Zeus. I thought you said you worked out? Libby, give her a hand."

Paige flinches as she and Libby struggle to handle the genoa sheets during the first tack of the day.

I tidy a wrench away and am about to offer to brew everyone some coffee when I have second thoughts. Do I really want to give Esther caffeine when she's in one of her driven moods? When Esther gets like this, I'm pretty good at letting it go. It's fine. These things don't get to me because I owe her. Esther made me feel human again after years of feeling like a mutant. For that, I can forgive her flaunting her wealth, her venomous comments and her general air of superiority. She can't help it, she's a Sagittarius – the archer – taking command is in her nature.

Herbal tea it is. No one wants an archer with caffeine jitters.

* * *

Jo

We're about to overtake another large yacht. She's a Bordeaux 60 with the name Actaeon painted in Cobalt blue across her white hull. Whether they realise they're in a race with us or not is irrelevant to Esther. Bacchus heels to thirty degrees or so and we gain on

161

them like the hunting dogs from the myth. It's a great story. The goddess Artemis was bathing in a river when Actaeon, a great hunter, came across her and saw her naked form. Artemis was furious and told Actaeon that he would be transformed into a stag if he ever spoke another word. Actaeon nodded his understanding and left Artemis to enjoy her swim. He wandered silently through the woods, searching for his pack of hunting dogs. When he heard their barks, without thinking, he called to them. The hunter immediately morphed into a magnificent deer with deep red fur and impressive antlers. Actaeon fled deeper into the woods until he found a pond. Leaning over the calm water, he saw his cervine reflection and moaned in horror. The sound came out as a stag's grunt and attracted the instincts of the pack. He was hounded, and ultimately, torn limb from limb by his own dogs.

It's the original *the hunter becomes the hunted* cliche. One of my favourite tropes in crime fiction: the detective is framed for murder; the serial killer who only targets other killers; the childhood victim who grows up and stalks her attackers. There's a reason these tales appeal to me.

"Jo!" Esther's eyebrows are an inch above her Chanel shades, almost reaching her hairline. "Earth to Jo. Mainsheet!"

I mumble something about not being able to hear her over the wind – it's about force five at the moment

– and grab a blue rope that attaches to the boom. I wrap it around a silver drum and tighten it up using a winch. The boom stops swaying and holds firm, increasing our speed further.

Frederick – God, I hate even thinking his name – watches cage fighting, or MMA, or whatever they like to call it. I know, it sounds like I'm going on a tangent, but bear with me. I think cage fighting is barbaric, human cockfighting if you ask me, but they have this saying: *don't leave it in the hands of the judges*. In other words, try to finish the fight by either knocking out or submitting your opponent before the time runs out. Otherwise, once the bell rings, the decision goes to the judges, and you never know how they may score it. The same can be said for life. How many times have people gotten away with rape, assault or murder? All the evidence was there, and yet, when their day in court arrived, they got away scot-free.

I shiver and nip below deck to grab a cardigan. With Bacchus rolling as I descend, I have to really take my time and make sure I'm certain of my footing with every step I take. I ensure I have a firm hold of one handrail before letting go of another. Shutting the door to my cabin, I rummage through my luggage looking for something that will both protect me from the wind and act as a comfort blanket. I find a beige piece of knitwear that will do the job.

Don't leave it in the hands of the judges.

We didn't leave it in the hands of the judges when was I was eighteen. It was the winter before I started at St. Andrews, and Big Manny James ran into the Black Swan with tears streaming down his ruddy face. He collapsed on the bar, begging for a shot of something strong. The bartender, Matthew Rowlands I think his name was, handed him a double whiskey, and he carried it in shaking hands, to a tartan-covered barstool. I'd never seen a grown man cry like that before, not one built like Manny. His closest friends, the guys he worked with at the airfield, gathered around him first, then the rest of the clientele followed. We all knew each other or knew of each other. It was a small place and everyone drank in the Black Swan. Everyone except the McPhersons. At first, we couldn't understand what he was saying between sobs. I thought something had happened at the airfield, a crash or a fire perhaps, but then he got control of his breathing and told us Tommy Ware, the football coach, had been abusing his boy.

Manny picked up a red, paper napkin and pressed it into his eyes. "He told some of the lads they'd never get picked for the first team again unless they …" He let out the sort of cry that pains you to listen to it. "Unless they did him certain favours. Said that's what all the Premier League players had to do. *You want to play in the Premier League, don't you?*"

Half the folk in the Black Swan had sons or little brothers who played for Longstone Dale under twelves.

No one said a word, no one took the lead – no one needed to. The hive mind was in operation. As one, at least forty of us emptied the pub and walked slowly and silently towards Ware's house at the far side of the village. Out of the square, down the unlit lane, up the bank, along the trail through the wood and under the viaduct. All the while, the McPhersons' manor was silhouetted atop the hill, its windows glowing with warm firelight. It was odd how calm we were; we just knew what had to be done.

I'm distracted briefly by the sound of Mabel and Paige laughing. We must have overtaken the other yacht, Actaeon, because I hear Mabel yell, "Eat our zero emissions!"

My eyes flicker to the ceiling and I decide to make some lunch. If nothing else, it will explain why I've been down here so long. There's no way I can socialise until I've dealt with this memory.

Ware's home was a one-storey converted farm building with thick stone walls and a chimney that hadn't survived the previous winter. From the end of his drive, we saw his outline in the light of his living room, a blue flicker from his television casting him a shade of cerulean. The sight of him incensed the mob. We broke into a sprint, threw rocks, hammered our fists into his front door. I remember the sound as

165

the window smashed and the door buckled under the weight of Harry Kings and Cliff Sheldon. Ware made a run for it, trying to reach his back door. He was fast, but the crowd were faster. They … *we*, I should say, were on him like animals.

I spent a summer in Belarus studying the Eurasian wolf. I've seen them take down prey in the wild. We were exactly like the wolves; everyone wanted their bit.

We beat him to death.

I was on the periphery, hardly touched him, but that doesn't matter, we acted as one. One pack. One mission. When it was over, we got up and left. No one called the police. No one said a word.

It was a week later when a relative raised the alarm and police came to ask questions. We hadn't seen a thing. Everyone in the village acted like they were shocked. *Who would do such a thing?*

"He was an upstanding member of our community," Harry told them.

"We're horrified something like that could happen in Longstone Dale," said Matthew while wiping down the bar.

Cliff finished his pint. "My fingerprints? Oh, you'll find everyone's fingerprints in Ware's house. He was the friendly sort, always inviting people over for a coffee, or a beer, or to watch the game. He was a *mi casa, su casa* sort of bloke."

I fix my mind on the task of making sandwiches and boiling the kettle. Bacchus lists right and left, and I'm thankful that my full attention is needed to stop jars slipping off the counter and the like. Nothing is simple in high winds; even the most basic tasks take twice as long when you're being bobbed from side to side.

When I think about that day, and the aftermath, I hate that I'm capable of such a thing, but I don't regret it. He was a predator who got what he deserved. Justice was served. The hunter became the hunted; we didn't leave it in the hands of the judges.

– CHAPTER 21 –

Mabel.

"Now this is sailing!"

I hold a metal shroud for support and extend my free arm to the side, feeling the wind as it whistles through my fingers and pushes my arm backwards. Turning my face skywards, I let fresh, cold raindrops hit my cheeks. It feels amazing. My hair tangles, my mascara runs, and my heart sings. In case it isn't obvious, I can be a bit of a thrill-seeker.

The sky's turned a gnarly shade of grey, like dark pewter, and these rain droplets are the size of grapes. No exaggeration. Each one hits the water with such force it looks like a miniature explosion. The waves are getting bigger as well; they didn't look like this twenty minutes ago.

Bacchus rises with the swell, and as she reaches the crest of the wave, the weight of the bow takes over and, in a seesaw motion, the front of the boat slams into the Ionian Sea. Salt water flows across the deck, over my bare feet and into the cockpit like a small tidal wave. Esther checks her watch.

"The rain's two hours early, and we're still three hours from Othonoi."

I shrug, climbing back into the cockpit. "Come on, you love sailing in conditions like this."

She does. I know she does; she revels in it. But today, her face is hard, and a line has formed between her brows, it's big enough to see over the top of her shades.

This isn't the Greece we knew yesterday. No bright blue seas or turquoise bays and coves. No azure sky or warm air. There's no need for sunscreen now. Jo and Verona are wearing caps to keep the rain off their faces, rather than protecting their foreheads from UV rays. The sea reflects the darkening sky, changing from Oxford blue to the colour of steel. White crests form on breaking waves, and the wind stings my face and muffles my hearing. This isn't the Ionian you see on postcards or travel shows.

Libby's been sat with her head in her hands for the past half hour. She lifts her face, which looks a little on the green side, and says, "Maybe we should anchor somewhere closer. We're not far from Paleo – Paleokastritsa."

Esther reaches over and strokes her dark, damp hair. "It's fine, darling." Turning back to me, she adds,

169

"I'm going to go batten down the hatches. Take the helm?"

"Aye aye," I say, grabbing one of the large wheels and spreading my feet to help my balance.

"And Libby, keep your eyes on the horizon, sweetie. It'll help with the seasickness."

Cruelly, as if Poseidon was listening, Bacchus arches over another wave and the horizon completely disappears from view.

Libby, looking even more queasy, lurches forward slightly then swallows hard. I have a horrible feeling she's just thrown up in her mouth. Fair play to her for drinking it back down. If she'd spewed on the deck, first, Esther would have lost the plot, and second, the rest of us might have spewed too. Isn't it weird how that happens? You see someone vomit, then you have to vomit. I wonder why that is.

While Esther scurries around below deck, making sure all the hatches are secured and the cabin doors are closed, I make the most of my time at the helm. Our passage plan calls for a heading of three-hundred and ten degrees. Bacchus pulls toward starboard, and I have to fight to keep her on course. The compass sways anywhere between two-ninety and three-thirty, giving my arms a workout as I try my best to steady her. Above me, our wind indicator vibrates nervously. I work in PR, which is cool. I love it when we pull off a major event, or I get to meet A-listers, but I haven't had a thrill like this in a long time. Excluding young Jorge, of course.

But as Esther returns, the wind gusts and I lose control of Bacchus for a second.

"Holy shit," I gasp. I have the helm turned as far to the port side as it will go, but the yacht still pulls hard to the right. "We need to trim the sails," I shout over the wind. "Take some power out of them."

"That'll slow us down," Esther replies. She grabs the cockpit table for support and shakes her head. "Speed before comfort."

Jo pulls the zipper on her waterproof jacket right up to her chin. "This is ridiculous, Esther." She grabs a furling line and begins to pull in some of the genoa, which I have to say is pretty damn ballsy of her.

The boat responds by listing slightly less than it was a second ago.

"And Libby's right," Jo continues, despite Esther looking like someone just pissed on her chips. "We should turn back and moor up on Corfu. It's silly us trying to get to some remote island during this weather. Let's get the engine on, get the sails away and get to shelter."

Esther folds her arms and adjusts her posture to look taller and broader. "No. Look, I'm skipper—"

"Yeah, yeah, you're skipper," mocks Jo as Bacchus crashes over another wave and another surge of wind has us reaching for handholds. She turns her back so Esther can't hear her over the wind, leans into me and whispers, "Is it just me, or is it starting to smell like a mutiny?"

The sky darkens further, and a rumble of distant thunder makes all our backs stiffen, even mine.

Within half an hour, the rain has increased to the point where it hurts my skin. Each droplet feels like a hailstone. Paige looks like she's crying. It might just be the rain, but her eyes are red, and she shakes from more than just the cold. She's scared, and I don't blame her. These aren't easy conditions, even for experienced sailors. The waves are now hitting us side-on, meaning we roll left and right like a giant rocking chair. I glance down at the instrument panel; we're being pounded by fifty-knot winds. With my eyes on the display, I don't spot the change in the water that warns me of an approaching gust. Bacchus heels dramatically until the top of the mast is less two meters from the drink. Everyone, including me, screams. Our water bottles and Verona's shades slide off the deck and disappear into the blue. After a moment, Bacchus rights herself, but it's still more than even an adrenaline junkie like myself can take. I have to admit defeat. I'm not having fun anymore.

"Skip," I call. "Sorry, Esther, I know you wanted to do this under sail, but it's getting silly now, and the others are frightened."

I press the pad of my index finger against the button that starts the engine. It grumbles and splutters. I try again, pushing harder as if that makes a difference. This time the motor doesn't make a sound, and as another gust of wind pounds us, I'm forced to turn to the others and shout the words no sailor wants to hear. "We have engine failure."

– CHAPTER 22 –

Mabel.

"What?" Esther shoves me out of the way as we dramatically heel over once more. She furiously pounds the button marked *Start Engine*. "This is ridiculous. She was serviced not long ago."

Libby, holding on to anything that's screwed down, tries to open the companionway doors.

"Where do you think you're going?" Esther asks, her voice higher in pitch than usual. She doesn't look the composed, put-together woman I'm used to.

Water hits Libby in the face as she tries to speak. "I'm calling the coast guard. We have engine failure."

Esther grabs little Libby roughly by the shoulders and almost throws her back into her seat. "Stay in the cockpit. You'll crack your head open down there."

"We need help," she pleads, her voice breaking with fear, and one by one, the other girls back her up.

"We should call it in," Jo screeches over the sounds of the storm.

Wind rattles through the rigging, thunder booms above us, and rain slams into the water as if each raindrop weighs a tonne.

"Are you kidding?" Esther opens a locker, pulls out straps attached to carabiners and begins to hand them out. "Clip on. We're not calling anyone. Do you know what happens when you call the coast guard? They won't just tow us to safety. They'll impound the yacht, launch an investigation. We'll have to pay this fee and that fee. We'll never get to Sicily on time."

By this point, I'm certain no one gives a flying fuck about getting to Sicily. We can fly home from any Greek or Italian hub.

"We're going to be fine. We can sail her in. We've done it before."

Jo finishes securing her carabiner clip. "We did it on Juniper, in force three, with the help of a shore crew. I'm with Libby. I say we head to Paleo-whatsit. V?"

Verona's face is almost set in stone. She looks from Esther to Libby, then back to Esther. She's clearly torn. "Let's head in."

"We can't," Esther shouts.

This bickering is doing my head in. Esther's lost control of the crew at the worst possible moment.

"Why the hell not, Esther?" I demand, wrestling with the helm as it spins violently back and forth.

"And don't give me any crap about needing to get to Sicily by Thursday. Your competitive spirit will get us all killed one of these days."

Esther pulls charts of the area from the table locker. They're covered in plastic sheeting to protect them from the elements. "It's too dangerous. Look at this marina at Paleokastritsa. It's too crowded. Rocks, reefs, islands … We'll be smashed to smithereens. But here, yes it'll take a while, but we'll be in open water, no hazards and the harbour will be quiet. Look, we can sail in here, it'll be sheltered, then the wind can take us onto the jetty side-to."

"Take the helm," I snap, grabbing the charts so I can see for myself.

I look up. Jo, Libby, Verona and Paige are staring at me. They don't want Esther's opinion – they want mine. Am I the new skipper? Jo said something about a mutiny, but she was joking, right? We all know this is Esther's father's boat; it's bad form for me to take over.

"Well?" Jo asks.

I pull on a cap and adjust the strap to stop it from flying off with the next gust. "Esther's right." As much as I hate to say it. "We need to plough on. If we had power, I'd say we should call it a day and head in, but we don't, and without power, there's no way we can make it into that harbour. Right, here's the plan. Paige, you have the best core. Go below deck and get six life jackets. Be careful, the rolling will feel worse down there. Are they still in the saloon locker, Esther?"

She nods but doesn't take her eyes off the compass.

Paige moves quickly to avoid too much water entering Bacchus's interior.

"Jo, reef the mainsail. Bring it almost all the way in. Esther, stay on the helm. You've got this. That's Othonoi, right? In the distance?"

The island is barely visible through the deluge. It's nothing more than a grey shape on a grey background.

Esther nods again. "Taking her to three hundred degrees."

"Libby, you doing okay?" She doesn't look well at all. Whether it's motion sickness or anxiety, I don't know. She needs something to do, something to focus on other than trying not to spew. "Can you find the storm anchor and set it?"

She stands, a look of purpose in her eyes that wasn't there earlier.

"And V, come over this side of the cockpit. Furl the genoa some more," I say, referring to the sail at the front of the vessel.

She grabs the sheet – a thin white rope with purple detail – wraps it around the drum and heaves. At the bow, I see the genoa begin to roll in on itself. I unclip from the safety rail that runs behind me and clip on to the starboard side. Paige re-emerges and hands out

177

the life jackets. Suited up, they take their seats in the relative safety of the cockpit.

I run my fingers over the clips on my life jacket, giving it a double and triple check. I don't get the luxury of staying the cockpit; I need to put the storm jib up. Which means climbing over the deck to get to the bow.

During a medicane.

- CHAPTER 23 -

Verona.

Caught somewhere between claustrophobia and agoraphobia, that's how this feels. Bacchus holds us prisoner, because to jump off her would be suicide, and yet we are completely exposed and at the mercy of the elements. As the storm rages, we're tossed about with such ease it makes me feel insignificant. Like we're nothing more than a plaything for the gods. Our faces are painted with distress. Paige's teeth chatter and Jo continuously tugs at her carabiner, as if she expects it to fail at any moment. With the exception of Esther, who is doing her best to hold Bacchus steady, we all have our eyes firmly on Mabel.

I often forget that Mabel can be an absolute warrior in times like these. She doesn't always portray herself in the best light, what with the way she dresses, her eyelash extensions, fake tan, and heavy makeup. I know you shouldn't judge a book by its cover, but we're all guilty of it when it comes to Mabel. She might like to play the Barbie doll at times, but she becomes more like Wonder Woman when the proverbial hits the fan. She shows no fear. I envy her. I wish I could be more like her in meetings. I used to be tougher and would hold my own with the board members, but that was before Daniel left. Now I'm becoming more of a pushover.

Mabel's wild, blonde hair is pulled through the hole in the back of her cap. Mascara and heavy eyeliner have left long black streaks down her face. I can't decide if she looks more like Brandon Lee in *The Crow*, or No-Face from *Spirited Away*. Her clothes are plastered to her, and she has a look of tenacity about her. Keeping her weight low, she holds the storm gib – a small, easy to manage sail – under her arm. Methodically, she takes one deliberate step at a time. She looks so vulnerable and unprotected over there. I can barely see her through the haze of rain and darkness that creeps around us. She's nothing more than a small orange glow viewed through a dark lens.

I don't know how long she's been out of the cockpit for, but I feel like we're all holding our collective breath until she gets back. Suddenly I recall the horoscope I read this morning – about challenging authority. Mabel has pretty much commandeered Bacchus. I try to put it from my mind. It might come back to bite us all later, but at least under Mabel's command, we've stopped quarrelling.

Mabel jumps back into the cockpit and glances at the control panel. Ahead, the orange storm sail billows from the bow. "How's that?" she asks Esther.

"Better," she replies. "The storm anchor's helping too."

The storm anchor, also called a drogue, is basically an underwater parachute that trails behind us. It reduces our speed but improves handling. We might be out here for longer, but at least Bacchus will respond to whoever is at the helm.

Mabel takes a long, deep breath and wipes water from her face, smearing her mascara sideways. Now she looks like a commando with mud stripes over her cheeks. She turns to the rest of us, looking each of us in the eye for a moment, assessing the emotions written on our faces. "Good work, team."

Those three little words warm me, and I don't think I'm the only one. We take our seats, shut our mouths and await our next instructions.

* * *

Esther guides Bacchus as close to the harbour wall as she dares. The winds are still high, and the rain lashes down upon us, but as we neared our destination, the island sheltered us from the worst of the storm. At least here, the rain is falling downwards, rather than driving sideways like it has done for the last few hours. A few hours? Was that all it was? I feel like I've been lost at sea for a week. Those were the longest few hours of my life.

We get into position, moving in a crouched formation to attach the fenders and get the warps ready. When we're within a few feet of the wall, Mabel gives a command, and Paige leaps like a long-legged antelope from the midship onto the stone pier. She lands in a deep squat before throwing her hips back and sprawling on to her belly. The movement gives her the most stability. The last thing we need is her losing her balance and falling off the other side of the wall. Libby tosses Paige a warp; she catches it and runs to the nearest cleat. Meanwhile, Mabel had done the same thing. They dig their feet against the cleats, using them for leverage. They squat and straighten their legs, using the power of their lower bodies to help as they lure Bacchus into her resting place for the night.

"Oh my goodness," Esther calls, her face brightening as the final warp is secured in a cleat hitch. "We did it. We did it, girls." She wraps the rope around metal prongs, then forms a figure-eight, before tucking the rope back under itself. She stands, pulls her shoulders back and bounces on the balls of her feet. Under her, pooled water splashes upwards with each bounce. She almost looks childlike, like a young girl testing her new wellies in the nearest puddle. She spreads her arms wide, waiting for hugs of relief.

When no hugs come her way, I unclip and offer her an embrace.

"I knew Pier Pressure could handle it," she whispers in my ear through my sodden hair.

One by one, the realisation that we are okay, that we're not going to die a watery death, washes over us and we pat each other on the back, squeeze each other and high five. After releasing Mabel, Paige climbs back aboard and offers Esther a fist bump. It's a test. She's waiting to see if she has another *urban* comment for her. After what Paige just managed, I think she'd be on the first plane home if Esther even dared.

We all watch, waiting to see what Esther chooses. Thankfully, she obliges, raises her fist and bumps her knuckles against Paige's. I'm pleased, but it does look odd. Royals rarely fist bump.

We come together, hugging in a circle around the cockpit table, our arms wrapping over the shoulders of the person on either side. We look like six drowned rats – drowned rats in orange life jackets. I'm between Jo and Esther, and I'm not sure which of us is shivering the most. We're all freezing cold and pumped full of adrenaline.

Mabel breaks the huddle first. "Want me to take a look at the engine?" she asks Esther.

Esther pushes strands of dark hair from her face. "After everything you just did?" She grabs Mabel's face in both hands and wipes her dirty cheeks with her thumbs. "You were a machine, darling. A machine! Put your darn feet up and relax."

I have to agree. "You're soaked through," I say. "Have a hot shower, and I'll fix you a gin and tonic."

This is music to her ears. She opens the companionway doors and gasps as she stares into Bacchus's interior. "Oh."

We crowd around to take a look. Bacchus looks like a bomb has hit her. The sofa cushions have slid to the floor; books are scattered everywhere. A galley locker has come undone, and its contents have flown free. The framed photos of the McPhersons at Sandringham has fallen from its hook. Plates are smashed like they were guests at a Greek wedding, a jar of olives is cracked in two, its briny fluid spread all over the galley floor, and green olives are scattered far and wide. Worse still, a bottle of red wine has broken into a thousand pieces. Streaks of crimson liquid make the cabin doors and benchtops look like they're part of a gruesome crime scene.

"Hit the showers, Mabel. That's an order." Esther claps her on the back. "Paige, Jo, we have some food on board, but not a lot. Are you okay nipping to the store? It's just over there." She points across the bay.

Paige and Jo look at each other and nod.

"We're already drenched," Jo replies. "A quick jaunt to the shop won't make a difference."

"The rest of us will get started on the cleanup."

Esther is clearly back in charge. Our time with Mabel as skipper is over.

184

* * *

By the time Paige and Jo get back from the shop, most of the cleaning is finished. We work in uneasy silence. Libby keeps glancing at me, and I think Esther is embarrassed, having lost our faith during the passage. She doesn't need to be. Part of management is knowing when to let the best person for the job take the lead sometimes. I don't do the design work for Lazy Llama foods because it's not in my skill set, I let someone more artistic handle that. Same with accounts and advertising. Our recipes are a different matter; they're my babies.

"We couldn't get much," Paige says. "Crisps and snacks mainly."

"As long as you have wine, we'll survive the night." Mabel emerges from her ensuite, and a billowy cloud of steam follows her.

Jo lifts a canvas shopping bag, and the reassuring sound of glass bottles chiming against each other is all the answer we need.

Mabel offers Paige the use of her shower as Esther disappears into her own, leaving Jo, Libby and myself sopping wet in the saloon.

"You go first," Libby tells Jo.

"Are you sure? You're shivering."

Libby picks up a shard of crockery from the floor and tosses it in the bin. "Go ahead. You've been out there longer than us."

185

Goody two shoes.

I finish scrubbing the last of the pinot noir from a cushion cover. It'll likely go musty overnight as we have no way of drying it properly right now. I'll give it another wash in the morning, then hang it from the guard rail before we set off.

Libby looks at me again, and I turn away. It's annoying. She makes me feel like one of her photography subjects. She wraps her arms around herself to keep warm as she goes back to scouring the floor for more fragments of porcelain and glass. Maybe if she cleaned a little harder, she'd have warmed up by now.

"What?" I finally snap when I catch her staring at me again.

"You've been weird with me ever since we met up in Kefalonia. Have I done something to upset you?"

Typical Libby. Always feigning innocence. "Like you don't know."

Esther chooses this moment to reappear. She's wrapped in a soft white towel; her damp black hair air dries, hanging loosely over her shoulders. "Who's next she asks?"

We both make a dash for it, but Libby gets there first. She's usually the polite one, the one who lets everything go in a desperate bid to show that northerners are the polite and friendly ones while the rest of us are rude savages. Not today. She practically barges me out of the way, and I'm left waiting for Jo or Paige to finish.

Mabel lifts a perfectly plucked eyebrow. "Everything okay?"

"Fine."

"Then where's that gin and tonic I was promised?"

- CHAPTER 24 -

Libby.

Like I don't know. That's what Verona said. The thing is, I don't actually know. I mean, I have an idea, but if it is that, well … well tough. That's her problem. I didn't do anything wrong.

I help Paige chop cucumber for a tzatziki dip. We have stuffed peppers in the oven, bowls of crisps and olives, and grated courgette ready to be squashed into patties and shallow fried. I forget how tall Paige is until I stand this close to her. Her head must be an inch from the ceiling, I feel like one of the seven dwarves in comparison. Maybe if I dyed my bob black, I could at least look more like Snow White that Bashful or Sneezy.

In the saloon, Ed Sheeran's voice sings a love song through Bacchus's sound system. Mabel looks a lot more relaxed now that she's had a gin and tonic; her feet rest on the dining table, and she has an arm around Jo's shoulders. Esther peers through one of the portholes. She wipes at it with the cuff of her sleeve and leans in closer.

"Another yacht's coming in."

"Let's hope this one has power," Jo says dryly.

Esther's promise of a cosy night in has come to fruition. Outside, rain pelts the deck and waves roll into the hull. They provide extra bass to the Ed Sheeran track, and somehow, Bacchus seems to be bopping in time to the music. The lights are dimmed, and battery-powered candles give the saloon a lovely glow, like a sepia filter. We're all in our comfiest clothing. For me, that's jogging pants and an oversized hoodie. For Esther, it's a designer robe and slippers that have the St. Regis insignia stitched into the instep. I wonder if she bought them, or if they come free when you stay there. I wouldn't know, I've never stayed anywhere like that. I've never even stayed somewhere that has valet parking. I'd ask, but after saying I thought classics was the study of Jane Austin novels, I think I'd better not.

Paige taps her foot against mine to get my attention. "What's Pete Tong?" she asks. "You have sad eyes."

"Oh, nothing. Just imposter syndrome."

A Champagne cork hits the roof just as the oven begins to beep. The stuffed peppers are ready. Paige removes them and places them to one side to cool. She takes a thick slice of feta, covers it in oregano and

189

black pepper, gives it a healthy drizzle of olive oil and sides it in the oven to bake.

"What do you mean?" she asks.

I stare down at my feet. "Just wondering if I'll ever fit in. Verona's … I don't know. I got my degree, got my dream job, live in London, have a great little flat, earn good money … Well, earn okay-ish money. But inside, I'm still the poor girl from the broken home in a forgotten borough. I know that's not the true definition of imposter syndrome; I'm just saying, I don't belong."

Paige tucks her index finger under my chin, lifting my gaze from the floor. She takes a deep breath before speaking. "Babe, there ain't a soul on the planet who don't feel like that from time to time. You do belong. Trust me. And hey, at least you have a real job – a respectable job. Look at Esther and me. We're the imposters. I model. I basically pretend to be happy, sad, shy, confident, whatever the shoot calls for. Not once has the way I felt on the inside matched the final image."

I drizzle balsamic vinegar on crusty bread and look around the saloon. "Imposters or not, there's a lot of wealth on this boat."

"Not as much as you'd think." Paige pauses while Jo hands us two flutes of Champagne. She waits until we have some semblance of privacy before continuing. "Jo's a vet, she'll be on fifty, sixty Gs a year. Maybe more. Good for her. I mean, she's a workhorse, she

190

deserves it. Mabel? She's probably on the same with her PR work, and she's pushed hard to get there. As for the rest of us, it's all show."

I don't believe her.

"Verona won't have much take-home pay. I know quality vegan food is in demand, but think about it, the margins must be so tight. Tesco will have negotiated the smallest price per unit possible, and forty per cent of her profits go straight to the Dragons. Staff, advertising, office space – it all adds up."

She has a point. My expenses are practically zero. If I'm booked to shoot a wedding, I make sure my transport is paid for, and I get to put some of my rent through my accounts as a home office. I pick up the stuffed peppers, tzatziki and crisps and take them through to the saloon. There's a faint smell of nail varnish as Verona paints her toenails a shade of light brown. No one seems to notice I'm there. There's only one *thank you*, and that comes from Jo.

Esther's back at the window. "They're nearly here," she says. I assume she means the other yacht.

I return to the kitchen area, appreciating the warmth that seeps from the oven. "You were saying?"

"As for our skipper, she might come from money, but it's not like she's worked a day in her life."

An immense thunderclap causes all of us to look to the ceiling for a moment.

"I was in Dubai, must have been a year and a half ago, because it was New Year. I got talking to this

Emirati who'd invested heavily in DYH Triton, you know, Mr McPherson's company. He sold his shares in the nick of time. The share price plummeted last year. He said the graph looked like the sheer face of a cliff. I think things are looking a bit better now, but yeah, they might look like they have loads of assets, but they also have a lot of debt. Mama McPherson was smart to get a prenup. She's back in Lagos and Papa didn't get a penny of the oil money. It's not like he's entitled to child support either. Esther's in her mid-twenties."

I check on the feta. It smells great but isn't quite ready. "I thought they were rolling in it?"

Paige shakes her head. "When her maternal grand-father dies, she'll be richer than God, but until then … She might have to think about getting a real job."

I snort. "I can imagine how she'd feel about that."

Paige laughs too but adds, "Not that I can't talk. Fame is fleeting; I'm smart enough to know that much. I need to earn as much as I can right now be-cause no one hires Instagram models once the wrinkles start appearing and let's be honest, my CV won't be up to much. I haven't had a normal job since we left Scotland. I try to top up my earnings here and there; I get a lot of free stuff for paid promotions, that sort of thing. When I'm done with them, I stick them on eBay."

My eyes widen. I never once considered that her modelling would have an expiry date, but it seems so

192

obvious. She's wise to bank as much as she can, while she can.

She leans closer, pretending to inspect the best before date on a bottle of Tabasco. "Want to know the juicy bit?"

"Does the Pope shit in the woods?"

"The Chanel sunnies, Esther's been wearing all week? There's a tiny chip on the right lens. You wouldn't notice unless you knew it was there. I noticed because I put it there when I flew down a chute at a water park on the Dubai trip I mentioned. Half the stuff I stick on eBay is bought by an Esther.MP97."

"No?!"

"Yes. And she has no idea that I know because I sell everything anonymously."

Childishly, this amuses me. It's not schadenfreude. I'm not happy at other's misfortune; it's just nice to know I'm not the only one who tries to keep up appearances.

When the oven beeps again, we remove the baked feta and take the last of the food through to the saloon. Esther is pulling on a t-shirt and some deck shoes. "Their fenders aren't at the correct height. And they're going to try and moor stern-to? Oh, for heaven's sake. They'll damage Bacchus."

She heads for the companionway doors, as she opens them, rainwater from the storm trickles down the stairs.

"Where you going?" Verona asks between coats of nail varnish.

"I'm going to give these jokers a hand. They can raft on to us."

Verona glances at the wet polish on her toes. "Erm … Do you want some help?"

"No, don't be silly," she replies. "Stay dry. No point us all getting drenched again."

I place the final bowl on the dining table. "Should we wait?"

"Dig in, darlings. I won't be long."

The door closes with a bit of a bump, and more water trickles in, flowing down the stairs like a lilliputian waterfall.

"I'll get a cloth," I say, going to mop up the mess. As I bend down and wipe the floor, something catches my eye. A brass bolt at the bottom of the stairs is undone. A small detail, one I wouldn't usually notice, except behind these stairs something very important is housed: the engine.

– CHAPTER 25 –

Mabel.

Now, this is the life – a bit of adventure followed by some pampering. I might be underplaying today by calling it a bit of an adventure. I was effing terrified putting that storm jib up – don't think I showed it though. I hope Esther isn't too pissed that I took over. To be honest, we really didn't have another option. Least we're all here in one piece. We're covered in bruises from top to toe, but we're here safe and well, and that's the important thing. I think Libby's still a bit shaken up; she seems out of sorts. She might still be feeling nauseous. It doesn't just magically stop once you moor up. I'll try and cheer her up later on; distraction is good for seasickness. Or maybe not, my attempts at humour never go down well with her.

Footsteps pad above our heads.

"How they doing?" Paige asks. Her face is covered in a mud mask – all of ours are. They're drying rapidly, and my face feels tauter with each passing minute. It's a pleasant remedy after being sprayed with seawater all day.

I swivel on my bruised butt and peer out the portside window. "I think they're nearly done."

"Can you see much?"

"Not really. Looks like four guys."

Jo frowns, or I think she does, we can't really move our foreheads now. "Christ, it's not the ones from last night, is it?"

I doubt it, but I cup my hands around my eyes and take another look just to check. My eyes find a red flag emblazoned with a black, double-headed eagle. "Nah. They're Albanians."

"Albanians?" The others crowd around the window as if our neighbours are exhibits in a zoo.

I look up and down their yacht. She looks reasonably new and in good nick. A thirty-eight footer if I'm not mistaken. Up the halyard, another flag flies below the Albanian one, this one's pale blue with a shield under what looks like a crown. It's probably a county or city flag.

"They don't have a Greek flag up," I say. "They're in Greek waters – they should have a courtesy flag flying."

Jo swallows an olive and drains the last sip of bubbly in her glass. "You might be comfortable scampering all over the deck during a storm, but most people are scared shitless. They'll probably sort it out when the weather passes."

I like that they think I was comfortable out there. It's not true, of course, but I like it all the same. A nervous skipper creates an anxious crew. You have to hold it together when you're in charge.

I wink at her then turn my gaze back to the window. A strapping man, topless with firm muscles, dark hair and stubble is stood at their bow. "Mmm, that one's tasty looking."

"Mabel!" Verona says it with a joking – but warning – tone to her voice.

"What?" I answer playfully. "I've never slept with a communist before." Then I think back. "No, wait, I have ... The Cuban."

I smile at the memory, and the mud mask begins to flake away around the creases in my cheeks – time to wash it off. I think the others have the same idea as we either scurry off to the heads or use the sink in the galley to clean the mud from our skin. Once clean, glasses are topped up and we listen as more footsteps plod above. I flick the kettle on; Esther will need a hot drink when she gets back in. Libby's eyes follow the sounds of footsteps as they move towards the bow. There's a high-pitched noise, followed by a heavy clunk a few moments later. It sounds like either the hatch to the crew cabin or the anchor locker has been opened then slammed shut.

When the doors to the companionway open, we all stop, stare and try not to laugh at Esther. If she wasn't soaked through before, she is now. Her t-shirt is see-through, and water drips down her bare legs, forming puddles by her feet. Goosebumps cover her arms and thighs, and bleached teeth chatter uncontrollably. As she moves down the stairs, the soles of her deck shoes squeak against the plastic steps. I hand her a dry towel and a steaming mug of hot chocolate.

She sniffs it. "Irish?"

"Naturally."

She cups the mug under her chin. Swirls of steam dance in front of her face as she takes a tentative sip, checking to see if it's too hot or just right. Satisfied, she begins to gulp it down.

"What are the Albanians doing here?" Verona asks.

"Same as us. Seeking shelter. Their English wasn't great, but I think they were returning from Otranto and decided to tuck in here for the night." She puts her mug down for a moment and squeezes her hair into the towel.

Libby picks up a crisp and crunches it loudly before asking, "We're you in my cabin?"

Esther looks up. "Yes. Sorry, sweetie. Should have asked, but I needed an extra warp. There was one in the storage locker under the bed in there." She gets to her feet. "I'm going to take *another* shower. Then how about we crack open another bottle of fizz and get this medicane party started?"

CHAPTER 26

Paige.

The sun manages to peek through the tiniest gap in the storm clouds. A slither of a reminder that above the clouds, the sun continues to shine, and the sky is still blue. It's completely thrown me because for the last couple of hours, it's felt like night. My body clock is suddenly off, and I feel weirdly jetlagged. I doubt yachtlag is a thing. Stormlagged? Now I'm just making up words. It's only been two and a half hours since we moored up on Othonoi, but it's been two and a half hours of alcohol, and we're all feeling worse for wear. Scratch that. We're smashed.

Esther has opened a bottle of fancy whiskey and is sharing it with Mabel. Jo's mouth is half pouting, half smiling, and it makes her look sort of frog-like. She's reclined so far that she's almost lying down. Libby is slurring her words, and Verona is drinking straight from a bottle of cabernet sauvignon.

The booze has hit us more than it usually would. We're dehydrated for one. During the passage, none of us took on enough water. Sure, we were splashed in the face with enough of it, but no one gave up their handholds to grab their water bottles. And once back on board, we were more interested in opening the bottles with percentage marks. Add to this the fact we haven't eaten enough. Libby and I did the best we could with what was available, but it was hardly a stomach-filling meal. Verona doesn't eat dairy. Without cheese, she's had about two hundred calories in food today – and about thirteen hundred in alcohol.

I've tried to slow down, but I'm a little on edge, and I always drink too much when I'm nervous. There's been a strange shift in the atmosphere over the last thirty minutes; I don't like it. We felt like such a team when we managed to moor up in those awful conditions, but the team spirit seems to have flittered away. I take another sip. I don't down drinks, don't do shots or play drinking games, but I keep sipping. Death by a thousand cuts; hammered by a thousand sips.

"Your step-mother designed the interior?" Verona says with a drunken drawl. "She has an eye for detail. It's lovely in here. Very tranquil. I can see why she'd use all these light shades. The pale-coloured wood fittings; they're almost grey. You know in colour therapy—"

Here we go.

"In colour therapy, grey symbolises stability. Stability? Yacht? Makes perfect sense. Your step-mother is a genius."

Esther blows a massive raspberry. "Hardly, darling. She couldn't add two and two together if you gave her a calculator and three guesses. And don't get me started on her latest business idea. Honestly, I've no idea what Daddy thought he was doing getting together with her."

"I'm sure she has some good qualities," Libby says, playing peacemaker.

"Pfft. She's half his age. It's embarrassing." Esther pours another whiskey and offers Mabel a top-up. She shakes her head. "Good qualities? Let me think. Well, I suppose she's into horses, and she's outdoorsy. Loves hiking and that sort of thing. You know, she reminds me of you, Jo."

Jo's glazed over eyes manage to focus on Esther. "Because she can't add up? I've never scored less than ninety per cent in a maths test in my entire life."

"No, no sweetie. The other things."

I don't think I've ever seen Esther this drunk before, and believe you me, we got into some states at uni.

"She's an animal lover, and she has the same figure you had when you were younger."

Ouch. That was a little harsh. I don't even think Esther realises what she just said.

"It makes sense," she continues, thoroughly oblivious to all our cringing. She holds her whiskey up to the light and admires it before swirling it around the tumbler and taking a long sniff with her eyes closed. Finally, she sips. "I mean, you are the reason he likes younger women, darling …"

Jo sits bolt upright.

"… Walking around my house in your flimsy little nightie."

Jo's hand slams onto the table hard enough to send the last remaining olive flying across the room. It misses Verona's head and lands in the sink in the galley. Under other circumstances, I'd cheer "Goal!", but I get the feeling I should keep quiet. I look to Mabel; she shrugs.

"It was YOUR flimsy little nightie." Jo spits each word. Her dark eyes are aflame with an intensity I've never seen from in her before. She pulls her silky hair back into a ponytail, rolls up her sleeves and jabs a finger in Esther's direction. "It was your nightie. You let me borrow it because you'd begged … BEGGED … me to stay over after Timothy Sutton dumped you for Kirsty Yorke."

"No, darling, I dumped him."

Jo stands up, her fingers clenched around the edge of the table, elbows locked to support her weight. "Don't *darling* me. He dumped you, and you spent all night crying about it. Do you think I wanted to stay over and listen to your drivel about how he was your soulmate? Of course, I didn't. I had mocks to study for but, oh no, you needed me, so I had to come running. I didn't work for your family, my parents did. So why was I always treated like staff?"

"I didn't treat you like staff," says Esther, still reclined and looking wholly relaxed. "Stop with the histrionics. You were my best friend."

"Bull shit. I didn't want to stay over. I didn't want to listen to your nonsense. And I didn't want your lecherous father to corner me in the kitchen and run his dirty hands up my legs and under …"

Tears flood Jo's eyes, extinguishing the fire what had burned just moments ago. She doesn't try to blink them away; she lets the tears fall onto her plate. They drip onto what remains of a slice of crusty bread that had hardened since we sat down to eat. Libby's next to Jo; silently, she lifts her hand to stroke Jo's arm but has it swiped away.

Esther's mouth curls and she makes a big show of lifting her gaze from her drink to meet Jo's. As if it's all such an effort. "Please. You were wandering around after dark, wearing black satin."

I wipe my brow; it feels clammy. "Bloody hell, Esther," I say. "Let's leave it there, shall we?"

Jo pushes her way out from the table and marches towards her cabin. I look to the others, my breath caught in my throat. We should stop her, call her back and try to sort this out.

"Jo?" I plead. "Jo, come back. We can work it out."

When she reaches her room, she stops, resting a hand on the door frame. She rubs her eyes with her free hand, her back shaking with anger or upset. Or both. When she turns, her cheeks are dark red, just like her eyes.

"I wasn't wandering around. I wanted a drink of water." She shudders. "And I was fourteen years old for fuck's sake."

The door shuts; we're plunged into silence.

My hand covers my mouth; I feel ill. This is awful. No one knows where to look or what to say. Poor, poor Jo. What a terrible thing to happen. I had no idea, and looking around, I don't think any of us knew that story.

"She never thinks about how *I* felt," Esther says, shaking her head dismissively. "Having to witness her trying to seduce my father. It's pathetic, really."

"I don't think that's Jo's version of events," Libby says, a quiet as a mouse.

"She was underage," I say. I can hardly believe what I've just heard. "There's no such thing as an underage seductress."

Esther snorts. "If it was oh so terrible, why didn't she say anything? Huh?"

We all know why. If Jo had kicked up a fuss, called the police or rang Childline, her parent's would have lost their jobs and their home. What an absolutely shitty situation for Jo to have been in, and at fourteen. I look around. Sitting in this pit of luxury, it all suddenly feels tainted. This is Mr McPherson's yacht, and it doesn't feel clean and expensive anymore — it feels gross and creepy.

Esther gives a dramatic eye roll when none of us answer. "Exactly. She didn't say anything because she knew she was in the wrong." She says this loud enough for it to be heard in Jo's cabin. Then, whether she really means it, or because she's just trying to see where our loyalties lie, she mutters, "Slut."

That's enough. I down my drink, ready to say my piece when Verona adds, "Well, she's not the only one."

"Hey!"

"Not you, Mabel." Verona blows her a kiss. "You're empowered, liberated, but you never take what's not yours." She blinks heavily and turns her gaze to Libby. "I loved Daniel. Loved him more than anything, and you stole him!"

Libby pushes her glasses up on to the top of her head so they act as a sort of hairband. "I didn't steal him. What are you on about? We bumped into each other by accident one day. I asked after you, but Danny said you'd been broken up for over four months. We went for a drink; we hit it off. It's not a crime."

"Wait!" Mabel puts her whiskey tumbler down on the table. The candlelight sparkles on the cut crystal glass but not as much as her eyes sparkle with the hint of juicy gossip. "You're with Daniel? Prince Charming Daniel?"

"Danny. He likes to be called Danny."

"I thought you didn't like cock?"

Libby glowers at her. "I'm bisexual, Mabel. Not a lesbian. How many fucking times do I have to say it?" Her northeastern accent is stronger when she swears. A lot stronger.

Tipping the bottle of cabernet sauvignon upside down, Verona realises it's empty and goes in search of a fresh one. I think she's had enough, but I doubt she wants to hear that right now. She looks triumphant when she finds a bottle of pinot buried deep in the fridge. It's probably warm now that Bacchus has been without power for hours. If the atmosphere wasn't so shit, I'd make a joke about having to drink it before it goes off.

Sauntering back to her space in the darkened saloon, Verona removes the cork using a waiter's friend and takes a swig. She licks wine from her lips before smirking at Mabel and Esther. "She might not be a lesbian, but she is a boyfriend-stealing whore."

"Oh, really?" Libby makes to snatch the bottle from Verona, but it's yanked just out of reach. "A whore? How did your drunk little mind work that one out?"

I like this Libby. Standing up for herself, not afraid to let her authentic voice shine. I just hate she's had to be bullied and insulted into it.

"Friends don't—" Verona hiccoughs. "Friends don't sleep with friends' ex-boyfriends. It's the rules."

Libby's mouth falls open, and she stares around the room, disbelief written all over her face. "It's the rules in crappy, American high school dramas. It's not a rule between real-life adults. Besides, it's not like you and I are actually friends. I haven't spoken to you since graduation."

Good for her, I think. I've only seen this version of Libby a handful of times but feisty Libby rocks.

"Look, it's not my fault you're still in love with Danny—"

"Daniel—"

"Oh, put a sock in it. It's not my fault he doesn't love you anymore. Instead of blaming me, maybe it's time you take a good look in the mirror." She points a shaking finger in Verona's direction. "If you put half as much time into your relationship as you did your vegan food empire, maybe you two would have stood a chance."

Esther lets out a snort. "Woo. Go, Libby."

I have to say, Libby's use of finger quotes when she said *vegan food empire* was a nice touch.

Verona takes another drink. It's less of a swig and more of a mouthful. "A whore would say that."

Libby doesn't need me to stand up for her; she's giving as good as she's getting. Regardless, I love Libby, more than anyone else here.

"That's enough, Verona," I say, with more growl to my voice than intended. "I'm sorry you still have feelings for Danny, but Libby hasn't done anything wrong. You're out of line. Stop calling her a whore."

She pouts, mocking me. "Why? Does the W-word hurt your feelings? Does it remind you of what you *really* are?"

She says *really* in a tone that causes Esther and Mabel to put their drinks down and lean in.

My blood runs cold.

"I saw the pictures in *Hello* of you cosying up to that sheikh."

No. Please, no.

"There was a story on BBC News last month. You must have seen it, Esther. *Influencers offered thousands for sex*. Fifty grand and as much shopping as you can handle?" She sniggers. "Just one catch: a non-disclosure agreement."

I can feel what little colour I have drain from my face. Prickles run up my arms and I begin to shake all over. It's like my body is about to crack open and spill my blood, guts and secrets all over the saloon floor. I put my glass down, sitting on my hands to keep them still. How on Earth could she know? A lucky guess? I should deny it, tell her she's being ridiculous, but I've already been quiet too long, and she can read it on my face. They all can. She knows, and she looks so bloody smug and high and mighty.

I feel so unbelievably cold now; every ounce of warmth has been sapped from Bacchus. Just because I did what they think I did, it doesn't mean I am what they think I am. I did what I had to do.

A voice in my head asks, So, why are you so ashamed?

Ice seeps from the top of my head, down my limbs to my fingers and toes. It's hate. Hate has filled my body. I loathe Verona more than I can put into words.

CHAPTER 27

Jo.

What a fool I've been. How could I have ever thought things would change and that Esther and I could move forward with our lives? Things never change; I will never be more than the help to her or the entire McPherson clan. I still remember my mother scolding me when I complained that Esther always chose which games we'd play.

"You are fortunate that Miss Esther plays with you at all. I don't want to hear that you have argued with Miss Esther or upset Miss Esther. My job, your father's job, both could be in jeopardy if you say the wrong thing. Do you want to be responsible for us becoming destitute?"

I shook my head.

"Know your place. Do I make myself clear?"

Know my place. Bloody hell, mother. I sit up in bed, the alcohol making my head heavy. I knew my place all right. Would I have kept quiet if I thought for a second my mother would stand up for me, or heaven forbid, just believe me? I love her, of course I do, but she's as complicit in this as Esther and her disgusting pig of father. She believed all that upstairs-downstairs nonsense. That some people were born to drive, others born to be driven. She actually considered herself – and my father and I by extension – less worthy than the people she worked for. We were servers, there to see to our master's every need. If that meant letting them walk all over you, or abuse you, then so be it.

I can hear them in the saloon. Paige and Libby are arguing with Verona. Esther giggles with Mabel every now and again. Shaking my head, I wonder if Esther and I were ever really friends. I think back, casting my mind to a time when we couldn't even reach onto the kitchen countertops. As children, I was a playmate, and though we went to the same primary school, I would tell people I was Esther's best friend; she'd tell people my parents worked for her parents. It wasn't all bad, I suppose. She did take me sailing on weekends, and on horse rides, and shopping trips. But when we became teenagers, it was clear I was nothing more than a confidante or someone to come crying to. She'd gone to private school by this point, but as we still lived on their land, I was still at her beck and call. My mother would come hurrying in, "Jovitha, to the big house. Quickly now, Miss Esther needs you."

I felt free when I got into St. Andrews. It was time to start afresh and meet new people; time to follow my own dreams and pursue my own interests. My parents were thrilled I was going to study veterinary medicine. "A vet. One day someone will clean your house. Imagine it, Jo." That was their idea of having made it: employing help of your own. I never did get a cleaner, it seemed silly when there was only Frederick and myself in the house. Besides, I find cleaning therapeutic.

Esther had never once considered going to St. Andrews. She'd mentioned Yale and Princeton, Harvard and the like, but we hardly spoke by upper sixth, so I never knew her plans. I'd meet friends in the Black Swan or stay in the village hanging out at the youth centre, anything not to go home. When I turned up at St. Andrews sailing club and saw her there, my heart just sank. So much for starting again.

She was so pleased to see me. Her face lit up, and she ran to me, introducing me to the squad. Now that I think about it, I wonder if she applied to go there because she knew I would be there. I've never considered that before. Maybe she needed me. Was I her safety net?

The bed linen in my cabin is silky. I can't stand it. Silk? Satin? It's all the same to me. The sensation of it against my skin makes me feel sick. I thrash my legs until the sheet is crumpled in the back corner of the cabin. Sitting naked is no better. Memories haunt me, and I feel unprotected. Fingers rummage in my suitcase, frantically searching for clothing. I grab trousers and t-shirts, layering them until I'm wrapped up enough to face a hike in the Highlands on a typical January morning. Here in Greece, despite the storm, I will overheat. I don't care. I'd rather be uncomfortably hot than feel silk creeping over my legs like imperial fingers.

Lying back down, it's hard to tell if the boat is wobbling, or if it's the alcohol making my head spin. Squeezing my eyes closed, a burning in my throat tells me I might see my dinner again, but I can't leave the cabin. I don't want to go back out there. I have to focus and try to get some sleep, but my mind keeps circling between this terrible night and the night we marched on Tommy Ware's house. I only touched him once; it was more of a slap than a punch. As much as I hated Tommy for what he'd done to those boys, it was Mr McPherson's face I was picturing as I stood by and watched the villagers punish him.

* * *

Libby

I pick up a few plates and move them to the galley before pouring myself a large glass of water which I down in one. I take my glasses off and clean the lenses on the loose fabric of my t-shirt. My eyes are tired and dry. After everything that's come out tonight, about Jo and what she went through, the allegations thrown at

Paige, I'm surprised I'm not crying. I think I only managed to hold the tears back because of Verona. I didn't want to give her the satisfaction. I won't apologise or feel bad. There was nothing between Danny and me when he was with Verona. We hardly knew each other back then, and I was under the impression he was a well to do trust fund boy, who wore pastel shorts and polo shirts. I'd judged him on his accent – something I was always assuming people were doing to me. I had him completely wrong. Danny's the sort of person to raise others up, not hold them back. He's the first man I've been close to who never questioned my bisexuality. He didn't call it a phase or make some lewd comment about just needing the right you-know-what to set me straight. He came to Manchester Pride with me last year and had a blast. Ariana Grande was the headline act; it turned out Danny had a massive crush on her. That made two of us.

With a sigh that makes me sound like I'm in my sixties, I rest my back against the cabinets in the galley. As eye-opening as this evening has been, it's time for me to get some shuteye. I can hear the rain as it hits the water outside. I'd look through the window, but I can tell from the sound that it's picked up again and is quite heavy. Besides, it's so dark I wouldn't be able to see anything anyway.

"Libby, where you going, sweetheart?" Esther looks concerned as I grab the rail at the companionway.

"Bed," I say.

214

"I thought you were bunking with me?"

Is she serious? I run a hand through my hair. She looks sad like I've stood her up or something. But I want my own space; I can't stay in here any longer. I actually want to get back to my poky little cabin.

"Thanks, but I'm beat," I say diplomatically. "I need to be alone."

I unlock the companionway and ready myself to move quickly. Even though it's Verona who's sleeping in the saloon, I don't intend on leaving the doors open longer than need be. I won't flood Bacchus just to annoy her – I'm above that.

"Oh, Lib, it's terrible out there."

I turn to face Esther and the others. "It's terrible in here."

I open the door and feel the force of the storm. Rain pelts my face and obscures my vision. A flash of lightning illuminates the sky, changing black to white for one brilliant moment. Esther rushes to her feet and is by my side, ready to close the hatch from the inside. She thrusts something into my hand.

"Clip on," she urges me.

I nod, and wave the carabiner to show I understand.

"Promise me."

"I promise."

Ascending the stairs, the sound of the wind howls in my ears and sends my hair flying in all directions.

"Libby …"

215

I turn, but I'm eager to get out of this weather. "What?" I almost have to shout it for her to hear me.

"I'm going to bed now. Knock on your wall three times. That way I'll know you're back in your cabin."

I agree and make a run for it. I clip on as instructed but still slip and slide on the slick deck. Esther acted all concerned by asking me to stay, telling me to clip on, and to knock when I'm back in. I glance behind me. No, I didn't think so. She's not concerned enough to wait and watch to see that I make it there in one piece. Perhaps I'm being unfair. Esther was out in the rain for longer than the rest of us when she went to help the Albanian's moor up. I'm not surprised she wants to stay indoors.

It's scary out here. There's not much light coming from the island. The only other colour in the total blackness comes from Corfu's direction. The faintest orange glow of light pollution shimmers over a northernly town. My foot slips again, only this time I hit the deck, literally. My knee lands on the metal diesel filler. Goddamit, that's going to form a nasty bruise by the morning. I've given myself a fright. My heart thuds with so much power, I can feel it in my ears. Though I was nowhere near falling over the guard rail, I have to fight to reassure myself that I'm not in danger.

Hatch open, I lower myself down the ladder, knocking my sore knee off one of the rungs. The catharsis of a few swear words helps relieve the pain. I

216

can't push the hatch back into place fast enough to stop cold water from pouring in after me.

Awesome. A wet bed.

I have a dry towel in my bag, so once I've squeezed the excess out of my hair, stripped naked and dried my body, I press it against the bed and try to absorb some of the dampness from the sheets and pillows. I ball my hand into a fist and crack it three times on the wall and wait until I hear Esther banging her wall in return.

A flash of lightning isn't immediately followed by thunder; there's a four or five-second pause. The storm must be moving away. Hopefully, the wind and rain will move on soon. I can't face a full night of Bacchus rocking back and forth, creaky noises and howling wind. Not on top of everything else that had happened tonight.

I lie down and wonder how I can possibly get any sleep when everyone seems to hate each other. Verona hates me and thinks I'm some sort of boyfriend-stealing bitch. Esther blames Jo for the breakdown of her parent's marriage. Jo's been holding on to that abuse for, God, it must be ten years. And as for Paige, I don't know what to think. I don't know whether she's caught up in something, is being forced into selling herself by her agent, or if Verona is just making up spiteful gossip.

I wipe my eyes as I stare at the ceiling; tears have finally come. I hope Jo and Esther can get past this,

217

and more than anything, I hope Paige is safe. Verona's probably just spreading rumours because she's miserable and wants everyone else to be too. Is it wrong that I hope she leaves at the next opportunity? Ideally, we'd all get on and finish this delivery together. Still, I can't see her having a change of heart overnight, and I can't face another week of her sneers and stares.

I place my glasses on the floor and feel around for a hairband to keep my fringe off my face while I sleep. *If* I sleep.

Rolling to my right, my face is inches from the wall, and I'm taken back to being stuck in the cupboard. Rolling to my left, everything feels achy. My hip isn't comfortable, it feels like there's a lump under my shoulder, and my feet feel higher than the rest of me.

Stupid crew cabin and its stupid cheap sheets and mattress. I stand, throw the sheets to the side and grip the edges of the mattress. Maybe it just needs flipping. *Three, two, one.* I give myself a mental countdown, then lift the mattress onto its side. It moves easily. Much lighter than I expected.

Not the only thing I wasn't expecting though.

A small holdall is stored under the bed. It's not mine, and curiosity has got the better of me. My head cocks to one side as I take the zip's pull tab in my fingers and slide it along the teeth.

I stare at the contents.

I thought tonight was bad.

What's in the bag is worse.

218

CHAPTER 28

Libby.

I should have given up on sleep. I could have distracted myself by reading a book, doing a crossword or doomscrolling through my news feed. But I thought rest would do me good, so I closed my eyes and persevered. The nightmares came in all shapes and sizes: monsters real and imaginary; faces from my past; my mother; my brother; Verona. In my nightmare, Verona had long canine teeth like some sort of vampire, and her eyes were an orangy-red. I'd been eating an aubergine, which was weird enough as it is as I don't even like aubergines. Vampire Verona stole it from me, shouting, "That's mine. That's mine." When I tried to take it back, she began to tear chunks from it with her teeth. She didn't eat it though, just spat the pieces on the floor, and hissed, "If I can't have it, no one can."

Boy, a shrink would have a field day with that one.

I pick some sleep from the inner corners of my eyes and jump from the bed as if it's on fire. Lifting the mattress and the MDF board it rests on, I check that I wasn't hallucinating last night.

I wasn't.

The bag is still there. It's contents as awful as ever.

I give myself a cat's lick wash using the little sink in my cabin. I can't hear any signs of life from the main part of the yacht. Some will be laying low, waiting for their hangovers to wear off. Others will be waiting for someone else to make the first move and emerge from their cabin to the communal areas.

It's gone ten. On any other day, we'd have been under sail at least an hour ago. Pulling on the handle to open my hatch, I blink as I see sunshine for the first time since yesterday morning. Squinting, I pop my head out of the hole like a dark-haired, bespectacled periscope.

It's as if yesterday never happened. The sun is bright and high in the sky, causing the water to sparkle as if covered by a million diamonds. Rainwater runs from higher land, down streets and alleyways until it reaches the sea. They act as substitute streams, guiding the water back to where it belongs. The water around Bacchus appears dirty, but it's only because the weather has stirred up the sediment. It will calm and be crystal clear again in no time.

Our neighbours are nothing but a distant speck on the horizon. At least I think it's them, I can't see a red and black flag from this distance. Ashore, a man in his late fifties sits at the end of the jetty. His legs dangle off the end, and he holds a fishing line made from wire wrapped around a square of cardboard in his hands. A clouder of cats surround him, edging their way closer in anticipation of a tasty breakfast.

"Morning, sailor."

Mabel lowers her shades. She's sunbathing across the deck, making the most of the sun before we get going. Topless, and wearing a pair of bikini bottoms that are smaller than most postage stamps, I make sure to keep my eyes firmly on her face. "Is anyone else up?"

"Esther's double-checking the course and the weather forecast," she says, stretching her arms above her head, then rolling her shoulders in circles.

I doubt anyone slept well last night. We'll all be full of aches and pains.

Mabel continues, "After yesterday, she doesn't want any surprises. She'll have her eyes glued to the instrument panel today."

I shake my head and suddenly feel as if my head is full of liquid. There's a good chance I still have motion sickness.

Mabel sighs and lays back down on her towel. "I can't get over last night."

"I know," I say, pulling myself out of the cabin so I can have a stretch of my own. "It was awful. Poor Jo. It must have been …" The words catch in my throat.

"And Paige. I can't believe Verona said all those things."

"Not that, silly." Mabel flashes me an unnaturally white smile. "I can't get over you being with Daniel. I thought you were all about the boobies."

It takes all my strength not to let my eyes flick south for a second. That's what she wants, and as gorgeous as she is, I'm not attracted to her anymore. Her ugly traits dampened any torch I once held.

Mabel May Sharpe knew exactly how I felt about her. She was such a flirt at uni; I thought she liked me back. She would always offer to help zip up my wet-suit. She'd brush my hair and braid it into two cute little pigtails, and she always paraded naked in the showers after training. When we were doing our day skipper course on Juniper, Mabel and I were alone be-low deck and I decided to go for it: I leant in to kiss her. It took all the courage I had, and she rejected me. Not a *sorry-I'm-just-not-into-you* rejection, a humiliating, soul-destroying rejection. She said, *urgh*, an actual *urgh* of disgust.

"What are you doing, Libby? I like men. And this university has a zero-tolerance policy when it comes to sexual harassment. It applies to men *and* women."

I was fucking heartbroken. Even now, thinking back, the emotion is still hard to comprehend. I love Danny. I have no feelings for Mabel whatsoever but, wow, that pain never left.

To my surprise, it was Esther McPherson, the girl I'd judged for buying her way into uni, who came to my rescue during that trip. She'd found me crying over the dishes.

"This is what Mabel does, darling. She likes the power. She leads people on, men and women, for the thrill of rejecting them." She put her arm over my shoulders and gave me a look of pure sympathy. "Gosh, you know who you remind me of? Clark Kent if he were female and fairy-sized. Adorable. Cute glasses. Anyway, I love Mabel dearly. She's a great friend, and goodness knows the woman can party, but you're not the first, and you certainly won't be the last. So, don't let her insecurities get to you. Now let's take your mind off it. Lift your chin up, finish these dishes, then I'll show you how to tie a Carrick bend."

It seems like a lifetime ago. I dust myself down in a feeble attempt to remove the creases from my t-shirt, step over the sun worshipper and grunt, "Grow up, Mabel."

"Oh, lighten up," she drawls. Then, when I'm almost at the stern of the ship, she calls after me. "Did you hear?"

"Yes," I say, snapping my head around. "You said, *lighten up*. Pardon me for not finding—"

She cuts me off. "Not that, snowflake. Did you hear the radio chatter? The pirates are back."

* * *

As the news of what Mabel has just told me sinks in, I look to the jetty and see Jo struggling with twelve bottles of water. She has a bag of six in each hand, her arms hang by her sides and the bottles take turns banging against her legs as she walks. Another twelve bottles stand next to Bacchus's passerelle; this must be her second trip to the shop. A stray dog with a gammy leg sniffs the air. I'd worry about him peeing on our water supply, but he's far more interested in the felines at the end of the jetty.

"Here, let me help." I jump ashore and help cart the water into the cockpit.

"Thirty-six litres should do it," she says with a yawn. She looks as refreshed as I feel.

Indoors, the atmosphere is tense, but thankfully I don't have to speak to Verona: she's still asleep. Sprawled across the saloon's sofa bed, she has earplugs in her ears and a silk mask over her eyes. I wonder if she's faking, to avoid us, but then she sucks in air and snores louder than a jet engine. Esther is crouched over the chart table, fiddling with a compass. Jo glares at the back of her head, while Paige tries to make coffee without getting in anyone's way. Her long, red hair is piled high on her head, and she's casually dressed in cotton shorts and a long-sleeved t-shirt. She hands Jo a cup with compassionate eyes and mouths to ask how she's doing.

Jo takes the cup but says nothing. I can picture her tossing the mug of boiling liquid over Esther. I'm pretty sure she's imagining the same thing.

Paige fills another mug, adds a splash of milk and hands it to me. "I checked the milk. The fridge had been off all night, but it's still good."

"Thanks," I say, my eyes searching hers. "You okay?"

"No." She folds her arms. "No, I'm not."

I need to speak to Paige, but Esther has just folded her chart away and has got to her feet. Now's my chance. I have to know what's going on. "Esther," I call. "I need a word. Can we speak in private?"

"Not now," she says, before entering her cabin and closing the door behind her. *Good morning to you, too.*

Paige nods her head towards the ceiling, a signal that we should go above deck. A prospect I'm more than happy with if it means being further away from Sleeping Beauty. Mabel is still sunning herself near the bow, so we stay in the cockpit and whisper.

"Listen, Paige, what Verona said last night. Whether it's true or not, it doesn't change anything. I know the real—"

"It's true," she says, cutting me off.

"Oh." I try to hide my shock but am obviously doing a terrible job at it. My brain searches uselessly for something to say. Paige sleeps with fans for money? I just … I just can't …

225

"It's not what you think, well I don't know what you think, but I know what Verona believes, and it's not as simple as that. It's because of Graham."

"Your brother?"

"His brain tumour. Well, the NHS are doing everything they can, God bless them, but it's getting worse."

"Shit. I'm sorry, Paige." I know how close she's always felt to Graham. Growing up with my demon sibling, I've really envied Paige's relationship with her brother.

"I've arranged for private health care so he can be more comfortable and have a private room, that sort of thing, but they can't do anything more than what the NHS have done." She blinks at the horizon. "Anyway, there's this new treatment. It's not available in the UK, but he could go to America and have it done."

Everything starts to make sense, and I nod to show I get it. "That sounds expensive."

"Expensive I can handle. But we're talking astronomical amounts, and no health insurance broker will touch him." She runs a hand over her jaw and takes a long slow breath. "Every penny I got for that trip to the Emirates went towards his medical costs. The stuff I sold on eBay too."

"How much more do you need?" Naively I think I can help. The girl who could only afford to go abroad this year because she'd be staying on her rich, uni mate's dad's boat. Like I could help.

Her gaze wanders over me as if she's gauging my expression, looking for disgust or judgement, but she won't find that here.

"I'm going to Moscow next month. For two weeks. It should cover it. After that, I'm done. Never again. But if Verona says a word and the press get hold of it, the deal will be off. These people require discretion."

I sit quietly for a moment, not sure what to say. Then I think about Esther cheering me up all those years ago and try to channel the spirit she put back into me. I put my arm over Paige's shoulder and kiss her on the cheek. "You're amazing. You know that? You're the best sister a brother could wish for, and frankly, Verona can go fuck herself."

Her solemn face cracks and breaks into a smile. She lifts her coffee mug and clinks it against mine. "Yeah. Fuck Verona."

– CHAPTER 29 –

He counts the bricks on the wall facing him. It's something to do at least. He's lost count twice already, but he doesn't mind. He'd rather count bricks than think about what the rest of the day has in store for him. Black Hood will be back, of that, he is certain.

He won't get breakfast, nor will he get lunch. Dinner will be small and bland. Last night it was bread; the night before he had plain rice. They'll give him enough calories and water to keep him alive, but not enough for him to have any strength.

Last night he had to listen to some fatso guard stuffing his face beyond the doors. Whatever he'd been eating, it smelled greasy. The thought of a dirty, grease-laden burger makes his mouth water. He swallows the saliva back down, not wanting to waste any hydration.

Somewhere down a dusty corridor, he hears a phone ring.

Please be good news.

Esther.

The troops, bar Verona, are gathered around the cockpit table. I can smell coffee and if I'm not mistaken, cigarettes. Must be someone on the jetty. My girls don't smoke, and if they did, they wouldn't smoke on Bacchus. Today is important to me; it's the first overnight sail I've captained in over eighteen months. I've tried to dress the part in tailored white shorts and a navy, off-the-shoulder top emblazoned with an anchor motif. It's vintage and very flattering. I've pulled my hair back into a chignon, which is a rarity. My hair can be very delicate, especially around the temples so I try to leave it down as often as possible. I hope by tying it back, I look like I mean business.

I put on my best smile and emerge through the companionway. "Morning, ladies."

There's an underwhelming response. Jo won't even look at me, and Mabel is watching a mangy-looking dog try to have his way with a fisherman's leg.

"Big day today. And I imagine some of us have fuzzy heads, so let's make sure we hydrate. Huge thank you to the lovely Jo for replenishing our H2O supplies."

Her lips pinch to the left side of her face, and I have the distinct impression she's literally biting her tongue.

"I also think we should keep a dry boat until we get to Le Castella." I make pointed eye contact with Mabel who puts her hand to her chest and lets her mouth fall open in a look of mock insult.

"Moi? Drunk? You must have me mistaken for someone else."

It's at that moment I realise that Mabel was the only one not involved in any drama last night. Jo and I, Verona and Paige, Verona and Libby. It was Mabel who kept her nose clean. I'm glad she knows I'm just teasing, because if she wanted to, she could remind me of that fact and then we'd all be going over all those arguments again, and that would be torture.

"Where was I? Yes. Le Castella. Have any of you been?"

Silence.

"It's stunning. Wait until you see the fortress illuminated at night. It's out in the bay at the end of a peninsula. The marina is easy to navigate, and there are tonnes of traditional pizzerias. The pizzas are to die for. If any of you even try to order a Hawaiian—"

"Esther?"

Paige's usually flawless face looks both tired and bored.

"Yes?"

"I'm sure the castle's lovely and all, but what about the pirates?"

"Ah, yes." I'd hoped they hadn't heard. "There was some radio chatter. I don't know the details, and no, I don't like it either, but I think the risks are minimal. We're in a busy stretch; we're more at risk from cargo vessels and cruise liners. That being said, we'll keep our wits about us."

God, my crew look unhappy. I've seen more enthusiasm from lame horses. It's my job to keep them onside and motivated, but I'm not sure I can. I know I played a part in Jo being so miserable this morning; I can be a big girl and admit that. But she's part of the reason my parents broke up. Why can't she just accept it? If she apologised, we could all move on. Libby is looking at me like I'm some curious object she wants to study. An alien seeing Earthlings for the first time. I've never seen this look on her before. It's unsettling. As for our sixth crew member, she's still in dreamland with her face buried in a pillow. This situation is stressful enough without …

Pulling my shoulders back and standing tall, I try to project an air of confidence. Fake it till you make it, that's what they say.

"Look, it's an easy sail this afternoon. Force four, south-westerlies. I'll be at the helm for most of the day so relax, sunbathe, whatever. I'll give you plenty of notice if we need to tack or gybe, but otherwise, enjoy a pleasant day at sea. Things will get more intense in the evening once the sun goes down and our shifts begin. We'll be operating three-hour shifts, and as Mabel and I have the most experience, I'd like one of us in the cockpit at all times.

Mabel nods her assent.

"From six to nine, I'll take the helm with Verona," I say. "If she's up by then, that is. Mabel, you've got nine to midnight with Jo. The wind may have increased to force five by then. Libby, you're with me after that; we're on until three a.m. That's a tough shift so try to catch some z's earlier on. Three to six is Mabel and Paige. The sun's due up just before six, and we should aim to arrive in Le Castella by seven. Any questions?"

Four hands shoot straight up into the air, and Mabel asks, "Aren't you forgetting something, Skip?"

I've covered the wind direction and speed, the passage plan, the shift schedule. "I don't think so. What is it, sweetie?"

They all answer at once. "The engine."

– CHAPTER 30 –

Libby.

Mabel – head down, arse up – examines the engine. It's stored under the companionway stairs, meaning those of us below deck can't escape for some fresh air, and those above deck can't escape the sun.

Esther and I peer over Mabel's shoulder.

"Give me some room. I can't see a bloody thing with all your shadows looming over me." She extends an arm. "Hand me a torch, Skip."

Esther does as she's asked. Mabel angles the torch around, trying to get the light to hit the various components from each and every angle.

"Odd," she says, putting the torch down only for as long as it takes her to remove a hair tie from her wrist and scrape her lion's mane back into a bun.

"What's the diagnosis?" Esther asks as she perches on the end of the sofa bed. Verona stirs and rolls over. Esther shakes her head and looks at the roof in exasperation.

"I can't see any obvious issues. There's a bit of corrosion here and over here, but nothing that should cause any problems. I'm going to give the whole thing a good clean, check the belts and oil filters and see what comes up."

She straightens up, stretches, and makes a soapy solution in a plastic tumbler. "Anyone want to sacrifice a toothbrush?"

Esther moves to her cabin and returns seconds later brandishing a green toothbrush. "I brought a spare."

It takes Mabel a further half-hour to give everything a good scrub. She removes a few items to examine with the torch and gives them extra attention. Finally, she wipes everything down with dry microfibre cloths, turns to us and shrugs. "Damned if I know."

When the stairs are replaced, we move to the cockpit. Esther hits the 'glow' button and the 'start engine' button. There's a loud pitched beeping noise followed by a rumbling noise and a purr as the engine kicks in.

"You're amazing, Mabel!" Esther beams, clapping her on the back. "Great work. Really great work."

Mabel pulls a confused face, sucking her chin down towards her chest and raising her shoulders. "I didn't really fix anything. Just gave her a good scrub."

"It's odd," says Esther, "but at least we're up and running. Take the credit, darling."

It's not odd. Not in the slightest. I turn away so no one can see my face while I hold my tongue and busy myself by tidying the sheets that control the mainsail. I thread each length of rope through my hands, making neat coils and storing them in mesh bags that hang on either side of the cockpit. I definitely saw the bolt out of position yesterday after we moored up. I didn't imagine it. And before Mabel started cleaning it, the engine was dirty. Grease and dust coated all parts of the engine bar one: the seawater inlet. Someone accessed the engine and closed the seawater inlet so the engine would overheat. Then at some point after we moored up, they opened it again, and flick of a magic wand, everything miraculously works.

Esther was so insistent that we sail on to the Faraway Islands despite the storm. Why was it so crucial for her to get to Othonoi? I'll tell you why. Because Esther had to collect something from the Albanians. That's why she tinkered with the engine and forced us to sail on when we wanted to turn back and find an anchorage on Corfu. It was the perfect excuse. That's why she went out to help them moor up. That's why she told us to stay warm and dry in Bacchus, and why she wanted me to bunk in with her.

* * *

Early afternoon and I've tried three times to speak to Esther alone. Three times I've been shrugged off.

"Not now."

"In a minute, darling."

235

"After we've tacked."

I swear if she dismisses me one more time, I'll scream in her face and tell the world—. Who am I kidding? People like me don't yell at people like Esther. I barely held it together with Verona. I let out a deep sigh and walk, head-bowed, to the front of the yacht, open my hatch and slip into my cabin like a workman disappearing down a manhole. I remove the black bag from under the mattress and psych myself up before opening it again.

Blank passports, hundreds of them. British, Irish, French and German. All bagged up in clear plastic pouches. And more cash than I can count. Thousands of euros bundled into neat stacks about an inch high and secured with thin strips of paper. I pick up a blank British passport in trembling hands and marvel at how authentic it looks. I take out my own to compare them and can't see a single fault. Perhaps it is real, stolen from wherever they're printed or stored. They look identical, save for the photo page which is blank, ready to be stamped with the relevant information. They'll need to backdated as they're the old, red kind, from when we were still in the European Union. I wonder who wants this passport. Are they trying to get into the UK for a better life? Or is it for some James Bond type who's off to conduct a top-secret mission that they need a fake identity for? An image of a seagull flies over the outline of Scotland on the official observation page. Turning it over, I think the

236

internal pages look just the same as mine. Who knows where this passport will take its new owner. I'd like mine to take me to Canada one day. I've always wanted to photograph moose and killer whales, that is if Esther doesn't get us all locked up because of whatever scheme she's pulling.

Tucking both passports in the back pocket of my shorts, I pick up a bundle of cash and thumb over the edge, feeling the slight draught caused by hundreds of pieces of paper flicking one after another. There's a zipping noise as each note slaps back into place. I've never held so much money at once. I remember having six fifty-pound notes after being paid in cash for a photographing a baby shower. That was nothing compared to this. Bundles of euros are stacked on top of each other like a rainbow. Twenty euro bills in bright blue sit next to orange fifty-euro ones. There are tens, maybe even a hundred, bundles of grass-green hundred-euro notes and fuck me, even two hundred euro bills in sunshine yellow. It's the most colourful bag of contraband I've ever seen.

Apart from the odd bag of weed or coke, it's the only bag of contraband I've ever seen.

I rifle through, looking to see how many bundles of two hundred euros there are when my fingers find something cold and hard. I push the money aside, like Moses parting a sea of cash, and stare open-mouthed at not one, not two, but three guns.

Not any old guns.

Fucking Uzis.

An abrupt sense of self-preservation hits me, and fuelled by panic, I begin to wipe everything I've touched clean. Using a corner of bed linen, I rub the guns barrels and the plastic bags that house the passports. I take each bundle of cash and wipe it on each side, noting the sum total as I go, before returning it to the bag.

Zipped up and safely stored back under the mattress, I rub a hand over my neck. It's clammy, and my forehead is icy cold. Last night, I slept on half a million euros.

What the – and I can't stress this enough – actual fuck is going on?

I want no part of it. Paige said the McPhersons were in debt, but surely there are other ways and means. This isn't *slap on the wrist* illegal. This is *never seeing the outside of a jail cell again* illegal.

Esther said Mr McPherson didn't want to hire a skipper to move Bacchus. Now we know why. After what Jo said last night, Esther's father sounds like a nasty piece of work. A user. Keeping his own hands clean while his daughter tricks her friends into helping her traffic blank passports and a shit load of money. And to Sicily of all places.

If this is a mafia thing and we don't show, or we're late … My mind runs away with me, and once more, the crew cabin suddenly feels claustrophobic and suffocating. I begin to imagine the most horrific things. I need to get out of here. I don't just mean this cabin, I need to get off this yacht and back to Danny. I've worked too hard to make something of myself to have it ruined by the bloody McPhersons.

* * *

A knock on the hatch above my head makes me jump out of my skin. I don't know how long I've been staring at the bed, fixating on what's hidden under it. Gathering myself, I reach up and turn the lever to open the hatch. I'm actually relieved to see Mabel. I'm not ready for Esther yet. I need to calm down.

Her tan seems to have darkened in the few hours I've been avoiding everyone. Perhaps she's doused herself in tanning oil.

"I made lunch," she says, all smiles. "Do you want it in your cabin?"

"Erm. Yes. Yes, please."

She hands me a bottle of water, a plate of sandwiches, and a fruit salad. I lift a slice of bread and see avocado, cucumber and watercress. Any other day I'd love how green and healthy it looks. Now I just see hundred-euro bills. "Thanks. Looks good," I lie.

"Listen, sorry for being a dick earlier."

I look up at Mabel. Behind her, the genoa flaps slightly. Whoever is in the cockpit quickly realises and tightens it up.

"You mean this morning or most of year one?"

239

She chews her lip for a moment. "All of it." Then, without further explanation, she stands and leaves. I'm left with an unobstructed view of the now taut genoa.

Unfortunately, Mabel, without some sob story or vow to make it up to me, there is no redemption arc. *Sorry* is just a word. I have a few words for her though: humiliation, heartbreak, suffering. I could go on.

* * *

When my alarm goes off shortly before midnight, I can still feel avocado and claggy bread stuck to the roof of my mouth. I run my tongue around the inside of my cheeks and over my teeth before reaching for my toothbrush. I give my face a quick wash and instantly feel more awake and refreshed.

Emerging from my hatch, the first thing I notice is how unbelievably dark it is. So far we've been hugging the Greek coast and hopping from island to island. We've never been this far from land, and in the dark, it's hard to tell where the sea ends and the shore begins. The darkness is peppered with tiny dots of colour: red and white navigation lights; twinkling stars; the orange sparkle of distant villages. None of these do anything to lighten the blackness that surrounds Bacchus.

"Is that you, Libby?" Mabel's voice rings out from the cockpit.

"Yes," I answer. "Time to change shifts."

"Clip on, and use a head torch. It's gusty."

When I reach the helm, I can tell Mabel and Jo are in good spirits. Perhaps the night sail has been good for Jo. With all that's involved with sailing in the dark, there's no way she'll have had time to dwell on her marriage being called off or the memories that got dragged up around twenty-four hours ago. Plus, Mabel does have a way of picking people up and finding a way to make them smile. That is, when she's not using you for her own sick game of who-will-fall-in-love-with-me-next?

"Evening, ladies." Esther emerges from inside Bacchus. Like me, she's dressed for the night sail. With no mountains to curb the wind, it's much colder this far from land. My jacket is a baby blue waterproof made by a brand you could find at any sporting goods store. Esther wears her trademark red with flashes of fluorescent yellow. It's a specialist coastal jacket, designed for comfort whatever the weather and is made by a famous sailing label. It probably cost at least four hundred quid. My mind flashes to those yellow two hundred euro notes stored under the bed.

"Report?" Esther asks Mabel as Jo silently returns below deck.

"We're doing a steady seven and a half knots. I'm keeping her on two hundred and thirty degrees."

241

"Conditions?"

"Good. A little gusty. Wind's coming from the south. The channel's busier than expected. We had to do some ferry-dodging earlier, but now it's mainly fishing vessels and cargo ships."

Esther takes the helm, nodding at the information Mabel has given her.

"We're around here," she adds, pointing to a chart in a plastic wallet.

The skipper and her first mate embrace before Mabel says she could kill for a gin and tonic, bids us goodnight and disappears into Bacchus for some shuteye.

Finally, I think as I inspect the carabiner clip that holds me to the guard rail. I have Esther alone.

CHAPTER 31

Libby.

The darkness is disorientating. It's hard to tell what's up or down, what's sky or water. Without the usual sights to ground me, I feel dizzy and unsure of my footing. Bacchus rises and falls with a rhythmic swell, but because I can't see the waves coming, each sideways roll has me reaching for handholds. This isn't something I'm used to, and though I know I shouldn't, I find myself continually grasping the carabiner clip, clipping and unclipping like a nervous school child clicks the lid on a pen. *Click, click, click.*

"Libby, dear, you sound like a metronome. It's annoying."

"Listen, Esther," I say, clipping back on before letting go of it. I brace myself for what I'm about to say. "We need to talk. I'm going to alight at Le Castella."

Even in the dark, I can see her brown eyes lift from the instrument panel to meet mine.

243

"There's a flight from Crotone to Milan. I can connect to London from there."

Esther engages the autohelm before folding her arms over her all-weather jacket. "Oh, don't be dramatic. Verona will come around. She's just jealous. She's redirecting her anger at you when really she's upset at herself for driving away the love of her life. She'll get over it."

She reaches out to me, her arms stretched to invite me into a hug. When I don't go to her, she pats my arm. "Don't let Verona ruin this trip for you. You're my friend, and I want you to stay."

"This isn't about Verona." The sound of my heart thudding, pulses in my ears. It's loud enough to hear over the wind and the noise of the sea beating against the hull. Confrontation is something I usually avoid like the plague. "It's about the passports."

There's a pause, then, "What passports?"

The pause gave her away. That, and the cautious look she's giving me. Esther knows precisely what I'm talking about. I reach into my back pocket and lift up the blank British passport. I hold it head height, between my thumb and index finger. The longer I hold it, the more I'm convinced they've been stolen from the manufacturer. A final run of EU red before the United Kingdom switched to dark blue. They even feel real. The texture is indistinguishable from my own.

Quick as a flash, Esther snatches it from me and pushes it into one of her many zip pockets.

"Look, Libby—"

"No, don't *look, Libby* me."

"Okay, calm down."

"CALM DOWN? No, Esther, I will not calm down. Seriously?" The thudding in my ears is louder and faster than ever. "Do you know what will happen to us if the boat is searched when we get to Catania?"

Esther battles to remain composed, but even through her thick, red jacket, I can see her chest lifting with increasing speed. She looks right and left, staring out to sea for a moment, then, thoughts presumably gathered, she places her hands on her hips – the same posture she always adopts when ready to talk down to someone.

"We're not going to Catania. What sort of halfwit do you think I am? We're going to a smaller marina down the coast. More off the beaten track."

"You're going to a smaller marina," I correct her. "We're not going anywhere. I'm leaving at Le Castella."

"It's not a big deal, Libby."

Is she for real? Does Esther McPherson actually believe this is no big deal? Perhaps she does. I mean, how often do we hear of politicians being let off some indiscretion in their expenses? Or members of the aristocracy circumventing inheritance tax? Celebrities getting away with who knows what because they can

245

afford the sort of lawyers that are off-limits to the likes of me – the likes of any working-class person. One rule for them; one rule for the rest of us.

"It's a huge fucking deal," I snap back. "Blank passports! Cash! And guns, Esther. Uzis. Fucking Uzis. I'm not rotting in some Italian jail for you or your father. We don't all have oil money to use as a get out jail free card."

Esther opens her mouth to argue, shuts it again and turns off the autohelm. Her mouth fixes into a hard line, and her eyes find the horizon somewhere in the darkness.

Quietly, barely audible over the rushing wind, she whispers, "It's not what it looks like. Daddy's in trouble."

She looks up, eyes glistening in the moonlight. "He was in debt. His business was struggling. He knew this man – an associate – he offered to help."

"An *associate*?" I echo, my head tilted to the side questioningly. "You mean a gangster?"

"No." Her voice is pained in a way I've never heard from her before. "Well, he didn't know it at the time. He knew this man, you see. They called him the Broker. He brokers deals between businesses, private citizens, even governments …"

I pace back and forth, unsure of what I'm hearing. The carabiner clip whistling as it runs up and down the jackstay, metal against polyester webbing. The

Broker? Brokering deals for corrupt regimes and dodgy companies.

"… He said he could fix it so that Daddy's main rival would go bust."

"Who was the rival?"

"Gimenez," she says into the collar of her coat.

Gimenez? Gimenez Energy. A memory tingles at the back of my mind. I've heard that name before. Yes. Jo and Verona were discussing how they lost out on some major tidal project while Mabel was flirting with young Jorge.

"The Solway Barrage?" I ask once the memory comes back to me.

"Yes." She wipes her arm over her face. "They planted porn on the CEO's computer. Deep in a hidden file where no one would spot it until the authorities were tipped off."

"Why would the authorities care about porn? It's hardly a reason to rescind on the deal or shut the whole company down."

"It was child porn," she says quickly. "He was arrested."

Suddenly I'm back in the business class lounge in Heathrow airport, feeling like a duck out of water, and scanning the headlines of the daily papers.

"Arrested? Esther, he's been locked up without bail for months. It's only now going to trial. Your father had that man's life and reputation ruined. Jesus, he framed someone as a paedo so he could nab their tidal

247

energy project. Esther, he could be killed in jail, and even if he's found not guilty, he'll never recover from that sort of allegation. Never."

Esther slams the helm then shakes her hand, having hurt herself. "We didn't know that's what they were going to do."

"Oh, that's okay then. The McPhersons didn't know. The McPhersons are totally innocent. You didn't do anything about it, did you? Just happily swooped in to finish the Solway Barrage while that man goes to jail. What's that project worth? What are the UK government – sorry, the UK taxpayers – paying DYH Triton?"

She shrugs. "The margins are thin. The manufacturing costs alone—"

"How much, Esther?"

"The project's expected to cost just north of a billion."

I have to sit down. I feel more disorientated than ever. In fact, I feel sick, and this time it's not the sea state making me feel this way. I'd chuck up over the side if I didn't think it would be blown straight back in my face.

"And let me guess," I start, speaking slowly in an attempt to keep bile from forcing its way up my throat. "This Broker didn't frame your father's main competitor out of the goodness of his heart?"

"Daddy was naive. When he asked how much he owed, he was told there was no fee. We secured the bid to finish the doomed barrage and business boomed. It was months later when the Broker got in touch and said Daddy owed him."

Minutes ago, Esther had the nerve to ask if I thought she was a halfwit. What sort of gullible moron makes a deal with the devil and doesn't expect the inevitable?

"His fee was half a million euros, blank passports and guns?"

If I was Esther's father, I might be tempted to think half a million was a fair price to secure a billion quid's worth of business for his company.

"Not quite. I don't know what this man did for the Albanians, but they owe them a lot. It has to be paid in a mix of currency, documents and weapons. Their vessel would draw too much attention in Sicily, but a yacht registered in Malta with—"

"With a bunch of young women having a girlie holiday wouldn't."

Despite the darkness, I see Esther flush. Guilt colouring her cheeks."

"It's called a triangle deal. Rather than paying them directly, we transport the fee of another party."

"I don't give a shit what it's called. We need to jettison this."

Esther's mouth falls open, and she slaps the auto-helm again. "We'll do no such thing."

"Why the hell not?"

"Because I told you: Daddy's in trouble. He didn't want to do the triangle deal. He said no. He didn't realise who he was saying no to, and when he refused, they took him."

My skin prickles as every hair on the back of my neck stands on end. "Took him?"

She blinks back tears that glisten in the moonlight. "He was in Naples when someone who works for the Broker met him for a drink under the guise that they could discuss a payment plan instead of the initial offer. He spiked Daddy's drink, put him in the back of a van and the next thing he knows, he's being held in some God-forsaken ghost town. He's being tortured in a dirty basement, Libby. They've only let me speak to him twice. Once to prove what they were telling me wasn't a sick joke, and once to confirm I was on my way to the collection point. I had to listen while they removed his fingernail with pliers, Libby. When I drop off the goods, they'll let me know where I can collect him from."

Though I fear I already know the answer, I ask, "And if you don't?"

"They'll kill him and come for me."

She says this with such a matter of fact tone to her voice, it makes what I've been trying to avoid come true in an explosive fashion. I turn to face the sea, lean over the guard rail and empty my stomach. I spit the last bits of sick from my lips. Using one hand to keep my glasses on my face, I wipe my mouth with the other, grimacing at the acrid taste of stomach acid.

"There's got to be another way," I say, gasping. "We can contact the coast guard."

"They OWN the coast guard."

She says this as if she's speaking to a simpleton. Of course, they own the fucking coast guard.

"You think we're the first private yacht to make this sort of delivery? They pay people to turn a blind eye. I've been assured no one is going to inspect Bacchus when we moor up."

Options run through my mind. "Then we go home and phone the police?"

"What will they do? They'll call the Italian police, and by then Daddy will be dead, and someone will be on their way for me."

Somehow, despite it all, part of me feels terrible for her. She's just doing what she needs to do to protect her father. I can't relate. I wouldn't do this for Mam or my brother, but I would for Danny. Though that's hardly a fair comparison because Danny would never do anything that would land us in this situation.

For a brief moment, I'm distracted by the sail at the bow beginning to flap. I think of the other's blissfully sleeping below deck. Paige and Mabel, Jo and Verona. None of us deserves to be in this position.

"Why are we here, Esther? Why drag us into this?"

The sail flaps again, this time more noisily. "Tighten the genoa," she says without skipping a beat.

"Tighten the genoa," I snarl back. "Ever the fucking skipper. Tighten your own bloody genoa." Then it dawns on me; that's why we're here. She can't sail Bacchus on her own. She's good, but she's not that good.

"I … I … Gosh, it sounds so stupid now, but I thought I could make the best of a bad situation. I thought having you all here would take my mind off what was happening."

"BULLSHIT," I scream.

"Keep your voice down," she hisses, her eyes flicking to the companionway.

"You weren't making the best of the situation. You needed a crew. You used us."

"Libby, I'm sorry, but—"

"You're not though. People like you are never really sorry." I shake my head. "Do they know we're here? The people who have your father. Do they know you brought us along?"

"They know I'm not alone. They don't know your names. I promise."

I don't know if I believe her. Do I believe any of this?

"No … I can't do it, Esther. Whatever you've gotten yourself into, I can't be part of it. We need to get these items off Bacchus or call the police. The *British* Police," I specify before she can tell me the Broker owns them too.

252

A fierce expression forms on Esther's face. "You need to stop worrying about what will happen if we make that delivery and start worrying about what will happen if we don't." She looks like a caged animal now. The poised woman I know is gone, replaced by someone more wild and ferocious.

"Yeah, I know, bad things will happen to you and your father, but you know what? That's not my concern. I'm leaving at Le Castella."

"You can't."

Not once has Esther asked me to go along with this. Not a single question or plea or beg. Only demands.

You can't.

You'll do no such thing.

Keep your voice down.

This is someone who doesn't ask for things, only demands them.

"Why can't I? You said they don't know I'm here."

"Because I don't trust that you won't run to the nearest police station. We stick together until the delivery is made and I have my father back."

"You don't trust me? That's rich." I turn, beginning to walk away. Walking away from Esther McPherson is something the lot of us should have done a long time ago. "You can't hold me captive," I say over my shoulder. Though standing my ground makes me shake with dread, I feel proud of myself: I'm taking control of this situation. "I'm making the call."

But that's the thing, people like Esther never relinquish control to people like me. I'm pulled off balance. Esther, fury radiating from every part of her, has followed me. She grabs my jacket from behind and pulls with all her might.

"You're ... not ... calling anyone," she hisses, tugging me back to the cockpit.

I push her in the chest, panicked by the sudden physicality. Up until now, our argument has been solely verbal. Now it's a fight. Her hand moves like lightening, slapping me across the face. I reach for my face, placing my hand over a patch of raw, stinging flesh. I feel like a child again and struggle to pull myself free as Esther grips the lapels of my jacket. I paw at her fingers, trying to pry her hands from me. When it doesn't work, I do something I've never done before. Without thinking, my hand balls into a fist, and I punch her in the stomach. She grunts and doubles over but refuses to let go of me, causing us to fall to the deck.

I find myself lying on my back with Esther straddling me. She grabs me by the hair and pounds my head onto the wooden deck. It makes me woozy for a second, then a surge of self-preservation takes over, making me fight back. I'm acting on instinct alone. I press my hand into her face, pushing the pads of my index and middle finger into her eyes. She twists her head side to side, trying to angle my fingers into her mouth. Her jaw snaps shut repeatedly as she tries to bite me. Finally, I muster enough strength to push her from me.

As Esther staggers back to her feet, I grab her leg, trying to leverage myself up. She slaps me again, in the same place as seconds earlier.

"I'm not having you get in my way," she seethes. Another hard push and my feet slip. There's a whooshing sound as the guardrail rubs against my trousers. My hands desperately grab for anything they can hold onto, because all too late, I realise that I'm falling.

Man overboard.

– CHAPTER 32 –

Esther.

As Libby slips ever closer to the edge of Bacchus, all I can think is, *how dare she!* I knew the moment I took that ghetto-dweller under my wing she'd be trouble. As if she has the gall to call my father a criminal. That's rich. I know all about the Bagshaw family and their criminal record. Her mother was done for drunk and disorderly, shoplifting and indecent exposure. I mean, can you imagine? And as for her brother, he's got a record for assault and possession of a bladed weapon. No wonder he's locked up. Long may it stay that way.

Libby doesn't understand. She sees everything as black and white; this is right, and that is wrong. She doesn't appreciate that sometimes you have to do bad things to get good results. All I've ever wanted was to keep my family together. First Jo, now Libby. All I'm doing is protecting my father. Perhaps she'd understand if she had one, but I don't think she knows who her father is. I doubt even her mother does.

Failing is not an option. It's not only my father's life on the line but also my family's legacy and reputation. They'll crucify us if word gets out. Gimenez and Triton, the barrage, the Broker, the paedophilic images. We'd never recover. It would go right to the top.

I can't let that happen, so with my last ounce of strength, I slap Libby across the face.

"I'm not having you get in my way," I tell her.

Then I push her once more.

Libby's scream dies in her throat as she stumbles over the guardrail. I didn't want it to come to this, but I've always been the sort to do what's necessary. To go one step further if it's required.

They say when you're about to die that your life flashes before your eyes and at that moment, I think I see the flood of flickering memories hurtling through Libby's mind. Her mouth is open, and the whites of her eyes are visible all around her irises. She looks like Edvard Munch's *The Scream*. Her arms flail forward, trying to act as a counterweight. Her hands grasp the air, fingers stretching and clenching as if searching for an invisible rope until they finally find something to seize.

Me.

She takes a handful of my jacket in each hand, and we fall together, into the unforgiving Ionian Sea.

The water feels like a brick wall when I smash into it. Frightened and cold, my legs kick out until my head finds the surface. I look around but can't see Libby.

Libby.

It's not the fall, but the sudden stop that knocks the wind out of me. My head hits the gunwale, the edge where Bacchus's deck meets her hull, causing me to groan in agony. I'm sore, concussed and disorientated.

But I'm alive.

Mabel was right to tell me to clip on, and true to form, Bacchus's carabiners are second to none.

Only my lower legs are in the sea, but the wake from the yacht kicks water all over me. It cascades over my head, and I fear if I hang here too long, I might drown. I reach up, feeling for the ledge, and when I find it, I dig my nails in. I'm no climber. I go to the gym, I work out, but I've never done a pull up before. My muscles scream, flooding with lactic acid as I try to heave my weight back aboard.

They say people find superhuman levels of strength under extreme situations, like a mother lifting a car off her child. Somehow, because I know I'll die if I don't, I start to move. My fingernails begin to crack and tear. Pain shoots through each knuckle of my fingers as my weight shifts from the carabiner to my hands.

Incoherent words leave my mouth. Guttural grunts and sounds that don't resemble any language I know. Panicked gasps of survivalism as I manage to get one elbow on deck. From there I pull the other arm over, hugging the deck to my armpits. The wake continues to splash over me, weighing me down and making each pull more tiring than the last. Still, Bacchus's teak decks have never felt so good.

Like a shuggy boat, I start to shift my weight right and left. With each swing my feet get a little higher, but the longer it takes, the harder it is to keep hold. Another nail is ripped from my finger, and I let out a throaty, pained sound. My hands plead for me to let go, to stop the pain. My survival instinct has to over-rule that voice, has to keep going no matter how many nails I lose or fingers I break.

One foot reaches the deck. *Come on, Libby*, I tell myself. *You can make it.* I hook my foot behind a stanchion, my bruised knee being pushed into the jammer for the genoa sheet. Once my right knee is up, dragging my left leg over the ledge is easier. I roll under the guard rail, spitting out some water that had forced its way into my mouth. I look for Esther. There she is, to the starboard stern. She's drifting further with each passing second.

She waves, "Libby. HELP!"

Esther.

She's made it back on board. She's standing. She's looking for me.

It's going to be okay. *I'm* going to be okay. I'm not far from Bacchus and I'm a sound swimmer. Yes, Bacchus is moving away faster than I could ever swim, but as long as I do my utmost, it will make it easier for the girls to pull me out.

I know they will. I know this for the same reason I was so annoyed at Libby moments earlier; she only sees black and white, good and bad, right and wrong. She knows the right thing to do – despite everything that's just happened – is to raise the alarm. Mabel will turn Bacchus around and have me back on board within minutes. I'm going to be okay.

Those words, *I'm going to be okay*, circle on repeat, like a comforting nursery rhyme. But in truth, I'm scared. My breathing is shallow and the near-black is suffocating.

The water's horrifically cold this far from land. My clothing helps, but not much. Swimming helps keep my body temperature up, but I need to be careful and not waste too much energy too soon. My fastest stroke is front crawl, but it's also more demanding. I switch to breaststroke, never taking my eye's off Bacchus.

"Libby," I shout her name, to help her track my location. "LIBBY!"

I switch to treading water so I can wave my arms above my head. Hopefully, my jacket is bright enough for her to spot. "OVER HERE."

She picks up the life preserver. *Yes. Good girl. Now throw it.*"

CHAPTER 33

Libby.

Shivering and soaking wet, I go into a form of autopi-
lot – or autohelm. The *man overboard* drill repeats in my
mind.

Alert the crew.

Hit the MOB button on the panel.

Throw a life ring.

Mark the position.

Prepare a line.

Although the yellow life preserver weighs next to
nothing, it feels heavy in my hand, anchoring itself to
the side of my leg as if I were dragging a suitcase. I'm
physically exhausted from heaving myself back on
board. Bruises throb on my shins and back, and my
throat stings from swallowing some salty water. I push
wet hair from my face, feeling the warmth of blood as
it oozes out of a cut on my hairline. The heat quickly

dissipates as it mixes with water and a chilly night breeze.

I scan the sea for Esther. I spot her struggling in the current. Splashes of water leap all around her as she waves her arms and shouts. I can't make out what she's saying, but her tone is halfway between fear and anger. Fearful of what is about to happen and downright appalled that it should happen to someone like her. McPhersons attend society balls, have private chefs, and hire mobsters to ensure rival companies go under. McPhersons don't leave their privileged lives in the hands of a poor girl who never studied classics. With each passing second, Esther's shouts become fainter, and within moments I can't make out a tone at all, only human noises muffled by wind and tide.

Alert the crew.

Turning to the companionway, I open my mouth but only "M … M …" comes out. My voice is caught in my throat. It's a pitiful real-life replay of a recurring nightmare where I'm too scared to scream. Only, I fear I won't wake up from this one. My mouth closes without a single audible word escaping it. My teeth chatter in rapid-fire bursts that only stop when they clamp down on my tongue.

Hit MOB on the panel.

I look back and forth between Esther and the instrument panel. Both blurred to me. Putting the life preserver down for a moment, I grab the helm with one hand, the index finger of my free hand hovers over the button. Even without my glasses, I can still read MOB written in thick letters.

Esther is harder to spot now. Her dark skin and hair blend seamlessly into the black of night, only her red jacket gives her location away. Reflective strips on her shoulders occasionally flash white as they catch the light from onboard.

A distant foghorn dwarfs Esther's final plea for help. She's too far for me to hear her now.

Throw a life ring.

Mark the position.

Prepare a line.

Esther slips under as a gust of wind fills Bucchus's sails. She's fifty feet away. Seventy. One hundred. A dot.

If I had my glasses, I still wouldn't be able to see Esther now. A surge of adrenaline makes my hands shake even worse than before, and it's a struggle to reef the sails. The lines slip in my wet hands, and each turn of the wrench takes all the strength I have. With the sails reefed we slow slightly and I try to gather my thoughts. I don't know if I'm crying or if my face is still wet from falling in, but my body aches from top to toe. Adrenaline does nothing to numb the pain I feel inside and out. Checking autohelm is still engaged, I sit in the cockpit with my head in my hands. I should turn Bacchus around, try to locate Esther. But it's too late; we'd never find her now.

Not alive anyway.

You should try, a voice in my head tells me.

I should listen, but if that voice is the angel on my shoulder, the devil on my other shoulder whispers, *What if you do find her alive? What then? She knows you left her for dead.*

Shit. I surge to my feet. It wasn't a conscious decision to stop and sit down. But I did. My dithering, my inaction, they both yield the same result – I left Esther McFuckingPherson to die at sea.

I didn't alert the crew; I didn't do any of the things I was supposed to. I just watched as we sailed away.

Panicking, I pace in the cockpit – two steps forward, two steps back. Would she have her father's associates come after me? Have them tie me up and torture me until I begged for death? She wouldn't even need the mafia, I realise. She could just tell the police, tell anyone. I'd be locked up for life. I can see the headlines now. *Jealous northerner tries to drown young royal, accuses her of smuggling.*

I don't even want to consider if allowing Esther's death would count as treason. She's not the sovereign, but she is related to her. She's in the line of succession. Oh shit, they can still hang you for treason, can't they? That's what Mam told me when I was a kid. She said we still had the death penalty for treason, piracy, espionage, and something else. There was four of them. Still pacing, I try to remember. Ah, it was arson in the Royal Dockyards. That was it – treason, piracy, espionage, and arson in the Royal Dockyards.

265

Christ almighty, I left Esther to die at sea. I'm – and I can hardly believe this – I'm a murderer. I didn't turn Bacchus around. I didn't throw a flotation device. I killed her.

A calm feeling in the top of my head seeps down me. Panic and self-pity will do me no good. It's time to use my only real strength: my mind. My eyes dry, my teeth stop chattering, and my hands stop shaking. I check the carabiner and walk along the deck to the bow, where I open the hatch to the crew cabin and grab the black bag.

Hauling it back to the cockpit, I spread the contents on the table. Plastic bags full of blank passports, multi-coloured stacks of currency and three fucking Uzis.

I chew my tongue where I bit it earlier. Massaging it gently between molars and contemplating what I'm about to do. I run every possible scenario through my head, imagining the fallout, the interrogations, the people who may come after me. My decision making is like a maze or a flow chart that I follow in my head. Each route that leads me to jail is discarded until I'm left with only one choice.

"No," I decide, saying it out loud as if verbalising my decision makes it more finite. "It's the only way."

The only way I get away with murder.

Because that's what this is. I still haven't alerted the crew, and it's a conscious decision this time. I gather myself and move to the companionway. The hatch

266

slides open with a thud. I waste no time opening the doors and flicking on the light in the saloon.

"Must you," says Verona. She rolls over and lifts her eye mask to glower at me. "Some of us are trying to sleep."

"Wake up," I snap. "Wake the others and get up here. We have a problem."

CHAPTER 34

Paige.

There's an urgent knocking on my door, then it creeks open and floods the room with light. The shock of going from deep sleep to fully awake so suddenly gives me palpitations, and I have to cover my eyes to shield them from the bright onslaught. I can't see, but I know by her voice that it's Verona.

"Get up. Something's going on."

We pile up the companionway and find Libby on deck. I can't quite believe my eyes. She's drenched and looks like she's been hit by a truck. Her face is swollen, and blood drips from her shivering hands. My first thought is that it's rained overnight and she's been hit by the boom or taken a nasty tumble. I look back below deck towards Esther's cabin. Why would she leave Libby alone during a night shift? That's hardly fair. If she wanted more sleep, she could have asked one of us to switch. I'm rested now, and Verona certainly got enough sleep earlier.

268

The thought dissipates. Esther's an experienced sailor; she *wouldn't* leave Libby alone during a night shift.

Worried, I turn back to her. Libby shakes her head, confirming my worst fears. "She's not in there," she says. "I'm not sure how to say this …"

Mabel frowns and begins to look around. She becomes more agitated with every second she can't find Esther. Dread forms on her tanned face.

Libby takes a deep breath before releasing what she has to say in one quick stream of speech. It's as if she's reciting a list of bullet points. Everything is short and to the point but without a single pause for breath.

"We had a fight. This trip isn't what we thought it was. Esther used us. We're nothing but her alibi. She slapped me, and hit me, and then—" Libby stops, her hand covering her mouth as she retches; nothing comes up. "Esther pushed me and I went overboard. She fell in after me, but I was clipped on. I pulled myself back up. Esther's still out there."

Though I had an awful feeling this was coming, it still takes a moment for the words to sink in. It's like my brain has frozen to protect me from the shock, and it not just me, we all stand like this. Fixed and silent.

Mabel is the first to burst into action. She grabs the metal rail that connects the sunshade to the cockpit. It supports her weight as she leans out, yelling for Esther. She turns to the helm, starts the engine and takes con-

269

trol of the vessel, turning Bacchus one hundred and eighty degrees.

"It's too late," Libby whispers, but Mabel's movement has kicked us all into gear.

Verona picks up the life preserver and pulls lines from the cockpit locker. Jo grabs a torch and begins to light the way for Mabel. A circle of light panning left and right as her eyes sweep the water for any signs of life. "Raise the alarm," I shout, turning on the spot, ready to run below deck and grab the radio. I'll hit the red distress button and broadcast on channel 16 for any boats in the area to help with our search.

"It's too late," Libby repeats, grabbing my arm. She looks dead into my eyes and says it once more, louder and with such deliberateness that I can't help but understand. "Paige, it's too late."

One by one, it dawns on the others. They stop yelling into the wind and running around with lines ready to toss. Jo's hand covers the crown of her head, her other arm wrapping around her middle in a self-soothing gesture.

"This can't be," says Verona. Her voice trembles as she says it and I spot her drawing the tiniest cross over her chest. "We have to try. We have to do something."

Libby's demeanour is eerie; she's not crying or panicking. She sits down in one of the cockpit seats, groaning in pain as she does so, and angles her head back to look up at us. She looks so different without her glasses and with her dripping hair pushed back off her forehead.

"We'll never find her," she says. "I didn't mark the position, and if we call for help …" She places her hand on a heavy-looking black holdall. "We'll need to explain this."

The cockpit table has foldable sides. Libby lifts one panel to create a larger surface area and unzips the bag. We all peer in.

* * *

There's an odd buzzing in my ears while Libby empties the bag, one awful item at a time. When she's finished, we stare silently at it. None of this makes any sense. Esther's gone. Apparently, she pushed Libby overboard. Apparently? Listen to me. Who am I more likely to believe? Libby, or the woman who tipped the press off about my abortion so she could make a few quid? So she could humiliate me? Feel some sort of power over me? And now there's more money than I can count, bags of passports and – I cough when I see them – guns. Real-life, could kill you before you could blink, guns.

"Libby?" Jo's voice wavers. "Are those Uzis?"

A trickle of blood runs down Libby's forehead. She wipes it away, wincing as her fingers rub over the open wound. Pulling her knees into her chest to keep warm, she starts to explain. She goes over finding the bag in

271

her cabin, and how Esther had wanted her to stay with her that night. She reminds us about Bacchus's engine failing in the middle of the storm. How it forced us to go on when we were all ready to overrule her and head into Corfu. She tells us about spotting the bolt on the engine access was out of position, and how the seawater inlet was the only part of the engine that didn't have a thin layer of dirt over it.

"Esther faked engine failure?" Mabel's forehead creases into parallel lines.

"She had to make it to the meeting point. Closing the saltwater inlet caused the engine to overheat and cut out. That meant we had to sail on to the Faraway Islands because we couldn't get a vessel the size of Bacchus into Paleokastritsa under sail, not in those conditions. It was the only way she could force us to go on to Othonoi. Esther must have got up during the night and opened the inlet again before letting you take a look at the engine."

Mabel puts a bag of passports back on the table and wipes her hand on her satin pyjama shorts as if she's just touched something dirty. "But why? Why would she do all of this?"

Verona picks up a bundle of hundred euro bills and begins tossing it from one hand to the other. I don't understand any of this but can see Verona's mind working in overdrive. "DYH Triton," she says, without using an upward inflexion; it's not a question.

Libby turns to face her and nods, "Bingo."

272

Jo disappears for a moment. I hear lockers opening below deck, then she hands us all blankets. I'm oddly reminded of the night we sat on deck while Mabel and Jorge got busy in her cabin. We looked at the stars, laughed, distracted ourselves. Then Esther pushed Mabel too far – like she pushes everyone too far – and I got a piece of glass in my neck. It seems like years ago now.

I wrap the blanket around myself and tuck my hair down the back of it. Other than Libby, we're all still in our nightwear. Not that Libby's clothes will be doing her much use; they're wet, and she's looking pretty pale. I think she might be in shock.

Pulling her knees in tighter and wrapping her arms around her legs to hold them in place, she goes on to tell us about DYH Triton, Gimenez Energy and the smear campaign against Gimenez's CEO. I recall the picture of him in the paper: Rowan something. He was being ushered into court with towels over his head while a crowd pelted him with bottles, cans, newspapers, anything they could throw. I remember being disgusted, thinking he deserved to rot in jail. Now I hear it was all the doing of this *Broker*.

"So," Libby says, as Jo lays a towel over her like a giant fleece tent, "we have some options. We can call for help, and try to explain that we didn't know what was being transported."

273

Verona snorts. "Yeah, like they wouldn't want to make an example of young women smuggling goods through Europe."

"Remember the Peru Two?" Jo asks, and I picture the two Scottish girls who tried to take cocaine out of South America, how they were paraded in front of the media. How no one mentioned the manufacturers, the dealers, or the real puppetmasters in the drug industry; it was all about the mules.

"Even if …" Libby swallows. "Well, I'd still be doing life for murder."

"Manslaughter, surely," Jo says. "She would have killed you if you weren't clipped on."

"Esther McPherson is thirty-eighth in line to the throne. There were no witnesses; it's my word against a dead royal. There's no way I'd get off on a self-defence plea. Then there's this Broker guy. This," she gestures to the bags of passports, "is all supposed to be delivered to some seriously bad people. If *we're* the reason they're not delivered."

"Yeah. We get it," I interrupt. "Option one is a no go. I don't want these geezers pissed off at us."

And Verona, who I suspect doesn't really care if Libby goes to jail, agrees. "Seconded. That doesn't work."

"What if we hoy it all overboard?" I ask. "Then when we call for help and report Esther falling in, we can deny any knowledge of this other stuff."

274

Mabel shakes her head. "The Greek authorities will definitely search the boat after a man overboard. They'll involve the police and look for evidence of foul play. Their records will show that no contraband was found on Bacchus. But, and this is a big but …"

"The Broker's Albanian contacts will tell him they definitely gave Esther the goods." Verona finishes. "Meaning, the Albanians will blame us for the failed delivery, and as far as the Sicilians are concerned, we'll owe them money and guns and more."

"Fuck," snaps Jo, burying her head in her hands and doubling over. "We're fucked. Fucking McPhersons. They use everyone and don't give a shit about the consequences."

We all sit and huddle together, partly for warmth, partly for reassurance. All seems lost. One friend is likely dead, and whatever option we choose, we're either at the mercy of this Broker, or my other friend is punished for someone else's crime.

Libby coughs. "There's another option."

Four sets of eyes find hers, and despite the ordeal, the grief and the terror she must feel, the corner of her mouth twitches upwards with a flicker of hope.

"Pirates."

275

CHAPTER 35

Jo.

"Mabel, how deep can you free dive?"

Libby's question seems odd. I'm not sure how it relates to anything that's going on right now. Unless – and I hope I'm wrong – she's going to ask Mabel to retrieve Esther's body. No, that's ridiculous; we're in half a kilometre of water. Not to mention it's pitch black and we don't know where the hell we'd find it.

Mabel shrugs and exhales through closed lips, causing them to flutter like she's blowing a raspberry.

"I'm out of practice. Maybe thirty-five feet."

A look of disappointment shadows Libby's face. "I thought you could do more?"

"I could. My best is fifty-five, but I trained for a long time to do that. Why do you want to know?"

Libby ignores the question. "What if you started training again? Could you manage forty-five in a few months?"

Mabel nods, and her blonde waves fall forward. "Yeah. I suppose so."

The answer seems to satisfy Libby, who stands, shuffles her way to the helm, turns the engine on and rotates Bacchus until her bow points east. She reaches into the bag and pulls out five or six wads of hundred euro bills.

"Jo, consider this compensation. The McPhersons owed you."

I look at the cash in her hand – green bills featuring a map of Europe flutter between Libby's fingers. If I'd made a fuss, or confided in someone, perhaps there would have been a case to answer. If I'd hired a lawyer … Hired a lawyer? I was fourteen, didn't have a penny to my name and didn't think my own parents would believe me. I know things turned out okay in the end, on the outside at least. I went to a top university and went on to become a vet. On the outside, everything looked great. On the inside …

Libby distracts me from thoughts of dark corridors and feeling trapped when she turns to Paige and asks, "Would this cover Graham's treatment?"

I can see the longing in Paige's eyes. Like an unloved puppy who needs a forever home.

She nods. "Yes."

"And you wouldn't need to go to Russia?"

"No. It would be enough."

I don't know what Russian trip Libby's talking about, but I'd heard Graham wasn't doing so well.

Paige starts to shake. Most people watching her would think she was cold. She is, after all, pale and annoyingly thin. I, however, can tell she's trembling from relief. Some stress she's been carrying around has been removed, and she's overwhelmed because of it.

"But we can't," she whispers, crossing her long legs. "There's no way we'd get away with it."

"We might," Libby says. She rubs her knee while she thinks for a moment. "And Verona, you could buy out a Dragon with your share. You'd be a step closer to owning Lazy Llama foods outright. It's your business, your brainchild, your hard work. You should own it."

Everyone looks uneasy. There's a definite smell of fear. Paige and Verona look tempted, but they're unsure of the morals and scared of any consequences. Mabel, who never seems afraid of anything, seems more excited than fearful. Like she's about to do something naughty, but she doesn't know what. As for Libby, I've never felt this energy from her before. She's usually the little one in the background. She's always been a quiet follower. I have to say, leading suits her.

I'm the first to break the silence. "They did fucking owe me."

I extend an arm and open my hand. Libby deposits the money into my palm. I feel it's weight, bouncing it up and down for a second; it's heavier than I thought.

Paige mimics me, allowing Libby to place a pile of money in her hand. She holds it to her chest like a

278

cuddly toy. "You know the lengths I'd go to for Graham. I just don't understand how … how we pull this off."

Libby glances back at the instrument panel, then up at the wind gauge before addressing us. "Here's the plan."

* * *

We sit, we listen, we nod.

It might just work.

Verona fetches a dry bag and some diving weights. The cash, every single euro of it, is wrapped in the plastic bags that had previously housed the blank passports. We place bag within bag within bag, like see-through babushka dolls. It's then placed in the dry bag, the ends rolled up to remove as much air as possible and then tied to the diving weights.

We each return to our cabins and gather everything of value.

"Make sure to complete factory resets on all your devices," Verona warns us. "Wipe them clean, remove your sim cards and toss the sims overboard."

I grab my phone and credit cards, then sit down on the bed for a moment. My engagement ring catches the light. I rotate it around my finger several times, wondering if I have the strength to remove it and finish that chapter of my life. Well, there's no time like the present, and if this is to work, I don't have much of a choice. I pull it up to my knuckle where it pinches the flesh and refuses to budge. My recent weight gain obviously isn't confined to my hips and arse. A drop of washing up liquid and some intense grimacing finally causes it to budge. Instantly, my finger feels weird and naked. My thumb moves to where the band should have been, but instead of massaging cold metal, it feels only warm soapy flesh.

I move through the saloon until I reach the door to Esther's cabin. Looking in the doorway, I feel as if I am invading her privacy. When I was little, I was never allowed in Esther's room unsupervised. In fact, I was never allowed in the big house unless she'd invited me over or mother needed an extra pair of hands with the laundry.

"Do you want me to do it?" Libby asks, a hand on my shoulder. "I don't mind. I mean, it was my idea."

I let out a deep sigh and shake my head. "No, it's okay. I've got this."

I step over the threshold and look around Esther's cabin. It's as immaculate as it was the night we were moored up in Gaios. The night Mabel, Esther and I drank gin and tonics on her bed. I open the first drawer in her dresser and pull out a hairbrush. To anyone else, it would just look like a family heirloom. It's clearly old. It's silver with a design of an elephant among swaying palm trees engraved into the back. Esther used to use this to brush my hair. I'd sit at her dressing table, and she'd stand behind dragging the soft bristles over my long dark hair. It felt so soothing, like a head massage. Then she would plait my hair into a long Dutch braid before pinning the braid into a spiral so it looked like a great big flower at the base of my head. It seems a shame, but I add the brush to the plastic bag that hangs from the crook of my elbow. It all has to go.

In the next drawer, I find her purse and passport. In the bag they go as well. I don't bother emptying her jewellery box; instead, I place the whole thing in the bag and feel the strain of the increased weight that pulls on my arm muscles.

A few designer items, some decorative figurines, a pair of Chanel shades and a Prada handbag; one by one, I stuff her things into the carrier. The plastic starts to dig into my forearm with not only the weight of our belongings but with the weight of Esther's disappearance. In a drawer next to her bed, I find the satellite phone she was so willing to show off to us. I turn the small receiver over in my hand, admiring the orange casing that's designed to keep the gadget safe whatever the conditions at sea. Was Mr McPherson really planning on crossing the Atlantic? *Was he fuck*, I think to myself. Esther only needed the sat phone so she could communicate with this Broker while we were miles offshore. Plus, she'd probably use it so she could stay off the radio channels as we approached whatever dodgy marina we were headed to.

As I leave to join the others on deck, I cast my eyes around the cabin once more, catching a glimpse of myself in the mirror behind Esther's dresser. I hardly recognise myself. Tired, my skin pale and lifeless despite the Mediterranean sun, dark circles under red eyes, and a posture that showed gravity was winning the war on my shoulders and knees. I'm a mess. Is this who I am, or is this what life has made me?

On deck, the holdall is filling. Libby's camera, her pride and joy, takes up most of the space. Verona's MacBook Air, iPad Pro and iPhone 12 are pushed into the gaps at the edges. Paige adds her Kindle and phone as well as some designer clothing.

I add my belongings, along with the items I took from Esther's room. Lastly, I toss in my engagement ring. It briefly catches the moonlight, a little sparkle as if it's winking goodbye to me. I feel Mabel squeeze me around the shoulders. She cuts up her credit cards, removing her name and adds the pieces to some of her jewellery.

"Passports," Libby adds. "In the newspaper, it said the pirates took the victims' passports."

We each retrieve our passports, tear them up so they dissolve easier, and drop them in the bag with nervous hands. Mabel tosses in a couple more diving weights before zipping up the bag and handing it to Libby.

"You're sure it will sink?"

"It'll sink all right," replies Mabel.

282

Libby can barely lift it, but she just about manages to carry it to the stern. She mutters, "Bon voyage," before tossing it over the guardrail where it hits the water with an intense thud.

Our ID, technology, the blank passports and those awful guns – they're all fish food now.

We wait in the darkness. I picture the bag sinking to the depths of the Ionian, wondering how long it will take to reach the bottom. If the distance were a road, Paige might be able to sprint it in under two minutes. I don't do running; I'd dawdle in five minutes later. The bag, I imagine, is sinking somewhere between those two speeds.

And strangely, the longer I stand here, thinking about the bag as it plunges into the depths, the lighter I feel.

With Esther having convinced Libby that her father's associates control some corrupt members of the Sicilian coast guard, we're headed back to Greek waters.

We're aiming for the Faraway Islands but, as it will take ages, Verona fills the kettle and makes us all coffee. We're in some dream-like alternate universe. Starved of sleep, too scared to grieve, and in self-preservation mode. Weren't we supposed to be enjoying the sunshine and having a catch-up? That's what Esther promised us.

I snort. I suppose we have caught up. Everyone's dirty laundry has been well and truly aired over the

283

past few days. Could it be that by the end of this, without Esther, we end up closer than ever? I'm mean, we all know each other's secrets, and we're bound together forever by doing what we're doing.

It's possible, but there's also a chance we'll never speak a word of it again.

– CHAPTER 36 –

Jo.

"Land ho," says Mabel without any of the energy or enthusiasm she usually exhibits while sailing. She points to a landmass that rises out of the water – an olive green triangle set against azure seas and clear skies.

The sun has been up for hours, and as Helios drives his golden chariot higher and higher into the atmosphere, so the air around us warms. We stopped shaking an hour or so ago, but my heart still races, and I still find myself jumping at the slightest noise. Paige is the only one of us who has managed to get some sleep. She was curled up on one of the cockpit cushions with her fleece wrapped around her when she nodded off. It wasn't long before she started dreaming and talking to herself. I couldn't understand what she was saying, but her speech was fast and excitable. I have a hunch she was dreaming about telling her brother he could go to the US for his treatment. The rest of us have managed to stay awake thanks to Verona's constant conveyor belt of coffee. She has us caffeinated up to our eyeballs.

"I take it you don't want me to head to the jetty?" Mabel asks.

Libby shakes her head. "Northern side. We need to find the right spot."

We're looking for somewhere off the tourist trail. Hardly anyone goes here as it is; it's a tranquil idyll. Still, we decide to avoid anywhere with caves or pretty beaches. We don't want to choose a spot where locals or sightseers would like to explore. There needs to be the right amount of depth too. Under fifty-five feet, but deep enough to mean the water isn't crystal clear.

"So, we're agreed?" Libby asks after we've cruised the northern coast twice in each direction.

"I think so," I say. It's taken hours, but I think we've found a spot that is as good as we're going to get.

Verona nods her assent. "It fits the brief. I checked Apple Maps before we dumped everything. Only two roads lead to this area, and I'm being pretty generous when I call them roads. They're barely walking trails. There are no houses, cafes or hotels around here. There's nothing marked as a scenic view or religious site."

"There's nothing to tempt sailors or divers," Mabel adds. "Sure you might get some boats sailing around just for the hell of it. Just to circumnavigate the island or having a pleasure sail, but that's true for anywhere. I think this is as quiet and as boring as we can hope for."

We're drifting near to steep rocks. An off-white cliff face looms out of the water, towering to ten or fifteen metres. Above the creamy stone, greenery takes over and thin dark pines jockey for the most sunlight, stretching their branches towards the sky. Other than the plants, and a wild goat that struggles with a limp, there are no signs of life.

I take a sizeable sand-coloured t-shirt and wrap it around the dry bag that contains the currency. The bag is bright red, like the jacket Esther was wearing when I last saw her. With this sandy covering, the bag will be less eye-catching if someone does come swimming around here, though scanning about, I don't know why they would. Everything of interest is on the southern and western side of the island. We have this place to ourselves.

In one quick movement, Libby tosses the bag overboard. We all lean over Bacchus, watching what looks like a large stone, sink until we can no longer make it out.

"Memorise the coordinates," Libby says. "Learn them by heart. We can't write them down."

When I was at uni, if I wanted to commit something to memory, I'd write it out five times, read it aloud ten times, and read it silently fifteen times. Without a pen or paper, I double up, whispering the numbers to myself over and over, then repeating them in my head until I reach thirty.

We all seem to have our own way of learning: Libby stares intently at the instrument panel; Verona closes her eyes, mutters something then reopens them; Mabel looks like she's counting on her fingers, but really each joint of her fingers represent different letters and numbers. I've seen her use this trick to remember anything from a handsome man's phone number to the first fifty digits of pi.

When she looks up again, she asks us all, "Ready?"

"As we'll ever be," I say. "How long until sunset?"

Libby checks the panel. "At least four hours?"

"We need to be quite far from land. Let's head south-east. The wind and current will bring us back west when we need it to."

* * *

More coffee. A micro nap. Another coffee.

We go over the plan time and time again. We quiz each other. Take turns testing the details and making sure there are no inconsistencies. We recite everything we can remember from the newspaper and online reports of piracy incidents. Weirdly, it reminds me of my old study group, but without the flashcards and textbooks.

"Paige," Libby says with a yawn. "Your turn, once more."

We all look like shit, even Paige. We've been awake so long I fear we'll mess up, start hallucinating, or forget the story. Thankfully, we should look like shit, and, though it scares me, we're going to look a lot worse when the time comes.

Paige sits up, makes her lip tremble and wrings her hands nervously. It's partly acting, but being honest, we all want to cry right now. "There … there were four of them. They kept shouting at us. They were so loud, and they grabbed me—"

"What did they look like?" I ask, playing police, or coast guard, or consulate official.

"Erm, I – I don't know. They wore masks; white masks with holes cut out for eyes. They looked horrible, like something out of a horror film. The tallest can't have been more than five-eleven, but they were all broad and stocky, and one of them had a belly that hung over the belt of his jeans. Wranglers they were."

Nice detail there. Verona remembered the daughter in the second incident gave a good description of the pirates.

"They were rough with us," she shrinks back into her seat. "We tried to fight, but they were too strong."

This goes on for another thirty minutes. By the time the sun sets, I'm certain we have our story straight. Unfortunately, now that it's getting dark, it's time to take care of the final details. I don't want to do this, but I have to. I stand up, turn the engine off and allow Bacchus to drift in the dark. We're at the mercy of the elements now. I give a quick prayer that Libby is right, and the wind will keep us in Greek water. Then I ball my hand into a fist, take a deep breath, and as hard as I can, I punch Mabel in the face.

Mabel spits up blood as well as a tooth.

"Oh, shit. Sorry, Mabel, I didn't mean to get your tooth." My stomach sinks with the same shame and pain of every fight I had with Frederick. I feel sick doing this to her.

Mabel rubs her face and calls me the worst swearword she can manage. I'm not offended. She growls to get through the pain then holds out her arm. I punch that too.

Libby, whose face is red and swollen, and whose limbs are already bruised, just adds a few scratches to the back of her hands.

Paige's turn. She scrunches up her face in anticipation. "Make it quick."

I hit her on the cheek before she can finish speaking. I didn't go hard enough to break it, but it will definitely turn yellow.

"How come she doesn't have to lose any teeth?" Mabel says with a slight lisp, examining the tooth between her fingers.

"*She* needs her smile back in time for I'm a Celeb," Paige says, her hand clamped to her face. "Don't say anything. We're not supposed to tell anyone until they do the big press release."

Mabel, despite her gruesome appearance, still manages to flash a wicked grin. "I knew it. You've got my vote, babe."

"Thanks," she says before sighing. "That's assuming we're not all in jail."

"No one's going to jail," I tell her firmly, but really I'm just trying to convince myself.

Once we're all bruised up, Verona takes some cooking string from the galley and begins to tie us up. She secures our hands behind our backs and ties tight knots. She has to override her training and avoid pretty sailor knots. She needs to make them tight but messy. We struggle against the string for a while, making sure it holds. Then Verona ties Paige to Libby and Mabel to me. We sit back to back on the saloon floor. It's uncomfortable, and my knees begin to ache within minutes.

Verona takes a stretch of string, holds one end between her teeth and the other in her right hand. Then she violently slides her left wrist down the length of the twine, giving herself a nasty friction burn. She repeats this on both sides of both wrists. Tiny droplets of scarlet flower on her skin, colouring the cooking string a dark pink. Verona wraps the bloodied cord around her thumbs and rubs it back and forth over the edge of the chart table. It doesn't take long for the threads to begin snapping, but it takes an age for her to get through the lot.

"My arms are burning," she says, massaging her triceps.

"Good," Libby says, and when Verona glares at her, she clarifies, "Your arms would be burning if you had to do that with your hands tied behind your back. They should ache."

Verona shakes her arms, loosening her muscles, and rubs at the burns on her inner wrists. A hush passes over the group.

It's time.

She wipes a tear from her eye and says with a sob, "I'll miss her."

Besides rehearsing what we're going to say to the authorities, no one has mentioned Esther in hours. Verona's words feel like a punch in the gut.

"We all will," I reply, surprising myself. "She meant a lot to all of us in one way or another." I blink back a tear of my own and conjure up an image in my mind of happier times.

"But what she did to you was unforgivable," Mabel says bluntly behind me. "I loved that woman. We got on so well, but she should have had your back, Jo."

I can't hug Mabel, but I can take her hand in mine. We squeeze each other's fingers until I give a yelp. My hands are beginning to feel the pain of hitting bony faces with bare knuckles.

"And you Libby," Mabel goes on, "She pushed you overboard. I'm not into all that karmic stuff like you Verona, but shit, cause and effect."

Verona takes a pillowcase from Paige's cabin and tears it into strips. She walks around us one by one, wrapping the fabric around our heads, forming gags. My hair gets caught in the knot as she pulls it tighter. It twinges and I crinkle my eyes in response.

"Sorry," she says,

I tell her it's okay, but through the gag, it's nothing more than a garbled sound.

"Is everyone ready?"

With wet eyes, I nod.

Verona gathers her strength. She takes a deep inhalation then slams a red button on the radio panel.

Vessel in Distress.

– CHAPTER 37 –

Jo.

Every sailor on every boat within range of us will be recoiling from the sound of the alarm. Loud and high-pitched yet slightly musical, the vessel in distress signal bleats like an offensive smoke alarm.

"All vessels, all vessels. This is sailing boat Bacchus, sailing boat Bacchus. Over." Verona almost yells as she speaks. She sounds urgent, scared, and most of all, just like we rehearsed.

When no one answers, she lifts the radio to her mouth again. "All vessels, all vessels. Please help. This is sailing boat Bacchus, sailing boat Bacchus. Over." She waits a beat, then screams, "PIRATES. Please help us. Pirates. Over."

The silence seems to last an age. I begin to wonder if anyone is even within range. There must be someone. In the Med, you're never really out of range of anyone. Between the sailboats, fishermen, tourist boats, ferries and cargo ships, someone's always going

294

somewhere. When the radio crackles, we all jump, none more so than Verona, who almost drops the receiver.

"Bacchus, Bacchus. This is catamaran Florence, catamaran Florence. Did you say pirates? Over."

The voice is female, the accent Scouse.

"Yes. Pirates," Verona squeals. "Please help. Over."

"Bacchus, are they still there? Over."

"No, they've gone. They tied us up. I've only just managed to get free. They've taken …" her voice is so distressed it will be near impossible for the sailors aboard catamaran Florence to understand her.

"Bacchus, what are your coordinates? Over."

Verona rattles off our location using the display on the navigation station.

There's a pause while Florence inputs the coordinates into their GPS. "Bacchus. We're not far away. We can be with you in twenty to thirty minutes. Do you have power? Over."

"Florence, Florence. Yes. We have power. I can meet you. Where are you?"

Behind me, Mabel squirms and mutters through her gag. "Can't believe we're going to be rescued by a twatamaran."

"Not now, Mabel," I hush.

Verona rushes into the darkness above deck, she starts the engine and directs Bacchus towards Florence. I hear a whooshing noise as she sets a flare, letting Florence, wherever she is, know our position.

After ten minutes, she shouts down the companion-way, "I can see their lights."

"You're doing great," Libby garbles through silky fabric. "Get a line ready."

Below deck, we listen as Verona starts speaking quickly and loudly. The sound of ropes being passed back and forth as the two vessels are tethered together can be heard. The voices are definitely from Liverpool.

"We reached the coast guard," I hear someone say. "We have a signal booster. We're to stay with you until they get here. Should be twenty minutes. Possibly less."

The silhouettes of two women appear in the companionway. Small, and in their sixties, they both gasp at the sight of us tied up and battered.

"Oh, you poor things." The smaller of the two runs down the steps and into the saloon. Her long hair is tied in a braid that reaches her waist. Light brown with strands of white, it swings behind her like a tail. She's dressed in plaid pyjamas with a Musto sailing jacket over the top.

"I tried to untie them," Verona says, her voice still quivering. "But the knots are tight, and I didn't trust myself with a knife; my hands keep shaking." She holds up her hands as evidence.

The lady with the long braid takes Verona's hands in hers, examining the friction burns on her wrists.

"Those burns look nasty. Come with me, dear. Let's get these under running water."

She turns on the tap in the galley and Verona winces as the cold water flows over her wounds. Letting go of Verona, our new guest takes a chef's knife from the top drawer and hands it to her companion.

"Here, Emily."

The slightly taller woman, who's sporting a silver bob pushed back with an Alice band, takes the knife from her and deftly cuts us free. That's when we yank our gags from our mouths and begining speaking at once. We cry about how they boarded so quickly that there was nothing we could do. We sob about how they hurt us and tied us up.

"Esther tried to stop them," I say.

"We told her to just do as they say," adds Paige, rubbing her face where I'd hit her. "But she never listens. Never bloody listens."

Mabel, making sure they can see the gap where her tooth should be, continues, "I said *be compliant, Esther. Keep your head down. Don't make eye contact*. She should have stayed quiet and done as I said, but she just wouldn't. She always knows best. She said, *Don't you know who I am? My father will make sure you rot in jail.*"

"Then that was that," Libby says, taking over from Mabel. "One of them recognised her and, what were they saying, Verona? Verona speaks all sorts of languages."

She turns the tap off and dabs a tea towel against her forearms. "Two of them spoke Turkish. I'm not fluent, but they definitely recognised Esther and, oh God, they took her. They tied her up, threw her in their boat, and they took her. One of them – the biggest one – he kept saying *fidye*. It means ransom."

The two women stand open-mouthed. Emily, the taller one with the bob had been examining Paige's face when Verona said this. She paused, Paige's chin still in her hands. "Oh, Christ. Sue, get back on to the coast guard. It's not just a *smash and grab*. They've kidnapped one of them."

Sue, with the braid, closes her mouth and reaches for our radio receiver. "What do you mean they recognised her? Is she famous or some—?"

As she asks this, her eyes land on the framed picture of young Esther with her mother and father attending St. Mary Magdalene's on Christmas Day.

Her eyes flicker around the expensive yacht, and before we can answer, she gasps, "Wait? This Esther? They've taken Esther McPherson?"

- CHAPTER 38 -

Four Months Later.

Libby.

The sun peaks over the horizon, though autumn has arrived, the sun still has enough ferocity to warm my face and flatten the goosebumps on my arm. I inhale, taking in the salty air and the aroma of fresh coffee. The villa Jo hired in the Faraways is spacious, basic, but most importantly, secluded. We arrived separately. None of us fancied running the gauntlet of press and nosy citizens by travelling together through the busier airports. I flew into Corfu airport two days ago and took a tourist ferry from St. Stefanos. Verona arrived on the next flight; she opted for Pegasus, a passenger ferry. She seems more like her old self. Her hair has grown a couple of inches, and it doesn't look like it's seen a set of straighteners in awhile. Her animosity towards me seems to have gone the same way as her shoulder pads and business attire. Thank goodness. When she arrived, she actually asked after Danny. I don't know if she was genuinely interested in us and our relationship or if she was fishing to see if I'd opened up to him about what really happened on Bacchus. But if she was looking for more information, she hid it well, and I choose to see the good in her.

Mabel emerges from our holiday let, carrying a silver tray laden with the fresh coffee I could smell. It's in a silver coffeepot that reflects the light of the sun. Next to it is a plate stacked with pastries.

"Sorry, V. I don't know which ones are vegan and which ones have cheese filling."

Verona laughs. "They're pastry. None of them are vegan."

Mabel's face falls. "Ah, crap. Sorry."

"It's fine, honestly. There's a nice loaf of crusty bread in the kitchen. I'll make myself some avocado on toast once I've had my caffeine fix."

Mabel chose to charter to her own boat and sail up the coast to meet us here. The sailing yacht she hired is a twenty-seven foot Beneteau. She's no Bacchus, but she's small and nimble, and Mabel can easily handle her single-handedly.

"I turned down the first boat they offered me," she told us when she moored up last night. "Yacht was called *Spoiled Princess*. Can you believe it? There was no way I could take her out of the harbour with a

300

name like that. A chill ran right down my spine. I made up some nonsense about wanting self-furling sails, and they offered me this baby instead: *Endless Summer*. Now that's a name I could get used to."

Mabel's teeth look perfect. You can't tell that one was punched out by a vet with a wicked right hook not too long ago. I don't know how her dentist fixed it, but it looks flawless.

The distant hum of an engine mixed with rubber tyres struggling for grip on gravel roads gets our attention. I pick up a mug of coffee and hold it to my chest in both hands, appreciating the sensation of heat seeping into my palms. Verona, Mabel and I turn our eyes to the dirt track that leads to the villa. We haven't been here long, but so far we haven't seen a soul in this area. We wouldn't have even known this place was here if we didn't have very specific instructions from the villa's owner.

The rumble gets louder, and a small plume of dust erupts moments before Jo's Vesper comes into view. She hired the tatty, old thing to ferry us back and forth between the town and our accommodation. Jo, dressed in a summery wrap dress, accessorised with a blue motorcycle helmet, isn't alone. Sat behind her is a tall figure in black.

Jo skids the Vespa to a halt, sending pebbles and gravel flying, and casting dirt into all our faces. I close my eyes and turn my mouth to my shoulder, breathing through the fabric of my T-shirt rather than inhaling

301

dust particles. By the time the dust settles the stranger in black has removed their helmet to reveal a long ponytail of luminous red.

"Paige," I exclaim, my face lighting up. "I didn't think you'd make it."

Mabel puts down her pastry, swallows what's in her mouth and asks, "Shouldn't you be on a plane to the jungle right about now?"

"I was dropped for a YouTuber with more silicon than she has brain cells," Paige says with a roll of her intensely blue eyes.

"Bummer."

I feel a tug in my stomach. "Didn't you need that money for Graham's BUPA bill?"

She shrugs. "Was only thirty grand, and I wouldn't have been paid until they wrapped filming. Bloody hell, listen to me, *only thirty g's*. If little Paige Vaughn from Hackney could hear me now." She shakes her head, admonishing herself. "I took out a second mortgage on my flat, sent the money straight to dad, and he's in the US now with Graham. He started treatment last week and seems to be responding already."

"That's brilliant," I say, and as I look around, we're all smiling at this bit of positive news.

"Yeah, I'm so pleased. Dad sent me a photo before I got on the plane. Graham looks pale and hauntingly thin, but there's a sparkle in his eye. He looks …" she pauses to search for the right word. "Cheeky. He looks cheeky. I haven't seen him that way for a long, long time. I burst into tears right there in the middle of check-in."

My face must be a picture of pity, because Paige laughs, and says, "Oh, it's fine, Libby. The woman on the desk took one look at me bawling my eyes out and upgraded me from business to first."

We call her various forms of *jammy git*, before she takes out her phone and shows us the picture of her younger brother. Graham's hair is a darker shade of red than Paige's and a large patch has been shaved off, revealing a white square of scalp. A nasal cannula delivers oxygen to his nostrils, but below the clear plastic tubing, his mouth is formed into a coy smile. Within seconds we're all either pretending not to cry or openly sobbing.

We spend the rest of the day going over the previous four months. We've only seen each other the once since the Greek coast guard rescued us. Rescued us? They didn't rescue us, though, did they? The longer I stick to this lie, the more I actually find myself believing it. I had a nightmare last week about the masked men boarding Bacchus. One of them grabbed me by the neck and slammed my head into the saloon table. He tied me up just as Verona had done. I watched him take Esther by the hair and drag her kicking and screaming up the companionway, her feet banging off each step as she went. When Danny woke me because I was screaming in my sleep, I had my own hand on my neck.

That wasn't the only night terror I had. In the first few weeks, all my nightmares were about The Broker and his, what should I call them? His colleagues? I dreamt of them grabbing me off the street, tossing me into a van with Paige and Jo. They drove us to some empty industrial unit in the arse end of nowhere and tortured us, demanding to know where the black bag was. The things they threatened us with … I'll spare you the details.

I ask the girls if they've heard of any more piracy incidents since we returned home. They haven't. Paige thinks it's because there was so much activity in the area with people out looking for Esther. Boats were searched at every port. Coast guards from almost all the countries around the Med recruited new staff and worked all the hours they could to find the missing royals.

Royals. Plural.

After her father couldn't be located, the theory changed. SO14, the Royalty Protection Group, suggested that they'd both been targeted by the same gang, and that they'd used the recent piracy in the Med as a cover, either by committing the previous events, or by using what they knew from the papers to have it blamed on them.

SO14 are right. Sort of. But it was us who used the recent piracy attacks to cover up Esther's death.

SO14 are still waiting for someone to make a ransom demand. When the Sun newspaper launched a ten thousand pound reward for information that led to her being found, all the chancers came out of the woodwork. The phones rang off the hook with people saying they'd seen Esther in the Romanian hills, or they'd spotted her in a strip club in Prague, or she was running barefoot down the street in Marrakech.

"You might be right," I tell Paige. "If I were a low-level pirate, stealing jewels and credit cards from yacht cruisers, I'd avoid the Greek Islands for a long time."

Verona coughs. It's midday now, and we're lounging in various positions in the garden. Mabel, true to form, is topless while she tops up her tan. Jo is engrossed in a book. She usually reads thrillers, but today she has something lighthearted with a picture of a cartoon pug on the cover. As for me, I'm letting Paige paint my nails a deep shade of berry.

"There's another reason the pirates have stopped targeting yachters around here," Verona says. "Think about it."

"The Broker blames them for the missing gear?" Jo asks, looking up from her book.

"Exactly. If they got wind of the sort of people who were looking for them, they'd be keeping their heads down for years rather than months. Because, as far as the Broker's concerned, the Albanians delivered the goods to Bacchus, Bacchus was targeted by pirates, and the coast guard didn't find anything untoward on Bacchus."

"Therefore, the pirates have the guns, the passports and the currency."

Paige finishes the second coat, and I lift my nails to admire her work, blowing on them to help the drying process.

"Everyone recovered from the vigil?" I ask, casting my mind back to the only time we've been together since the police separated us for our interviews.

"Oh, Christ." Mabel looks up. "I felt like the whole world was watching me."

"They were," I say.

"How do you do it, Paige? It was creepy. Everyone knew my name: the pastor, the family, the randoms lining the road outside the church. Urgh, and the press. *Mabel, Mabel, where do you think they took Esther?*"

Paige considers the question. "You don't get used to it. I thought that after a while, I'd learn to tune it out and it would just become white noise. Haven't managed it yet."

None of us wanted to go to the vigil. It was organised by Esther's step-mother. Her birth mother had flown over to attend, so it was awkward, on top of everything else. I'd rather have pulled my own teeth out, but we decided it would look weird if we didn't attend. We arrived together for support, speeding past the photographers and the public to sit at the back out of everyone's way.

The church was dark and candle-lit, and though large, the number of people who'd been invited made the whole thing claustrophobic. The Liverpudlian ladies who'd responded to our SOS call were there too. We made small talk and let them fuss over where our various bruises had been. We made all the right noises, dabbed our eyes when we should have cried, said amen when it was called for. In short, I tried not to act guilty about letting one of our nation's sweethearts drown.

It was self-defence, I tell myself again. I've had to remind myself a lot recently that *she* pushed me overboard.

Afterwards, Sue and Emily, the Scouse ladies, gave an interview to Hello magazine. We haven't spoken to the press, we don't want to draw attention to ourselves, but Sue and Emily are free to do so. They were only with us for forty minutes aboard Bacchus and maybe another twenty minutes at the church. Still, in that time it would appear they became our best friends and know everything about us. They described us as looking like we'd been in a car crash. Bruised, cut, traumatised. They called me brave, said Verona was inspirational, and that Mabel looked shell-shocked. I'm not sure what they had against Paige, but they told Hello that *she's not as pretty in real life* and that she *should have some elocution lessons*. Being a Mackem, I find it hilarious that a pair of Scousers think a Cockney needs to address her speech patterns. Us Brits and our accents.

After another few hours, of hydrating, sun-worshipping and general chit chat, Mabel checks her watch. "I think it's time."

The sun is lowering in the sky. There's no dusky pink yet, but the heat of the day has diminished, and the tourist boats will be long gone. We dress and begin walking down the dirt track. Mabel and Jo go ahead on the Vesper, Mabel's golden waves billowing out the back of the spare helmet.

It will take us the better part of an hour to reach the marina. After twenty minutes, the path changes from a worn trail to one resembling a mosaic. Flat white stones sit at odd angles, dark stripes of uncovered dirt running between them. On either side of the track, spiky yellow shrubs erupt in bunches, tickling our bare legs as we walk. We mainly walk in silence, watching bees the size of ping pong balls zip from flower to flower, and listening to the breeze as it whistles through taller grass.

"Jo's been quiet," I say after forty minutes.

Paige agrees, saying she hardly said a word when she met her from the ferry.

"She just wants this whole business over with," Verona says, kicking a pebble out of her sandal. "I know, we all do, but I think … Well, her relationship with Esther was pretty toxic, and it doesn't sound like she ever spoke to her parents about what happened. Then there's the break down of her relationship with Frederick. I imagine she wants a fresh start. You know, she told me she's thinking of using her *compensation* to go to South Africa. She wants to spend some time volunteering in a wildlife sanctuary, try and get herself a permanent paid position in a national park."

The image of Jo finally getting to work with big game is a pleasing one. As we fall into silence again, imagining Jo helping a sedated lion with a sore foot or saving an elephant from poachers, it occurs to me that I too should think of my share of the cash as compensation. I plan on cleaning it through my photography business. Make up a few international clients each year who pay me in cash. It will take years, and yes, I'll be paying tax on it, but it's doable. Verona has a similar plan. She recently opened an eco store in Camden; some zero waste, zero plastic venture. They sell bamboo toothbrushes, shampoo bars, plastic-free detergents and organic grains. Like many businesses in London, she accepts various currencies. When she's managed to launder it all, she'll be able to buy back a substantial slice of her vegan food business.

The marina is starkly different from how we saw it during the storm. The sea is flat and calm, peppered with white dots where gulls relax between meals. There are no cracks of thunder or flashes of lightning. The sky isn't black; the wind doesn't howl. Endless Summer doesn't rock back and forth; she doesn't battle the elements as Bacchus had to.

Mabel extends a hand and welcomes us aboard.

309

"Cosy," Paige says, looking around the tiny saloon and galley.

"She's no Bacchus, but we are supposed to be keeping a low profile."

"Mabel Sharpe? Keep a low profile?" I say with a smirk.

She laughs. "Stranger things have happened. Anyway, the wind's a bit crap so we'll be motoring round to the north. Hopefully, it will pick up in time for us to sail back."

She presses two buttons on the instrument panel, causing Endless Summer's engine to growl.

"You know, I still can't believe Esther let me clean the entire engine when she knew there was nothing wrong with it."

"I can," Jo says flatly. "It was Esther. She managed to get us to Othonoi and got her engine cleaned for free. She'd have thought it was brilliant."

Mabel's tanned shoulders lift and fall in a resigned shrug. "True. But I take umbrage with you saying Esther got us Othonoi. She may have tricked us into coming here, but *I* got us here."

"Too right you did," Verona says in agreement. "You were a machine."

I climb out of the cockpit and head to the bow to raise the anchor. There's no hatch at the bow, no crew cabin, no poky little room to stick the northerner that no one wanted to bunk with.

310

I look back to the stern as the whirring noise of the windlass tells me the anchor is being hoisted from the seabed. I look at Mabel joking around with Verona and realise I hold no ill will towards them. There's no ache when I look at Mabel, no awful pit of rejection eating away in my stomach. I'm not mad at Verona either, after all the names she called me. After the huffy comments and dark looks. I was more upset about the things she said about Paige, to be honest. But now … Well, I can't complain, can I? They've all stuck by me. They listened to everything I told them about Esther, her father, the Broker, and the poor bastard who ran Gimenez Energy. And just like when we sailed through the storm, we did what we had to do to survive. We got on with it.

– CHAPTER 39 –

Verona

"Here we are."

Mabel switches the engine to neutral while Libby drops anchor. We wait for what little breeze there is to swing Endless Summer nose to wind, and when Mabel's satisfied the anchor is holding, she switches the engine off.

Silence.

I've missed silence since returning to England. First, it was the constant questions from the authorities, then the endless phone calls from journalists, investors and family. The noise in the factories where we mix ice cream and the buzz of jigsaw blades while joiners fit out the new store. Traffic, car horns, text messages, the tube. It's nonstop. It's overwhelming. Coming back here means I can appreciate the quietude once again. I must make an effort to get out of the City more often. I think of the meeting I need to get back in time for, the supermarket bosses I need to charm next quarter and the investor who wants our latest accounts.

Hmm. Rather than get out of the City more often, I think I need to get out of the City full stop.

I'm a skilled chef. Granted, I'm not classically trained, but I know my vegan cuisine inside out. I can whip up a meat-free, dairy-free lasagne that would fool even the most hard-core carnivore. Perhaps, once I've cleaned my share of the money, I should take a sabbatical. I could head overseas and open up a little vegan cafe by the sea. Thailand? San Francisco? I suppose the world's my oyster. Or my mushroom-based oyster substitute to be precise.

Mabel strips out of her shorts and vest and pulls on some three-quarter length leggings and a long-sleeved neoprene top. She must be expecting the water to be colder than when we were here last. She takes a belt and attaches diving weights to it before fastening it around her hips. Standing tall, Mabel starts practising breathing exercises. She breaths in as deeply as she can, holds it for a second then inhales some more. It's amazing how much extra air she can fit in her lungs.

While Mabel prepares herself, I look around, checking for other boats. All of us together at the villa is one thing. If anyone asks, we can say we came out to remember Esther, hold a vigil of our own. But out here, bobbing about in the water? I'm not sure what excuse we could give then. I suppose we could say we wanted a sunset sail. Say we were honouring Esther by doing something she loved. Yes, that might work. Regardless, I'd rather word of this didn't end up in the press. We don't want the Albanians, or the Broker getting wind of it. They might put two and two together.

After five minutes, Mabel lowers a swimming platform and ladder that are attached to the back of Endless Summer. She fits a dive mask to her face and dips her foot off the edge, testing the water temperature.

"Fuck me. It's freezing."

"St. Andrews in January freezing?" asks Libby, knowing fine well the answer is *no*.

Mabel mock shivers. "Nothing's that cold." She steps off the platform, entering the water feet first. She waits a moment while she finds her buoyancy and takes a few more deep breaths to acclimatise in the cool Ionian sea. On her next breath, she tips forward, angling her head downwards and she dives into the blue as smoothly as any marine mammal. Ripples of water expand from her point of entry, but there's not a single splash.

"She swims like a fish," murmurs Jo.

"Do you think she'll find it?" Paige asks. Her eyes lose focus as she looks off into the distance and I wonder if she's worried about the consequences if the money isn't there and she can't repay her second mortgage.

"Might take her a few goes," I say. But if it's there, she'll find it.

314

Libby suddenly, and loudly exhales before sucking in more air in frantic gasps.

"What are you doing?" I ask. "You gave me a heart attack."

"Seeing if I can hold my breath as long as Mabel."

"You don't stand a chance," Jo says, then she bursts into hysterics. "Did you hear about the guy she met in Ibiza?"

"No."

"This was years ago. They were fooling about in the pool—" She stops herself. "Put it this way, she can hold her breath long enough to—"

Libby's face is a picture. "You're joking?"

Before Jo can say if she's joking or not – she's not, I've heard this story from the horse's mouth, so to speak – we hear a splash. The four of us peer over the guard rail and see Mabel's infectious grin.

"Bingo!" Her arm thrusts out of the water, her scarlet-polished talons gripping a bright red dry bag.

"Holy shit," gasps Jo. "You did it." She takes the bag from Mabel, who swims to the rear of Endless Summer and pulls herself up the ladder to the swimming platform. She sits for a moment and catches her breath.

"I didn't think I'd make it," she pants. "Deeper than expected. Not quite where we left it … Shifted."

Mabel is back-slapped and hugged. We wait for her to peel off her wet clothes and wrap herself in a towel before we dare open the bag.

"Go on," says Mabel. "I can't stand it any longer. What if we open it up and it's just a pile of soggy mush? Just put me out of my misery."

Libby takes the bag. Her face is peaky and she's sucked her lips in, forming her mouth into a thin line. She presses the edges of a black plastic clip until the two slides come away from each other. Her hands shake as she unravels the folds of the bag before coaxing the zipper open. She peers in.

"Libby, I'm about to have a breakdown. Is it dry or not?"

Libby looks at Mabel. The former giving nothing away, while the later twists her wet hair, wringing water from it on to the deck of Endless Summer.

Drip, drip, drip.

"LIBBY!"

Libby's face cracks and she tips the bag upside down. Bundle after bundle of perfectly dry currency falls to the cockpit table. Paige scoops up a handful and holds it to her chest before kissing it. Tears swell under her eyes before spilling down her cheeks.

I pull her into a hug. "He's going to be okay."

She nods, unable to speak.

I pass a few bundles to Jo. "Compensation."

"Compensation," she repeats back to me. "And a new leaf."

Libby picks up her share, counting each bundle as she goes. "Thank you," she says quietly. "All of you. You didn't have to stand by me."

316

"Yes we bloody did," Jo says. "This wasn't your doing, Libby. The McPhersons only had themselves to blame. Greed, greed and more greed. That selfish old pervert started all of this. Causing Gimenez to fold, ruining a man's reputation and causing countless people to lose their jobs. He could have repaid his debt to the Broker, rather than involve his daughter. Esther didn't have to involve us. She didn't have to try and throw you overboard. They could have stopped this shit show in its tracks at any moment, but they didn't. They did this to themselves; we took the only option left to us."

"And now?" Libby asks, wiping sweat from the back of her neck.

"Now, we sail back to port," I tell her. "We walk back up to the villa, pour ourselves a large glass of something strong and try to get some sleep. Tomorrow, we start the rest of our lives."

CHAPTER 40

Jo

It took a few more months, but eventually, the press stopped calling. Esther stopped being classed as *abducted* and was instead referred to as *missing, presumed dead*. SO14 had a few more questions for us, of course, but we handled it. Stuck to the same story. I haven't seen the Pier Pressure girls since we left the Faraway Islands for the last time. There was mention of us having a reunion in five years, but I'm not sure anything will come of it; we're all trying to move on.

Bella begins to stir. Her anaesthetic is starting to wear off. The white rhino calf is already over sixty kilos and is possibly the cutest creature I've ever seen. Checking her vitals as she lays on the baked, sienna earth, I see her heart rate and blood pressure are perfectly fine. She'll be running about her paddock with her best friend, Katie the warthog, in no time.

We got the call the day after I arrived. Even though I hadn't changed time zones, the long haul flight and the culture shock meant I still felt like I had jet lag. Jumping into a 4x4 and off-roading it into the bush to meet a gamekeeper named Elvis certainly helped wake me up. Bella's mother had been targeted by poachers. Elvis and his crew had fought them off and transferred her so she could be operated on. It didn't end well for Bella's mum; she'd been shot twice, and they'd already started to remove her horn. Thankfully, we were able to save Bella. Bella is thriving at the wildlife rehabilitation centre where I'm based. She had a nasty cut on her leg when we brought her in, which is why I sedated her; I had to replace a few stitches. She's all cleaned up now, and I've given her a cocktail of antibiotics.

She opens her ginormous, brown eyes and blinks. I've never been the maternal sort, but I know I'm going to shed a tear when Bella is big enough to be released. She's still bottle-fed at the moment, and as feeding her round the clock is one of my jobs, I guess she's my baby.

My heavy, grey, wrinkly baby.

I heard on the grapevine that Libby and Daniel are engaged now. Before Libby left for Corfu airport, she took ten grand from her pile and gave it to Paige. *"Just in case."* Then she handed a few more to me. *"Consider it interest on the compensation payment."*

I told her not to be silly, to keep it or hand it over to Paige. A qualification like mine means I'll be absolutely fine – financially anyway. But, she insisted. That little Mackem can be quite stubborn when she wants to be.

The news feed on my phone still bombards me with stories from home. I scroll through each morning, dreading the news that Esther has washed up somewhere, or that Mr McPherson escaped from Sicily. This morning, my newsfeed included election news, a political scandal and the reveal of this year's *Strictly* contestants. My fingers kept sliding up, moving from story to story, but I'm sure I saw a flash of red hair and porcelain skin between the sequin-clad celebrity dancers. I paused at a sailing story. The image of a sailing yacht caused me to almost drop my coffee. My fears were unfounded, though. It wasn't about pirates or anything dodgy washing up in the Mediterranean. It was a story about Meditide, a charity that takes children and teenagers with mental health problems on sailing expeditions. They'd received a *sizeable donation from an anonymous source*.

Mabel, I think, smiling to myself. Had to have been Mabel.

Bella's thick legs begin to twitch and kick, so I clear the area and help roll her back to her feet. It's not easy given her weight, but I'm not complaining. I'd rather be doing this than dealing with the cats and dogs at

Forest View, not to mention bloody Lydia. No Frederick, no Patricia, and so far, no one has peed on me.

Inspired by Mabel's philanthropy, I think of the extra money Libby gave me. There's a women's centre in the nearest town. They provide healthcare, contraception and a safe bed to any local women who need it. I'd planned on volunteering on my days off, but it turns out the wildlife rehabilitation centre is a full-time gig. Babies like Bella need feeding day and night. Instead, I'll drop off a few hundred-thousand rand, anonymously of course. That will help keep a lot of women safe.

I like the idea of donating the money Esther was transporting to free her disgusting father to a women's centre. There's something poetic about it, and I think Esther would approve. I mean, she's a feminist, is she not?

Bella staggers off as if she's drunk. She follows the wooden panels that mark the perimeter of her enclosure as if she might have to stop and lean on them for balance. Katie scampers over to greet her, her little tasselled tail high in the air like a hairy antenna. The piglet is a third of Bella's size and she makes the most adorable squeaking noises. Bella is already as big as a fully grown female warthog. I wonder if that's why Katie loves her so much. Is Bella her substitute mother in the same way I am to Bella?

I might be reading too much into it, but anthropomorphising aside, there's a real sense of family here. I haven't been here long, but I already feel more at home than I ever did living on Esther's estate, at St. Andrews, or at Forest View.

I tidy up my equipment and exit the paddock. It's a lovely evening, and some of the volunteers are meeting at the lake for sundowners. I'll only be having one drink as we have a big day ahead of us tomorrow. We're releasing a male buffalo shortly after sunrise. He weighs over half a tonne so we'll need to have our wits about us. A radio in the distance crackles and I tilt my head in its direction, awaiting the evening update. Elvis's heavily-accented voice reports that all's well in the lower grasslands. All rangers are in position, and there have been no reports of poachers.

All creatures great and small can sleep soundly tonight.

Including me.

- The End -

– MESSAGE FROM THE AUTHOR –

If you have two minutes, please head on over to Amazon and leave a review for Dead In The Water. The support of my readers means a great deal.

If you'd like to be kept up to date with future releases, join my mailing list at betsybaskerville.com

Connect with me online:

Web: betsybaskerville.com
Twitter: @B__Baskerville (double underscore)
Facebook: B Baskerville - Author
Instagram: b_baskerville_author

Writing Dead in the Water has been an absolute pleasure, but not as much of a pleasure as researching it was.

When the muses came calling and told me to set a murder mystery on the high seas, I could picture it: a sailing yacht, six university friends, turquoise waters, balmy nights, and a storm that brewed literally and figuratively. A classic six people get on the boat, only five get off deal.

I had a plot, characters, and location. What I didn't have was any technical knowledge. If the Pier Pressure ladies knew how to sail, there was only one thing for it … I needed to learn to sail! Luckily, my partner knows how to handle a yacht, so Rob and I packed our bags and headed to the Ionian.

After arriving in Corfu, we got acquainted with our boat; she was named Pindos, after the Pindos mountain range. The first thing I needed to get used to was sailing terminology. I thought I'd travelled to Greece to learn to sail, not to learn a new language. Bathrooms are called heads, bedrooms are cabins, the kitchen is the galley and don't get me started on the word *rope*. The wheel is the helm, the entrance is the companionway, and the doorframes are called *&%$ £$! because try as you might, you will stub your toe, or bang your head on them at least once a day. I'm 5'5", imagine how 6'2" Rob felt.

Terminology mastered, it was time to get under sail. Each day followed a similar routine, one I don't think I could get bored of. We would start with a briefing to find out where we were headed, what the conditions would be and if there were any hazards to be aware of. Next, we'd get shipshape, have a cup of tea and head off for our day's adventure. In the evenings,

Rob and I would go exploring before sitting down with a glass of white on the water's edge to watch the other boats come in and discuss my writing. We'd make notes on our surroundings including the sights, sounds and smells. I'd bombard him with technical questions about the weather and the engine, and we'd discuss the importance of waterways and naval strength in days gone by. In fact, the prologue to Dead in the Water was written while we drifted in the doldrums somewhere between Meganisi and Kalamos.

After two weeks in paradise, I wouldn't call myself a sailor, but I had enough knowledge to plough on with the important task of actually sitting down and writing.

I'd like to thank Rob for his continued support. He never tired of me picking his brains and asking sailing questions during this process. I'll always remember sitting in Pindos's cockpit while we spitballed ideas in the midday sun. Or when we wandered through the Roman cemetery in Fiskardo and discussed Persephone's abduction to the underworld.

A big thank you also goes to Joe, Meg and Cian, the crew of lead boat Vassia during our flotilla trip with Sailing Holidays. Joe was an excellent, patient skipper who taught me the portmanteau *twatamaran* (a definite candidate for word of the year!) He also didn't laugh too hard when we dropped a fender and had to go on a walk of shame to retrieve it once it washed ashore. And Cian, thanks for not giving me too much suspicious side-eye when I asked how one could fake engine failure. I only asked for research purposes. Honest.

Finally, a word of caution. Dead in the Water is a work of fiction. There's no black holdall full of passports and Uzis at the bottom of the Ionian. There's no dry bag full of cash weighted to the seabed off the Faraway Islands. If you go looking for them, you will be disappointed.

– ABOUT THE AUTHOR –

Betsy was born and raised in Newcastle upon Tyne. She describes herself as a crime fiction addict and UFC geek of epic proportions.

When not writing, Betsy loves hiking with her boyfriend and their very naughty Welsh terrier.

IF YOU LIKED DEAD IN THE WATER, MEET ATHENA FOX...

"Hooked from the first page."

"A gripping original thriller."

"Couldn't put it down. Engrossed from start to finish."

ALSO BY B. BASKERVILLE:
THE DCI COOPER TRILOGY

"Gritty characters and intriguing storyline."

"Keeps you guessing. A real page-turner."

"Felt totally immersed… Would make a great TV drama."

Printed in Dunstable, United Kingdom